Sudden Silence

The Case of the Murdered Band Leader

By Cortland FitzSimmons

Originally published in 1938

Sudden Silence

© 2015 Resurrected Press
www.ResurrectedPress.com

Published by Resurrected Press

This classic book was handcrafted by Resurrected Press. Resurrected Press is dedicated to bringing high quality classic books back to the readers who enjoy them. These are not scanned versions of the originals, but, rather, quality checked and edited books meant to be enjoyed!

Please visit ResurrectedPress.com to view our entire catalogue, and like us on Facebook at Facebook.com/ResurrectedPress to stay updated!

ISBN 13: 978-1-943403-02-8

Printed in the United States of America

Resurrected Press Books in *The Ethel Thomas Detective Story* <u>Series by Cortland FitzSimmons</u>

Resurrected Press Books in *The Chief Inspector Pointer Mystery* Series

Death of John Tait
Murder at the Nook
Mystery at the Rectory
Scarecrow
The Case of the Two Pearl Necklaces
The Charteris Mystery
The Eames-Erskine Case
The Footsteps that Stopped
The Clifford Affair
The Cluny Problem
The Craig Poisoning Mystery
The Net Around Joan Ingilby
The Tall House Mystery
The Wedding-Chest Mystery
The Westwood Mystery
Tragedy at Beechcroft

RESURRECTED PRESS CLASSIC MYSTERY CATALOGUE

Journeys into Mystery
Travel and Mystery in a More Elegant Time

The Edwardian Detectives
Literary Sleuths of the Edwardian Era

Gems of Mystery
Lost Jewels from a More Elegant Age

Anne Austin
One Drop of Blood
The Black Pigeon
Murder at Bridge

E. C. Bentley
Trent's Last Case: The Woman in Black

Ernest Bramah
Max Carrados Resurrected:
The Detective Stories of Max Carrados

Agatha Christie
The Secret Adversary
The Mysterious Affair at Styles

Octavus Roy Cohen
Midnight

Freeman Wills Croft
The Ponson Case
The Pit Prop Syndicate

J. S. Fletcher

The Herapath Property
The Rayner-Slade Amalgamation
The Chestermarke Instinct
The Paradise Mystery
Dead Men's Money
The Middle of Things
Ravensdene Court
Scarhaven Keep
The Orange-Yellow Diamond
The Middle Temple Murder
The Tallyrand Maxim
The Borough Treasurer
In the Mayor's Parlour
The Saftey Pin

R. Austin Freeman

The Mystery of 31 New Inn from the Dr. Thorndyke Series
John Thorndyke's Cases from the Dr. Thorndyke Series
The Red Thumb Mark from The Dr. Thorndyke Series
The Eye of Osiris from The Dr. Thorndyke Series
A Silent Witness from the Dr. John Thorndyke Series
The Cat's Eye from the Dr. John Thorndyke Series
Helen Vardon's Confession: A Dr. John Thorndyke Story
As a Thief in the Night: A Dr. John Thorndyke Story
Mr. Pottermack's Oversight: A Dr. John Thorndyke Story
Dr. Thorndyke Intervenes: A Dr. John Thorndyke Story
The Singing Bone: The Adventures of Dr. Thorndyke
The Stoneware Monkey: A Dr. John Thorndyke Story
The Great Portrait Mystery, and Other Stories: A Collection of Dr. John Thorndyke and Other Stories
The Penrose Mystery: A Dr. John Thorndyke Story

The Uttermost Farthing: A Savant's Vendetta

Arthur Griffiths
The Passenger From Calais
The Rome Express

Fergus Hume
The Mystery of a Hansom Cab
The Green Mummy
The Silent House
The Secret Passage

Edgar Jepson
The Loudwater Mystery

A. E. W. Mason
At the Villa Rose

A. A. Milne
The Red House Mystery

Baroness Emma Orczy
The Old Man in the Corner

Edgar Allan Poe
The Detective Stories of Edgar Allan Poe

Arthur J. Rees
The Hampstead Mystery
The Shrieking Pit
The Hand In The Dark
The Moon Rock
The Mystery of the Downs

Mary Roberts Rinehart
Sight Unseen and The Confession

Dorothy L. Sayers

Whose Body?

Sir William Magnay
The Hunt Ball Mystery

Mabel and Paul Thorne
The Sheridan Road Mystery

Louis Tracy
The Strange Case of Mortimer Fenley
The Albert Gate Mystery
The Bartlett Mystery
The Postmaster's Daughter
The House of Peril
The Sandling Case: What Would You Have Done?

Charles Edmonds Walk
The Paternoster Ruby

John R. Watson
The Mystery of the Downs
The Hampstead Mystery

Edgar Wallace
The Daffodil Mystery
The Crimson Circle

Carolyn Wells
Vicky Van
The Man Who Fell Through the Earth
In the Onyx Lobby
Raspberry Jam
The Clue
The Room with the Tassels
The Vanishing of Betty Varian
The Mystery Girl
The White Alley
The Curved Blades

Anybody but Anne
The Bride of a Moment
Faulkner's Folly
The Diamond Pin
The Gold Bag
The Mystery of the Sycamore
The Come Back

Raoul Whitfield
Death in a Bowl

And much more!
Visit ResurrectedPress.com
for our complete catalogue

LIKE us on Facebook for upcoming release
announcements!

Facebook.com/ResurrectedPress

FOREWORD

If *Sudden Silence: the Case of the Murdered Band-Leader* reads like a treatment for one of those 1930's mystery films, it shouldn't be surprising. Almost from the beginning of his career he was associated with the film industry. One of his early books, *70,000 Witnesses: a Football Mystery* was turned into a movie of the same name to be followed two years later by the novel and movie *Death on the Diamond: A Baseball Mystery*. At least four of his mystery novels were turned into films and he worked as a screenwriter on a number of other movies.

Mystery films were a popular staple of the movie palaces during the 1930's with some of the biggest stars of the day included in the casts. Many of the best combined murder, romance, witty dialog and comic relief. Possibly no film of the era epitomized this more than *The Thin Man* starring William Powell and Myrna Loy which was based on the novel of the same name by Dashiell Hammett one of the creators of the hard-boiled school of detective fiction. This film, with its cast of colorful characters headed by Powell and Loy in the roles of Nick and Nora Charles was such a hit that it inspired many subsequent imitators.

Cortland Fitzsimmons was well equipped to follow this trend. He had already produced two sports themed mysteries that had been made into movies and would go on to write a number of other novels based on the popular culture of the time including ones base on magic, movies, and music.

Sudden Silence has all the elements of a successful film. It starts out with Hal Harrison, a popular band leader who has been warned not to play a series of shows in San Francisco. To this is added a love interest in the form of Joan Paxton a wealthy socialite from New York whose mother has been trying to get Harrison to play a benefit concert. The two have an on again off again relationship spiced with plenty of witty dialog, while the mother provides the comic relief. Added to this is a murder that happens on stage in front of a large audience. Joan assumes the role of detective to prove the innocence of Harrison. Needless to say, the ending is happy for everyone except the murderer. The surprising thing is that this book was never made into a movie. It would have been a natural.

Cortland Fitzsimmons is not particularly well known today, which for lovers of 1930's films is a shame. *Sudden Silence* is sure to entertain fans of the genre, and Resurrected Press is pleased to offer this new edition of this 1938 mystery.

About the Cover

The cover of this edition incorporates re-worked elements of the original dust jacket used on the first edition of this book, published in 1938.

About the Author

Cortland Fitzsimmons was born in Brooklyn, New York (possibly Queens) on June 19, 1893 and died July 25, 1949 in Los Angeles, California. After attending New York University and The City College of New York, he worked for some time as a salesman for several book distributors and publishers before turning to writing full time in 1934. Most of his works as a writer were mysteries, a number of which were based on sports themes such as *70,000 Witnesses: A Football Mystery*, *Crimson Ice: A Hockey Mystery*, and *Death on a Diamond: A Baseball Mystery*. A number of his novels were made into films and he moved to Los Angeles to work as a screenwriter. His last book was a cookbook that he co-wrote with his wife Muriel Simpson *You Can Cook If You Can Read*.

Greg Fowlkes
Editor-In-Chief
Resurrected Press
www.ResurrectedPress.com
Facebook.com/ResurrectedPress

CHAPTER ONE

By a clever ruse Hal Harrison and his orchestra had left the hotel avoiding the mobs of curious people and autograph seekers who were as constant as the changing tide whenever he made a public appearance. But in spite of their trick and the vigilance of Maxie Blake, his business manager, the telegram, which was a prelude to adventure and the cause of much of the trouble which followed the murder, was delivered to Hal Harrison in person at the railroad station in Portland, Oregon.

Maxie was busy directing luggage laden porters when he saw the messenger boy approach Hal and deliver the message. Hal tossed the boy a quarter, ripped open the envelope, read it quickly, crumpled it angrily into a tight ball and jammed it into his coat pocket.

"Now what?" Maxie mumbled as he watched Harrison, expecting a tirade to break over his head at any moment. In his long experience with famous musicians, stars and great impresarios he had learned to expect and deal with temperament. In fact, anything which deviated slightly from the normal, no matter what it was, Maxie called temperament.

Hal Harrison had none of the traits of a bad tempered prima donna. To his credit let it be said that his temper was quick rather than bad. Small things did annoy him and most of all he resented the incursions into his private life which had followed his sudden rise to fame, not only in the United States but, because of radio, all over the world. He was constantly besieged and beset by fanatics who wrote, wired and tried to see him personally. Except for sentimental women, most of the people who annoyed him had something they wanted to sell or some worthy cause which they hoped to promote with Harrison's money.

As Maxie waited for the angry storm which did not break, he dispatched the last load of luggage toward the train. As he hesitated a moment before approaching Hal, he saw him take the message from his pocket and reread it. Maxie moved forward doubtfully, not quite certain of the reception he would receive. Hal's eyes and the slight twist of his mouth indicated bitter resentment. When Maxie reached his side Hal turned and said with icy calm, "Let's get aboard," and moved down the long platform toward the car which had been reserved for himself and orchestra.

"Well, we fooled the crowds this time," Maxie remarked with satisfaction as he climbed into the car behind Hal and looked back at the few scattered groups of people who seemed totally unaware of the fact that the famous Hal Harrison was boarding the Cascade Limited on his way to San Francisco.

Hal mumbled a reply—a bad sign. Maxie was determined to make conversation, hoping in that way to make Hal forget the thing which was so obviously annoying him.

"That dummy bus idea of yours was great, Hal," he said flatteringly. "This is the first time we've been able to leave a town comfortably on this whole trip. I don't see why you didn't think of it before," he prattled on as they moved down the aisle of the car past chatting groups of musicians who were busily preparing for their night's ride.

Hal made no reply as he moved toward his drawing room. The knotted wad of paper which his fingers rolled about in his pocket was occupying his thoughts. In the drawing room, with the door closed behind them, he refused to speak. He paced up and down the narrow space, bumping into Maxie, who had given up his efforts at conversation and was vainly trying to stow Hal's personal luggage.

With the last piece of luggage beneath the seats, Maxie flattened himself against the side wall and demanded, "Why don't you spill it? There's no point in letting one telegram eat you up. What's in it?" He had reached a high point of annoyance with Hal and his gloomy silence.

Hal drew the ball of paper from his pocket and tossed it to Maxie, who caught it in mid air. Maxie smoothed the crumpled wad and read:

IF YOU VALUE YOUR LIFE STAY AWAY FROM SAN FRANCISCO

Maxie's amazed whistle was long and loud. He reread the warning before he handed it back to Hal.

"Well?" Hal demanded.

"Nothing to worry about," Maxie said thoughtfully with an assurance he did not feel. "It was probably sent by some nut."

"Then it's the first of its kind."

"Why should anyone send you a telegram like that?" Maxie insisted. "It may be some guy who is jealous because his girl raves about you."

"I wish I thought so."

"Say, are you taking it seriously?" Maxie demanded. "I thought I was the gloomy one in this outfit."

"I don't like it," Hal replied.

"Neither do I, but hell, it's just one of those things. Why, it was sent by a piker!" Maxie said disparagingly. "There's less than ten words in the message. A man who counts his pennies over a thing like that isn't really serious."

"It's a very exact message. 'If you value your life stay away from San Francisco,'" Hal quoted, counting the words on his fingers. "It just fits the case. No more words were needed."

"Yeah, but who do you know in San Francisco?" Maxie demanded.

"Chubby Carlton, Rex Kingford, Chick Stoner and Phil Martin," Hal replied.

"They might be a little jealous of your success as compared to theirs," Maxie admitted, "but they wouldn't want to murder you. Not even Phil Martin, who has always been a sore head."

"He wouldn't have nerve enough, but Kingford might."

"What would he gain by it?" Maxie demanded. "Listen, you're tired. You shouldn't let a thing like this get under your skin."

"Would you like to receive a message like that?" Hal demanded. He opened the door leading into the main part of the car and looked down the aisle.

"Aw, somebody's trying to scare you, if anything!" Maxie deprecated.

"Scare me?" Hal demanded. The thought was a new one.

"Sure. To keep you away from San Francisco for some reason or other."

"As if I'd let a thing like that scare me!" Hal said, his mood changing.

"Well, what are you gonna do about it?" Maxie asked.

"Do? We're going to finish our tour in San Francisco as advertised. What did you think I'd do, turn tail and let my public down?"

"Oh, I knew we'd go on," Maxie replied brightly. "I was just wondering what you'd do about the message. Forget it, will you?"

"That won't be so easy."

"But you don't have to run around San Francisco trying to find out who sent it."

"Then you noticed that it came from there?" Hal demanded.

"Sure, I noticed. I thought maybe it was sent from here."

"What made you think of that?"

"Because it was delivered here at the station when it should have been sent to the hotel."

"A person in San Francisco might do that," Hal reflected. "You don't suppose there's a leak in the orchestra, do you?"

"In the band?" Maxie was surprised. "Don't be silly!"

"If there is, I'd like to know it," Hal insisted. "We live too closely to have a squealer in our midst."

"Now, don't start trying to run the thing to earth," Maxie begged. "Haven't we had trouble enough?" he demanded as he tentatively fingered a bottle of aspirin tablets which he always carried in his coat pocket. Maxie was an aspirin addict. He took a pill on the slightest provocation, believing they helped to keep him calm.

"Are you trying to suggest, in your sly way, that we quit?" Hal asked with a smile.

"Quit?" Maxie repeated. "I'm no quitter. I like a fight as well as the next one," he said defensively. "Only—"

"Only what?"

"Enough is enough. If we get into a jam in San Francisco, we'll lose out on your new contract. Higgins is a queer man. He'll stand for no nonsense."

"Let Higgins go fly a kite!"

"Now, you don't mean that," Maxie remonstrated. "You're not big enough, yet," he added quickly lest he offend Hal. "Every radio star in the country would like to get the Higgins spot and you know it. You can't afford to have Higgins let you down. It would give everybody the idea that you were slipping."

"Me slipping!" Hal scoffed. "I'm on the way up!"

"That's just the point," Maxie agreed. "You've got a long way to go if you're careful and you've got to be careful. You can't fool with a man like Higgins. He doesn't care who you are. He puts up the money. He runs his business and his hour the way he wants it run because of the purity of his product. We can't have anything go wrong now. As it is, we're cutting things too fine. We get into San Francisco tomorrow evening, play two nights and then fly back to New York. Suppose there's fog or bad flying weather, we'll be late, and if we are, Higgins will cancel the contract. You know he didn't want you to make this trip."

"And what has your sermon to do with the telegram which we were discussing?" Hal asked with an amused grin.

"I don't want you going around San Francisco sticking that telegram under people's noses and asking them if they sent it. Try to control your temper, will you?"

"You know it's only the small things which really make me mad," Hal replied.

"Yeah, I know it, but does anyone else when you fly off the handle?'"

"Can't I live a life of my own? Can't I have any normal reactions? Do I have to submit to this sort of thing without taking action?" Hal demanded.

"You do when you're a 'dream man,' " Maxie answered with a slight smirk which curled the corners of his otherwise gloomy mouth.

"One more crack like that and I'll treat you to a display of my temper," Hal warned. The one thing that annoyed him more than anything else since his rise to fame was the appellation of "dream man" which a gay young reporter had used after Hal's first big public appearance. The name had stuck, other reporters had pounced upon it, and during Hal's early days of popularity over the air announcers had used it until Hal's protests became more than mere vehement utterances.

Maxie pulled back out of Hal's reach. "You're too free with your fists," he said with a wary eye on those hands which he had seen fly into action too often to suit him. "Fighting don't prove nothin'."

"It's the only language some people understand. I'm going to San Francisco and I'm not going to be mollycoddled by you, understand?" he demanded. "Thought I'd quit, did they?" He returned to the thought of the telegram.

"May I come in?" a cheerful voice asked from the doorway.

"You are in," Maxie replied sourly. "What do you want? Didn't we give you all the news you wanted up at the hotel?"

"Sure! Sure! And don't ever let anyone tell you that Roger Brown doesn't appreciate a break. That's why I'm here. Those people waiting up at the hotel are going to be awful disappointed, Mr. Harrison."

"Why ain't you up there to write a story about their sorrowful faces when they learn that the great Hal Harrison slipped away from them?" Maxie asked.

"I'm gonna write that. Don't worry, Maxie old boy. That'll be in, but at the moment there's other fish to fry." He pulled some papers from his pocket and sorted them quickly as he talked. "We just had a dispatch from San Francisco. I wanted to get the lowdown on it before you left town." He handed Hal a slip of paper on which several lines of tape message had been pasted. "Take a look," he suggested to Maxie who was bending over Hal's shoulder to read.

PHIL MARTIN, POPULAR SAN FRANCISCO BAND LEADER AND ONE TIME MEMBER OF HAL HARRISON'S ORCHESTRA TO BRING SUIT AGAINST HARRISON FOR ONE MILLION DOLLARS. DAVE FIELDS, MANAGER OF THE CRYSTAL GARDENS WHERE HARRISON IS TO APPEAR FEARS HARRISON WILL NOT KEEP HIS SAN FRANCISCO CONTRACT.

When Hal looked up from the message Brown asked eagerly, "Did I just overhear you say you wouldn't quit?"

"I'm not quitting. I'll be in San Francisco. This is the Cascade Limited, isn't it?"

"Sure, but you could arrange to get to Sacramento and go East from there."

"I'm not going East. I keep my contracts. It'll take more than Phil Martin to keep me out of San Francisco. If he's looking for trouble, he's going to get it this time. I'm getting sick of him and his suits. If he isn't careful, he'll be sorry he ever tried to cross me. I'll fix him!" he ended with grim determination.

"Is that a statement for the press or just blowing off steam among friends?" Brown asked with a grin.

"It's steam," Maxie said quickly, scowling at Hal.

"It's a statement," Hal contradicted, ignoring Maxie's hush hush signals.

"No!" Maxie cried.

"Go ahead," Hal instructed Brown. "Get it in the morning papers, then Martin and all of San Francisco will know exactly how I feel."

"Don't print that!" Maxie continued to protest to the reporter.

Brown hesitated.

"Go ahead!" Hal repeated. "Spread it!"

Maxie had been fumbling with his bottle of aspirin tablets. He extracted one from the bottle and flipped it into his mouth. With a gulp he swallowed the dry pill. "You're crazy," he muttered. "Plain stark crazy!"

Further discussion of Hal's sanity was cut short by the cry of, "Board, all aboard!" which came faintly from the platform below.

"Thanks, Harrison," the reporter cried and scuttled for the door as the train began to roll.

Maxie flattened his nose gloomily against the pane and saw Brown racing across the station platform. "Now you've done it," he complained. "The fat's in the fire for sure. Why couldn't you have kept quiet? There's no point in making things worse than they are. They get bad fast enough!"

"How do I know that Martin hasn't been the cause of all the trouble we've been having en route?" Hal asked.

"How could Martin have done those things?" Maxie asked with disgust.

"You can frame anything these days if you know how to do it," Hal replied, "and you know it. That woman in Detroit who insisted I was the father of her unborn child could have been a plant of Martin's."

"I thought Higgins was through with us when that

broke," Maxie laughed. "Was he burned!" His smile faded. "The woman was a nut; Martin had nothing to do with it."

"How about the pest who wanted an X-ray of my throat?"

"She was just another nut."

"And the riot in Chicago? Those frenzied women who tried to tear me limb from limb. Who started the riot? Some women or woman who was planted in the crowd, of course. Women never acted like that before. And what did the papers call them?" he demanded. "'Hungry Hearts Seeking Their Dream Man,' " he repeated with disgust. "I tell you Martin has been trying to queer me all along the line and now he threatens to bring suit hoping in that way to keep me out of San Francisco. He's afraid of being shown up. He doesn't want to sue," he ended positively.

"Don't be too sure of that," Maxie protested. "Martin's always had a yen for money, your money."

"Well, he won't get it! I'll see to that! Trying to queer my tour and spike my guns with Higgins!"

"You're just loco on the subject of Martin. You know very well he had nothing to do with the young debutante in Cleveland who threatened to commit suicide unless you married her on the spot. And," Maxie raced on as Hal tried to argue, "do you think Martin is behind Mrs. Llewellyn Paxton and her crazy idea that you must play for that goofy Benefit of hers?"

"She's a nut, but she's perfectly harmless," he dismissed Mrs. Paxton. "I'm not talking about silly women. Just the ones who have tried to hold up the trip," Hal explained.

"And what of Mrs. Paxton's daughter?" Maxie demanded.

"A nit wit, just like her mother, only prettier, of course," Hal replied.

"You're wrong, definitely wrong." A voice startled them from the doorway. "She's prettier than her mother, I'll admit that, but she isn't like her mother, not a little bit. Mrs. Paxton is a flutterer, but the girl knows definitely what she is doing and gets it done. You don't suppose for a moment, do you, that the ingenious tricks pulled by those two women were the product of Mrs. Paxton's thoughts?"

It was Mary Dale who spoke. She was a blonde, slim and trim as a racing craft. Her soft husky voice and warm friendly eyes had made her the leader of the famous Dale Sisters Trio which had been associated with Hal from his early days. As Hal's popularity increased, the Dale Sisters became proportionately famous.

Hal smiled a welcome to her. "Come in," he invited.

"For a moment," she replied.

"Sit down," Maxie suggested. "You certainly polished off the Paxton women."

"I'd like to know the girl better," Mary said.

"Well, I wouldn't," Hal muttered. "She gets in my hair, and while we're on the subject," he gave Maxie a sharp look, "it's up to you to see that I'm not annoyed by either one of them again."

"I guess we've shaken them at last," Maxie said hopefully. "I didn't see them in Portland at all. They weren't at the station. They've probably given up."

"After having followed you across the country?" Mary cried. "Not if I know the type and I think I do. You'll hear from them again," she asserted positively.

"You learn about women from women," Hal told Maxie as he tried to stifle a yawn.

Mary jumped to her feet. "You're tired," she said. "I just dropped by before turning in to ask you how you liked the new number."

"It was fair," Hal replied. "It needs pepping up. You didn't seem to have your mind on your business tonight. We'll have a rehearsal in the morning."

Joe Stevens, Hal's pudgy arranger, poked his head in at the door and cried, "Listen to this, Hal." He began to hum a few lines.

Hal stopped him immediately, saying, "Joe, you're a musical pirate. That's not new! It's part of a Chopin waltz."

"Ha, ha!" a chorus of voices cried from the aisle. "We told you so!" Disgruntled, Joe Stevens turned from the door and shoved his way through the group.

Mary slipped away also, with a soft "good night" as they all wandered off to their berths. As Maxie closed the door something on the floor caught his eye. He had a mania for tidiness. He was constantly picking up after Hal, who carelessly dropped his things wherever they happened to fall. The boys laughed at Maxie but not even ridicule could change a lifelong habit of neatness. Bending forward, Maxie picked up the strip of paper. Perhaps it was the color of the paper or more likely it was the long string of letters which attracted his attention and was responsible for his reading the words which said:

KEEP HIM AWAY FROM SAN FRANCISCO

There was no doubt in Maxie's mind about the message of the telegram, part of which he held in his hand. He closed the door and handed the slip to Hal.

"Then there is a leak in the band," Hal cried. "Who is it?"

Maxie shrugged.

"Where did you get this?"

Maxie explained.

"Who was at the door?" Hal demanded.

"Mary, Joe, Buck, Charlie, Scat Miller and Tony. Oh yes, Jerry was there too but he was in the back."

"Well, Mary and Joe are out. It must be one of the others. Keep your eyes and ears open. Don't let on that we suspect anything and we'll catch whoever it is, cold. I don't want anyone who's mixed up with Martin in my orchestra."

"And after the royal way you treat the boys too," Maxie muttered. "I don't see how one of them could do it."

"Never mind that. I'm not looking for gratitude but I do expect loyalty as long as I pay them a salary. Forget it!

I'm turning in."

As they undressed, Maxie said thoughtfully, "I wish you hadn't spoken so openly to the reporter. It won't do no good."

"It's always a good idea, Maxie, to carry the fight to the other man's corner," Hal said with a grin. "Don't talk any more. I'm tired."

He spoke the truth. He was worn out. It was his first trip across the country with his famous Harmony Men. It had been a long series of one and two night stands playing to capacity houses, to say nothing of the curious public which dogged his steps wherever He went. Since his sudden rise to fame he had received thousands of requests for his photograph, but he had had no idea that in every village, hamlet and farm he was the phantom lover, the Prince Charming of the air. He knew that women liked him but until he made the trip he had no idea what their adoration could be like.

At heart Hal was an ordinary man with a fairly good singing voice. He had not planned to become a celebrity. When he left college he hoped to make some money, marry, settle down and raise a family. But fame, overtaking him unexpectedly, had spoiled his plans. At first he liked and enjoyed his popularity. Then it began to make his life involved. The money he made so quickly became a great responsibility in itself and necessitated his keeping a staff to look after his affairs.

As his fame increased, his private life vanished, taking his dreams with it. He became a public figure. No matter where he went he became the center of an eager, curious crowd. He once said to Maxie that he was heartily sick of seeing so many tonsils which were always on view as people gaped up at him, their mouths open.

There were times when he thought he would retire, he had enough money, but it wasn't as simple as that. There were about a hundred people who depended upon him for their livelihood. He knew he couldn't quit and leave them dangling in mid air looking for work. As long as the public demanded his particular talents he felt he must carry on.

There were times when he was very lonely in the midst of the crowds which constantly surrounded him. There is no warmth or companionship in a mob of people. Maxie was always with him and Maxie was all right but Maxie was a business man thinking of box office first, last and always. Hal wanted a home. He wanted real friends.

He had acquaintances, countless numbers of them, but they were just people who used him. He met hundreds of women, but they seemed to be interested in Hal Harrison the orchestra leader, the man with the dream voice rather than the Hal Harrison he knew still lived and waited behind the wall of publicity which had been built around him. Hal wanted some girl to love him for himself and not for what he had or represented.

Secretly, he was romantic enough to believe that some day, somewhere he would find the girl. His father had once said to him, "Son, when you find a woman who'll go through hell's fire for you, get married. If you'll take my advice, which I doubt, you'll wait. It's worth it. Your mother was like that."

Hal had waited. There were times when he thought he would go off alone somewhere and meet people as a plain ordinary man. He wanted to convince himself that he still had those qualities which make a person interesting to others because of what they are rather than what they do.

Before he fell asleep that night he thought of San Francisco, the romantic city of the West. All his life he had wanted to see the Golden Gate. It would take more than Phil Martin and a threat to keep him from realizing that dream.

Late the next afternoon before they pulled into Oakland, Maxie glumly handed Hal a copy of an early evening paper, saying, "Now, you've done it. Wait till Higgins sees that. He'll probably cancel our contract."

Hal smiled as he read the paper. It contained a

rehash of the old quarrel between himself and Phil Martin and ended with Hal's threat greatly enlarged and elaborated.

"What are you crabbing about?" Hal asked with an amused grin. "You're always looking for publicity, aren't you?"

"Yeah, but not this kind. Remember now, no matter what happens I want you to hold your temper, no fights."

"I'm rested, Maxie. I'll be good," Hal promised.

"Even if he calls you a sissy?" Maxie insisted because he knew that was the one thing that infuriated Hal more than anything else.

"Well—" Hal temporized.

"You don't want us to go on relief, do you?" Maxie asked.

"I'll be a good boy, Maxie. Don't worry about me. I had a good sleep. I'm feeling fine and just across the bay is the Golden Gate and one of the most romantic cities in the world."

Maxie peered through the window. Across the bay the slanting rays of sun painted buildings and housetops in a bath of orange gold. Behind the city the fog rolled in from the Pacific, trickled over the Twin Peaks, blocked out the sun and changed the golden light to drab gray.

"I don't like it," Maxie complained.

"But you haven't seen it. There are all sorts of things to do and see. I'm going to be very busy. I've always wanted to see Chinatown."

"I don't mean the city. I mean that fog bank rolling, in shutting out the sun. It's a warning. I wish we'd never come to this town. The minute I saw that cross eyed girl this morning at breakfast I knew we were heading for trouble," he replied dolefully.

"Forget it!" Hal was all agog as he watched the changing skyline across the bay.

"Do you think I ought to tell the police?" Maxie asked.

"Tell them what?"

"About the threat, of course!"

"We've nothing to worry about," Hal assured him brightly. "We weren't wrecked coming down. We'll be in the midst of a crowd of people once we get off the train."

"Yeah, but he might try to do something to you. You never can tell."

"Not Phil! He's too smart! He'll pick a nice quiet time when he'll be perfectly safe, that is, if he does anything at all, which I doubt."

"I wouldn't be too sure of myself if I were you," Maxie advised gloomily as he turned to direct the porter with their luggage.

"A murder might liven things up a bit," Hal suggested.

CHAPTER TWO

There hadn't been as much excitement in San Francisco since the opening of the bridges. Hal was impressed and pleased with his reception. Dave Fields, the manager of the Crystal Gardens, was in Oakland to meet him with some city officials.

When the ferry docked at the foot of Market Street, it took a determined police escort to get him safely from the boat to the waiting limousine. Not even the mobs in Detroit or St. Louis could compare with the horde of frenzied women eagerly waiting to catch a glimpse of him. While Hal was being delayed by the official reception Maxie and the band preceded him to the hotel.

From the Ferry Building to the Palace Hotel, Market Street was lined with curious crowds. Across the widest and busiest street Hal had ever seen, great banners swung from building to building. They read:

Tonight and Tomorrow Night
at the Crystal Gardens!
HAL HARRISON
and
HIS HARMONY MEN
In Person!

The police escort with sirens screaming cleared the way. They passed signs, placards, posters and huge billboards from which Hal's picture smiled down at the packed throngs lining the curbs. It was a great reception and a grand show. Hal bowed and smiled, outwardly pleased. Inwardly, however, he sighed. Two nights in San Francisco and then he'd return to the comparative peace and quiet of New York. Only two more days of being a goldfish, he kept assuring himself as they neared the hotel.

The police and hotel staff did their best to keep back the surging, excited autograph seekers, but in spite of their efforts Hal lost his topcoat and hat before gaining the security of the elevator on the ground floor.

When the lift stopped at the fourth floor, he heard the tinkling notes of a piano. He knew what that meant. The members of the band had preceded him from the station. Maxie would be holding one of his usual publicity receptions for the members of the press.

He was right. His suite was a mass of musicians and reporters. Joe Stevens, the pudgy arranger, was pounding out a new orchestration to give the assemblage color. Maxie, glum as usual, was like a spectre at the feast as he scurried about pouring conviviality to the members of the press.

Hal's appearance was greeted by a shout and a toast proposed by Jimmie Farr, crack reporter on San Francisco's leading paper, the Crescent.

In the next ten minutes, Jimmie Farr managed to get Hal into a corner and asked him if he had any statement to make relative to Phil Martin.

"None," Hal replied.

"Phil Martin says if you're looking for trouble, you'll get it," Farr offered suggestively.

"I'm not looking for trouble," Hal replied quietly. "There is no reason why my two night stand in San Francisco should cause any. I'll mind my business and if Martin keeps quiet, everything will be all right."

"Do you want to deny the statement published in the Portland paper?" Farr asked.

"No. Let that stand. I meant it. If you want to print something new say I'm looking forward to my stay in San Francisco and am happy to be here."

"How about that threatened suit of Martin's?" Farr asked.

"Just a bluff. Makes nice publicity," Hal replied.

"The old bologna, eh?" Farr grinned.

Hal's attention was diverted to a man who stepped up and called him by name. Always polite, Hal greeted the newcomer cordially. His quick temper flared the next minute, however, when he realized that the smooth stranger had just served him with a warrant in connection with Martin's suit.

"Then, it wasn't a bluff, after all," Farr chuckled.

"He'll wish it was!" Hal stormed. "I'd like to have my hands on him right now!"

"Easy, easy!" Maxie cautioned, rushing up. "Remember your promise."

"Promise be damned! Clear these people out of here. I want to think!"

"I'll be seeing you!" Farr flung over his shoulder as he made for the door.

Maxie was an excellent manager. He knew when to do as he was told. He began moving the guests toward the door. In a few minutes the sitting room was comparatively empty. With a sigh of relief Hal sank into an easy chair. Joe Stevens was still pounding away at the piano. He paused for a moment, looked across at Hal and asked, "How do you like this?"

His fingers rippled over the keys as he vamped into a chorus.

Hal listened attentively for a moment, then shook his head wearily. "It's always been good, Joe. Verdi wrote it first. Try something that isn't quite as well known, for a change."

Joe crashed to an annoyed end.

Maxie offered Hal a telegram. "I knew it. You've gotta be more careful. Higgins is warning you to keep clear of unsavory publicity."

"Nice of Higgins! I'll be good," Hal promised with a grin as he returned the telegram. "Better have dinner sent up," he suggested.

"And you'd better be getting dressed. We haven't much time. Boy! We'll need the reserves to get you out of here!" He simmered with enthusiasm. Maxie never boiled about anything but his own ailments. "What a town! What a town! I wouldn't be surprised if we do seven grand tonight!"

"I thought you didn't like this town," Hal teased.

"I don't feel right about it, but business is business and we're here to make money. I have a feeling we're headed for trouble, the cross eyed dame, the fog and all. Maybe, if you'll just keep your head, we won't have no trouble. Remember your promise," he cautioned as Hal rose from the chair, pulled off his coat, slung it on the couch and began to undress as he advanced toward a door. "This my room?" he asked.

Maxie nodded.

Hal's shirt was already off as he opened the door. For one unbelieving moment he paused, then recoiled as if stung. He blinked twice to be sure that his eyes had not played him a trick. Mary had been right, after all. There could be no doubt of it. Mrs. Llewellyn Paxton, glistening with diamonds, wearing a smart tailored suit, Paris hat, her mink coat thrown open, was standing in the middle of his bedroom floor. And to make matters worse she stood there in his very own pet fleece lined bedroom slippers. His eyes held on those slippers a moment as a wave of anger and resentment flashed over him. Hal hated people to use his personal things. Boiling mad, his eyes flashed back to her face.

She gave him a placating smile. "Hello," she purred, "my feet were simply killing me!" She pointed down with a vague fluttering gesture before his wrath exploded.

"Get out of my slippers!" he bellowed. "And get out of this room!"

Mrs. Paxton reacted to the angry orders immediately. With a gasp of amazement she leaped clear of the slippers. They were elevens. She plumped to the floor. She winced with sudden pain, then turned on Hal, her anger nearly matching his. "Don't shout at me, young man!" she cried. "I won't move a step until you—"

"I'm not going to play for your Hands Across the Sea Benefit! For the hundredth time—No!" he shouted, thoroughly incensed.

Maxie came bustling to the door. "What's the matter?" he asked.

"Didn't I tell you to keep that woman away from me! Get her out of here!" Hal bellowed. "Do something to earn your money!" He stepped back into the sitting room and slammed the door with a bang, enclosing Maxie and Mrs. Paxton in his bedroom.

He leaned against the wall and groaned. Joe Stevens looked across at him from the piano and asked, "Woman?"

"Yes."

"Boy, you've got what it takes!" he said enviously.

"You can have it!" Hal said bitterly. "I can't even have privacy in my bedroom!"

Maxie opened the door, fanning himself with his hat. "Okay, Hal. The dame's gone."

"See anything of her nit wit daughter?" Hal demanded.

Maxie denied the daughter's existence with a shake of his head.

"Are you sure?" Hal insisted.

"Positive. Get dressed, will ya?"

"I expect you to protect me from such things," Hal said as he strode across the room.

"I try. I didn't know she was in there. How could I? I can't do everything, be everywhere," Maxie complained.

"You sound like a woman," Hal scoffed.

"And you promised to hold your temper," Maxie retorted.

"What would you do if you found a woman you hated standing in your slippers?" Hal growled.

"I know," Joe Stevens said with an amused chuckle. "He'd faint."

Hal paused at the door. "Call the manager and tell him he's got to get me out of here through some alley. I'll be ready in ten minutes."

"But dinner!" Maxie protested. "I've ordered it!"

"Cancel the order. We'll eat at the Gardens. You arrange to get me out of here. I can't stand the sight of another woman right now!" The bang of his door gave added emphasis to the statement.

Mrs. Paxton had begun her attentions in New York when she tried to persuade Hal that he should play for her Hands Across the Sea Benefit. Hal had refused then but Mrs. Paxton had not believed him. Her persistency was most annoying. She asked him again and again until he hated the very sight of her. The one thing Hal did not know about Mrs. Paxton was the fact that she had made a bet with some of her friends that she could get Hal Harrison to play for her Benefit and she wouldn't have to pay a cent for his services.

Hal fumed about Mrs. Paxton as he dressed. It was twenty minutes rather than ten before everything was arranged for Hal's exit from the hotel. One of the musicians was to wear Hal's familiar camel hair coat. With collar turned up and hat brim pulled down over his face, the musician was to brave the crowds in the lobby and on the street. Hal, alone, was to go down in the service elevator and out through the alley to a waiting car.

When Hal and his double were ready, Maxie peered cautiously into the corridor. The musician stepped into the hall followed by Maxie and moved toward the elevators. When the lift door closed behind them Hal flashed down the corridor and popped into the waiting service elevator. The door closed promptly. The lift started with a jerk.

Hal gave a low moan when he saw that he was not alone with the operator. Mrs. Paxton's lovely daughter had him cornered! She was really a beautiful, glamorous girl but Hal was too provoked to see or think of anything but the fact that the Paxtons had outwitted him again.

Joan Paxton folded her arms and regarded him appraisingly as he tried to ignore her presence. A soft ermine wrap fell away from her smoothly rounded shoulders, revealing a slim body in a pale blue evening gown. A silver slippered foot took a step toward Hal.

"Stay away from me!" he cried. Then, "Let me out of here!" he bellowed at the operator.

A dangerous glint appeared in the girl's eyes as she seized the lapels of his coat. "Afraid, eh? Well, you don't get out of here until I say so. We're riding up and down together, you and I until you promise to play for Mother's Benefit. Remember, I've followed you and her three thousand miles and have been forced to look at you and your banjo eyed public until I'm sick to death of the sight of both of you."

He was impressed by her grim determination. He knew, and knew that she knew, that he could get out of the lift if he wanted to do so badly enough. He didn't want to get out for a moment at least. She had flecked him on the raw with her last remark. "Banjo eyed, eh?" he repeated.

"That's what I said. And I've had enough of it. Now if you'll just give me your—"

"I said 'No' in New York. I repeated it in Buffalo, I shouted it in Chicago. I had you both arrested in Cleveland, and detained as a public nuisance in Salt Lake City. Do you know what I'm going to do here?" he demanded threateningly.

"Say 'Yes,'" she breathed hopefully, ignoring his serious manner.

"No!" he cried. "Do I have to put it in writing?"

The car reached the basement and started on another upward trip. "You've got to play at Mother's Benefit!" she repeated desperately. "We can't get married until after you've played for it."

He stepped back, alarmed. The girl was really mad. "Married!" he repeated.

The car bumped, stopped and started down. Hal grabbed the operator by the arm. "If you don't open that door when we reach the bottom, I'll have you fired. I'll have you boiled in oil, or better yet I'll take a good sock at you. You don't want to force me to marry a mad woman, do you?"

Joan glared at him. "You certainly hate yourself, don't you? Marry you! Why, I wouldn't marry you if—"

"If I were the last man on earth," he finished the quotation, dimly aware by this time that she was extraordinarily pretty as she stood facing him, eyes flashing.

"Well, I wouldn't! I don't like your looks! I don't like your band and I don't like your public! And I think your voice is terrible!" she added as an afterthought.

"I'm sorry," he said, concealing his secret amusement. "I didn't know you cared."

"The conceit of you!" she stormed. "I don't!"

The car bumped to a stop. The bewildered operator glanced at Joan.

"Let him out!" she ordered.

Hal stepped aside for her to leave the car first.

"Why can't you be reasonable?" she argued. Her mood changed to a softer note as she explained, "I didn't mean all the things I said about you. I suppose you're all right in your own way. I'm not after you, really. I want to get Mother settled. I can't do a thing while she's gallivanting all over the country."

"But you said those things. You must have thought them whether you meant them or not. They can't be taken back. You can't recall the spoken word."

"Very well, I'm sorry."

"I suppose you're excited and upset about the man back in New York. What you really want is for me to help you get married, is that it?" he asked.

"I don't want to get married," she denied.

"But you just said—" He stopped and faced her.

"I said there was a man in New York who wanted to marry me," she flashed back.

"That's understandable. Why don't you go back to New York and marry him?" he snapped.

"It's none of your business and you don't need to throw me a few back handed compliments. The man in question happens to be another of Mother's ideas. She picked him out. As you may have guessed, my mother is a very determined person once she makes up her mind."

"I'll say she is," he replied grimly.

Joan giggled. His remark was so heartfelt. "I know how to handle Mother—and the man," she added. "She keeps urging, he keeps asking and I continue to say 'No' to both of them. They wait hopefully. You see, the reason I want to get this Benefit thing settled is this: I won't be able to travel, marry someone I love or have a moment's peace until your corny band has played for the Benefit."

To tell an orchestra leader that his band is corny is like waving a red flag at a bull. Her remark was most unfortunate. He had been softening toward her, feeling a little sorry for her, but his old anger flared.

"Corny?" he echoed indignantly. "I'll never play your Benefit. And that's final. You can die an old maid, for all I care." He jerked at a door which faced them at the end of the corridor.

"Of all the unreasonable, stubborn—" she cried.

He stepped through the door. She tried to follow him. He shoved her back gently, saying, "This is the end of the line." He let the door close between them. He sprinted down the alley.

Joan pounced out of the door and darted after him. She caught his flying coat tails as he stepped on the running board of the waiting car.

"Not so fast!" she cried.

"Let go of me!" he stormed.

"Do you take me with you or do I scream?" she challenged.

"Go ahead and scream," he said indifferently.

"You asked for it," she replied. "And wait till your public hears about you waylaying an innocent girl in a dark alley!"

She took a deep breath. Her chest swelled. Her mouth opened but the threatened cry died unborn. Hal suddenly remembered that telegram from his sponsor, Higgins. His hand went over her mouth just in time. He pushed her into the car.

She sat back and watched the road as they were whisked along.

"You understand that I don't intend to have you tagging along behind me all evening," he said, exasperated by her sullen silence.

"I'm just as determined as my mother. You've got to give in."

"No!" he shouted and burrowed into the corner of the seat.

A mile from the Crystal Gardens they were caught in a traffic jam. For that night, at least, all San Francisco seemed Hal Harrison conscious. The roads were blocked with cars. Harried police tried to hold back the mobs and clear the traffic snarls at intersections.

After one very long wait, Hal leaned out of the car and called to a policeman. "I'm Hal Harrison. Can you get me through?"

"Yeah?" the policeman retorted. "Well, personally, I'm the Sultan of Siam and—" He stopped in mid speech as he compared Hal's eager face peering out of the car with the same countenance which smiled down at him from a nearby poster tacked to a telegraph pole. He blew his whistle shrilly and waved down the line of cars.

In a few minutes, with a motorcycle clearing the way, they crawled toward the Gardens. A brilliantly illuminated sign ran the full length of the world's largest dance palace, reading:

FOR TWO NIGHTS ONLY . . . HAL HARRISON IN PERSON!

As the car crept to the entrance of the jammed parking lot, two policemen boarded it, trying to ward off the people who ran up to flatten their noses against the windows. Hal glanced at the girl.

She said, "Beautiful spectacle, isn't it? There's something about the human nose when flattened that—"

"But have you ever noticed their tonsils," he asked, "or their adenoids? Much more interesting."

She made no effort to conceal her contempt for his gaping public.

A long line of eager customers snaked away from the box office waiting their turn to buy tickets. It was a good natured crowd shoving and jostling as it strove to hold its place.

"Look at your public," she scoffed as the crowd surged forward. A woman tripped and fell. She screamed in terror as it seemed inevitable that she would be crushed under the advancing feet. Quick hands yanked her upright.

The car crawled to a stop at the roped entrance. Hal stepped out, followed by Joan. "I'll leave you here," he said.

Her reply was drowned in shouts of, "There he is!" There was a great shout, a combination of ohs and ahs. Hal's face broke into a wide, prop smile. A schoolgirl ducked under the restraining rope and ran to his side, breathlessly asking for an autograph. Hastily he scribbled in her book, then started for the door. He bowed and smiled and waved his hand as he advanced toward the entrance.

Joan was at his heels. "That's right," she sneered, "eat it up!"

He glared at her for a split second, then dashed up the remaining steps as the rope strained under the heavy load of pushing, shoving humanity. Joan sped after him. "Do you play the Benefit?" she demanded.

"I do not!" He turned to the special policeman guarding the door and said, "There's ten dollars in it if you'll keep this woman out of my hair. She's just escaped from her keeper."

"Oh," cried Joan, "I could kill you for that."

Hal glanced at the policeman. "You see? She's absolutely violent."

The policeman's burly arm caught Joan as she tried to follow Hal through the door. "Be a good girl and go home or I'll have to run you in," he warned.

"I won't go home!" she flared.

He took a good look at her ermine wrap and said, "If I see you and that white overcoat around here again, I'll lock you up for disturbing the peace. A nice girl like you ought to be ashamed!"

Joan was defeated for the moment and beat a hasty retreat. She had a plan but it would have to wait until her mother arrived.

At the entrance Hal was greeted effusively by Dave Fields, the husky owner of the dance palace. Fields face broke into a broad grin as he pumped Hal's hand. "Welcome!" he cried, and then, "Have I fixed things for you?"

Hal looked over the gaily decorated entrance. "You've spread yourself, Dave. It looks fine. I see you've even decorated yourself. You shouldn't have done that." Fields' hand went to his discolored right eye. "What did you do, run into a door?" Hal teased.

"As a matter of fact, that's exactly what I did do, only nobody believes me," Fields replied as he fingered the sore spot under his eye.

"They never do," Hal agreed with a laugh.

Inside the hall, Hal was greeted with loud applause. Debs from Nob Hill were rubbing elbows with the girls from Woolworth's as Fields led him to the table which was reserved for him and the other band leaders of the city whom he had invited to be his guests. The hall was packed. Waiters wormed their way through the crowded aisles while bus boys rapidly set up an extra row of tables on the edge of the dance floor, a thing unheard of at Crystal Gardens.

"Where were you?" Maxie demanded. "I thought you had been kidnaped."

"Same thing," Hal explained briefly. "Where's my dinner? I'm hungry."

At a signal from Maxie, waiters began serving a simple meal. Fields left to superintend activities.

Hal was enjoying his steak when a voice burst upon his ear. "Now, Mr. Harrison, about my Benefit—"

Mrs. Paxton and Joan were standing beside him. Joan gave him a triumphant smile. With one comprehensive glance he knew how she had passed the policeman at the door. Instead of her ermine wrap, she wore Mrs. Paxton's mink. She had also twisted a scarf over her silky hair.

Hal ignored them and said tersely to Maxie, "Call the cops!"

"If you have me arrested again—" Mrs. Paxton began.

Maxie looked at her sadly. "Listen, lady. The jails in this town are terrible. Won't you please scram? We don't want no trouble, but you're asking for it. Is it the cops or —"

Mrs. Paxton sniffed, beckoned to a waiter and trailed off.

Hal's table began to fill before he had finished his dinner. Phil Martin, the Crystal Gardens' own maestro, sauntered up. For a moment the crowd hushed, waiting, hoping to see a row right then and there. Hal greeted Phil cordially and invited him to sit down. With a cocky, self assured smile, Martin seated himself in full view of the audience. The others came quickly after that. Chubby Carlton, Rex Kingford, Chick Stoner and several lesser luminaries arrived. There was an air of tense expectancy about the group as they drank quietly.

Maxie tried his utmost to dispel the weighted atmosphere. "Remember your promise," he whispered to Hal as he passed beside him.

Hal nodded.

Rex Kingford, tall, thin and suave, had had his eye on Phil Martin's spot at the Gardens for a long time. Kingford knew he was a better band leader than Martin, but San Francisco and Dave Fields, the manager of the Gardens, had failed to recognize the fact. Kingford made no effort to conceal his interest in Martin and Hal. Martin, for all his debonair attitude, was nervous in the presence of the man he so widely imitated. To cover his feelings, he drank steadily.

Kingford looked over the hall with an appreciative eye and asked acidly, "Don't you wish you could pull 'em in like this, Phil?"

"You'd be satisfied with my audiences," Martin retorted.

"Let's keep personalities out of this, Kingford," Hal suggested hastily.

"Might as well try to keep bees from honey," the cherub faced Chubby Carlton chuckled.

Dave Fields hastened to the table. His face was beaming. He rubbed his big hands together with satisfaction as he stood and surveyed the packed house. "How do you like our place, Hal?" he asked and then turned to Maxie. "Didn't I tell you we'd pack them in?"

Dave Fields asked many questions but he never waited for an answer. His questions were punctuations in a monologue. With his habitual lack of tact, he threw his next question at Phil Martin. "When are you going to be as good as Harrison?" He chuckled as he winked at Maxie. "I hear the boys are calling you 'The Number Two Company.'"

"When you—" Martin started to reply but was interrupted by a round of clapping from the audience. The Harmony Men were trooping onto the bandstand across the hall.

As the applause died down, Hal said to Fields, "You've certainly got a friendly house here, Dave. It must be capacity."

Phil Martin looked up from his glass and said sourly, "It is. All my friends are out to get a load of you imitating me!"

"Cut it out!" Hal warned quietly.

"So you don't like it?" Martin sneered. "The truth hurts, does it?"

"Wait until you're sober," Hal advised.

"What are you afraid of?" Martin went on. "Was that statement in the paper just a lot of your usual hot air?"

"Cut it," Hal warned a second time, his voice edgy.

"Now, now," Maxie stepped into the gap, "remember where you are."

"I know where I am," Martin retorted. "And where I ought to be if it wasn't for that double crossing—"

"Easy, Phil." Dave Fields' deep voice growled a warning.

Maxie, sensing what was coming, took an aspirin and was gulping it down as Martin replied, "He fired me the minute he began to get the breaks and then he stole my style of singing. Why, even his band copies mine!" he cried.

Hal rose to his feet and shook off Maxie's restraining arm. Several reporters circled the table listening. "You know why you were fired from my band and you know why I've never mentioned the reason. Would you like me to break that silence?"

"Because you double crossed me with—"

"Don't say it!" Hal threatened.

"The purity boy doesn't want dirty publicity, does he?" Martin taunted.

"I gave you a beating when I fired you and if you say what you were going to say, I'll finish the job I started then. If you want it, just start something." Hal's eyes were flashing as he leaned over Martin.

Fields grabbed Hal by the arms. "Forget it! No fighting here. Do you want to ruin the show?" He tugged at Hal. "They're waiting for you. You'd better get going. We do a sustaining broadcast at eight thirty."

He led Hal to the floor. Hal's drummer, on the watch for their entrance, rolled the drums. Dave advanced to the center of the floor. With hands upraised to command silence he shouted, "Ladies and Gentlemen! I give you the one and only Hal Harrison!"

There was a tremendous burst of applause as Hal, bowing, crossed to the bandstand.

"What an ovation!" Chick Stoner shouted to the other band leaders at the table.

Phil Martin's darkly handsome face was sulky. "What's he got that we haven't got?" he asked bitterly.

"Nerve and a couple of million dollars!" Chubby Carlton answered.

"Are you going over to take your bow, Phil?" Rex Kingford asked.

"I suppose I'll have to do it or be called a sorehead," Martin grumbled. "I've half a mind to tell that crowd about the dirty—"

"You overestimate your mental capacity," Chubby Carlton taunted good naturedly. "Why don't you tell the crowd? You wouldn't want these people to think you were a sore head. Just tell them why you hate Harrison."

"You mind your own business!" Martin jumped to his feet snarling.

"Sit down, you fool!" Dave Fields ground into his ear as he pushed him back into his chair.

Martin grumbled to silence.

Across the hall the Harmony Men were ready. Hal, adjusting the microphone to his height, glanced at the control room where the announcer was introducing the program. Hal, while waiting, took his first comprehensive look at the Crystal Gardens. It was the largest razzle dazzle resort he had ever seen, done in the latest style of modern architecture. The room was a great oblong. The special features included hanging balconies on all four sides with private deluxe accommodations, a dance floor equipped with indirect lighting, a receding roof which lifted gently and slid out of sight, a moving bandstand which rolled silently out onto the light studded floor.

There was an expectant hush over the auditorium as Hal with baton lifted waited the sound engineer's okay. Suddenly the red bulb beside the microphone glowed. Hal's baton came down and the Harmony Men swung into their famous signature.

In a moment the floor was filled with gently swaying couples who seemed to be gliding on an inverted sky as they revolved over the light studded floor. In two minutes, hundreds of couples were jammed into a slowly undulating mob at Hal's feet.

During the second number, Joan whirled up in the arms of an awe struck youth and planted herself directly in front of Hal. She kept demanding, "When are you going to give in?" The young man stared at her as Hal shook his head grimly and looked off across the hall.

The crowd would not be satisfied. They demanded more and more at the end of each number. The demand for encores grew tiresome. In desperation Hal called his trio down, the famous Dale Sisters, headed by Mary. They sang the final chorus.

During the short intermissions between dance numbers, the bars were busy. Laughter and excited chatter rippled through the great building. At eleven o'clock, when the boys were badly in need of a rest, Hal announced a special number.

"You must keep off the floor," he warned. "This is a show feature and your own maestro, Phil Martin, has promised to take a bow and sing a chorus for us."

As Phil Martin stepped to the floor, there was a good natured cheer and a spattering of applause. Phil crossed directly to the stand. Hal stepped to one side, giving the stage center to Phil. With a nod from Hal, the music started. The house lights began to dim until only the exit signs glowed in the darkness. A baby blue spot centered on the floor, picked up the members of the chorus, as the girls danced in, swaying in rhythm to the waltz tune. Then Phil Martin's voice, sweet and surprisingly clear, added a final touch to the caressing music. He had never sung as well.

Hal moved across the platform to the outer edge to give Phil the complete spot when the lights would come up. As he neared the edge of the platform he felt a tug on his trouser leg and Joan's voice demanded, "Are you going to say 'Yes'?"

"Quiet!" he whispered.

The next instant Joan had scrambled to the stand beside him. "Promise," she insisted.

"No!"

"Then I'll make a scene and they'll say you did it on purpose because Martin was singing so well," she threatened.

"I don't like men who beat women," Hal growled in a heavy whisper, "but I'm beginning to understand why they do it. I'd like to take a sock at you right now."

Joan giggled. "Why don't you? It would be wonderful publicity."

"Pipe down, will you?" Hal cautioned as the Dale Sisters swung into the second chorus, their rich voices harmonizing with the rippling music. The chorus went on with their ballet routine. The Dale Sisters finished and moved away. Phil Martin took the next chorus alone, his voice rich, caressing and powerful until it stopped suddenly with a startled, gasping, throat closing "Uggh!" Coming over the microphone it sounded like clotted surprise.

Always on the alert for the unexpected in connection with his orchestra, Hal sprang forward before the strange gurgle had died away. In the dim blue light coming from the spots on the floor he could see Martin's body beginning to sag. With outstretched arms, Hal caught Martin as he gave a final slump, swung him around toward his tenor sax, Scat Miller, and whispered, "Take care of him! I think he fainted."

Being a showman first, last and always, it was only a moment later that Hal's voice filled the crowded room with its haunting quality as he picked up the song that had died on Martin's lips. Women sighed and snuggled a little closer to their partners. Men returned the pressure of trembling fingers as Hal's voice drifted slowly away, lingering in memory only. With the last bars of the music the chorus vanished into the darkness. There was tremendous applause. The lights came on slowly, almost reluctantly, as the girls pranced back to take their bow to the unending applause. Hal beckoned to the Dale Sisters, who took a bow. Then he swung round hoping that Martin had recovered.

Martin was on Scat Miller's lap, head sagged forward, body careening tipsily. Hal motioned to Scat to get Martin on his feet. Scat tried. Martin's body stretched across his lap. Scat moved his hands, gave a startled cry and jumped from his seat. Martin's body slid to the floor, falling with a dull, echoing thud. Hal stepped back quickly, aghast at what he saw.

Mary Dale had moved down front. She covered her eyes and screamed. Her voice, amplified by the microphone, shrilled, echoing and reechoing through the hall.

The crowd jumped to its feet and surged forward.

Hal leaped into action before panic could spread. "Get him out!" he cried to two of his men. "The rest of you play. Now! Swing it out!"

As the body was carried behind the stand, only those people in the vanguard of the onrushing mob could see the thin knife protruding from Martin's back.

CHAPTER THREE

Hal kept the band playing. The floor filled with dancers. Some of the people who had surged forward toward the stand after Mary's scream began to mix with the dancers; the others, eagerly morbid for further details, moved off after the body, which was being carried into Fields' luxurious office on the corridor at the rear of the building near the bandstand.

Fields dashed up, tossing the curious aside as he crammed his bulk through the door just ahead of Johnson, who was in charge of the special detail of police sent out to the Gardens to preserve order. Maxie rushed in just as the two musicians laid the body face down on the floor.

"What happened?" Johnson demanded.

"I don't know, but it looks like murder to me," one of the musicians replied, pointing at the knife handle protruding from Martin's back.

"What an escape!" Maxie exclaimed.

"Escape? He's dead, ain't he? What are you talking about?" Fields demanded.

"I meant Hal," Maxie replied, and took an aspirin. "That knife was meant for Harrison!"

"What's that?" Johnson demanded.

"Don't ask questions! Do something!" Fields shouted. "Get the murderer! Do you want to ruin my business?"

"Who did it?" Johnson asked Maxie.

"I dunno nothing about it. Ask Harrison, he was out there," Maxie replied evasively.

"Go get him!" Johnson ordered.

"No! No!" Fields shouted. "He must keep playing or the crowd will wreck this place!"

Johnson began barking orders to several of his men who had managed to follow him to the room. "It's murder!" he cried. "Stop anyone who tries to leave the hall! Keep the band playing! Get a doctor! Call Inspector Burke at once!"

The officer who had been instructed to get a doctor used his head wisely and made his way toward Hal on the front of the bandstand.

Although Hal had attempted to conceal the murder, there had been some people near the stand who had actually seen the knife in Martin's back. The news ran through the building like wildfire, passing from group to group, from table to table. "Martin's been murdered! Martin's been murdered!" The words were passed along until they reached the crowd on the outside of the building. Several people hurried toward the exits, but were turned back by Johnson's men, who began blocking the doors.

As the officer approached Hal he called, "We need a doctor! See if there is one in the house!"

Hal brought the number to a close and made a short announcement: "Is there a doctor in the house, please? If so, go to Fields' office on the side corridor. The waiters will show you the way. Hurry, please! Phil Martin has had a sudden heart attack. Will the balance of you keep dancing or return to your tables?"

There were some unbelieving jeers from the crowd, which were lost in the quick rush of the music as Hal returned to leading the band.

With callous indifference, most of the people continued to dance. There were, however, many who followed the policeman back to the area near the office and pressed against the rope which had been strung up to keep the crowds back.

The doctor was finishing his examination when Inspector Burke, gruff and blustery, arrived with assistants and a stenographer to make notes. Burke's series of questions were as sharp and rapid as the rattle of a machine gun. In a few minutes, he had things moving rapidly.

His questions bore immediate results. He sent for Kingford, Stoner and Chubby Carlton. He dispatched two men to search Martin's apartment, telling them to hurry back. He refused to permit Maxie to leave the room. Mary Dale, her face white and strained, came in and sat in a big chair. Scat Miller, looking a little ill and whiter than ever, stood near the door. Dave Fields paced up and down in front of his desk, where Burke's assistant was busy taking notes. When the band leaders were brought in Burke snapped, "That's enough for a starter."

"We have three people who tried to get away from the building. What'll I do with them?" Johnson asked.

"I'll attend to them later," Burke answered. He turned to Fields and demanded, "Why was he murdered?"

"How do I know?" Fields answered with one of his habitual questions.

"You knew him pretty well, didn't you?" Burke snapped.

"Would I pay him six hundred a week, if I didn't?" Fields retorted.

"Come on, Fields, don't hedge!" Burke urged. "Tell me what you know and don't ask questions. That's my job."

"Do I know any more than the rest?" Fields replied. "Is it right for me to be saying things that may hurt innocent people?"

"What things? What people?" Burke barked.

"Anything, anybody," Fields grumbled.

"Did Martin have any enemies?"

"Don't all band leaders have enemies?" Fields asked.

Burke tried to be patient. "What sort of enemies?" he insisted.

"Other band leaders, of course. Aren't they all jealous of each other?"

"You've got a nerve to say a thing like that," Chubby Carlton spoke up indignantly.

"Who are you?" Burke asked.

"Carlton, a band leader."

Burke swung back to Fields. "Come on, be specific," he ordered.

"It don't seem right, just the same," Fields protested.

"I'll be the judge of that. What did you mean when you said he had enemies?"

"Well, Kingford and Martin didn't get along, doesn't . . .?"

Kingford interrupted to shout, "Is that so? You were always fighting with him yourself!"

"Oh, you were, were you?" Burke hammered at Fields.

"Sure, sure," Fields agreed. "That's right. Doesn't everybody have arguments with musicians? Ask Maxie here, he knows that." He pointed a finger at Maxie.

"Keep me out of it!" Maxie cried.

Fields' remark gave Johnson an idea. He stepped forward and whispered something in Burke's ear. Burke nodded and then went back to questioning Fields. "What did you argue and quarrel about?" he demanded.

"Music, numbers, floor show and all that sort of thing. Aren't all artists temperamental?"

"Was it temperament that gave you that black eye?" Kingford challenged.

Fields rubbed the discolored eye tenderly with his finger. The skin had been broken and was crusting with blood. He winced as his finger touched the sore and cried, "Didn't I run into a door? Doesn't everybody know that?"

"I heard different. You had a row with Martin and he socked you," Kingford accused.

Fields spread his great hands under Burke's eyes. "Look! I could break Martin in pieces with my two hands. Would I let him sock me?"

"Did he try it?" Burke's question startled Fields, who replied, "It was a door, I tell you."

"Where were you at the time of the murder?" Burke went on.

"I was on the way to my office when I heard his voice break right in the middle of the song. I ran out front to see what had happened."

"Did anyone see you?" Burke asked.

"How do I know? Did I know there had been a murder? Was I thinking of an alibi? I was worrying about my business and the success of my show. I wanted to know what had happened."

"And you found out?" Burke suggested.

"Not then. Harrison was singing when I got round to the front. Everything seemed to be all right until the lights came on and I saw Martin on that fellow's lap." He pointed toward Scat Miller.

"But you didn't do anything about it, did you?" Burke insisted.

"No."

"Why not? Didn't you realize that there was something wrong with Martin?"

"Sure I realized that."

"Then why didn't you take some action?"

"A lot of reasons. Martin had been drinking heavily. He was sore. He and Harrison had had a fight."

"What about?"

"Everybody knows there was bad blood between them."

Maxie jumped to his feet and protested loudly, "You can't say things like that, Fields!"

"Sit down!" Burke barked at Maxie.

"Fields is right," Johnson offered. "There was something in the paper about a row between Harrison and Martin. Martin was going to sue Harrison for a million dollars and Harrison threatened him."

"It was newspaper stuff, publicity!" Maxie cried.

"Quiet!" Burke growled.

"Shall I put him out?" Johnson asked.

"No. They give themselves away in a crowd like this," Burke answered. He turned to Fields. "What do you know about this feud between Martin and Harrison?"

"He can tell you more about it. He's Harrison's manager." Fields evaded the question by throwing it to Maxie.

"Tell me." Burke swung on Maxie.

"Martin has been sore at Harrison ever since he was fired from the Harmony Men," Maxie replied.

"But what about this suit for a million dollars?" Burke insisted.

"You see it's like this—" Maxie floundered for words. "Martin was a good band man but he didn't have the stuff to make a leader. He was never satisfied while he was with us and when Harrison caught him in something shady he fired him."

"What had Martin done?"

"I dunno. Harrison never told me."

"But what has all this to do with the suit for a million dollars?"

"I'm trying to tell you if you'll let me. Martin got his own orchestra together and finally located out here. He's been doing Harrison's stuff and he's been doing it so long now that he thinks he's the one who originated the idea. He's been claiming that Harrison copies him and it's just the other way around. That's what the suit was about, but it was only a bluff to try and scare Harrison, to keep him away from San Francisco. That's all."

"Harrison was served with papers tonight. It says so in the *Crescent*," Johnson cut in.

"Oh, it does, does it?" Burke said gleefully. "I guess we're getting hot!"

"But the knife was meant for Harrison!" Maxie cried. "They killed the wrong man."

"What are you talking about?" Burke demanded.

Maxie told him about the arrival of the telegram in Portland and the threat which it carried. Since Burke listened so attentively, Maxie told him about the slip of paper he found in the car corridor. "There's someone in the orchestra who is in league with Martin," he stated. "Harrison isn't afraid of the suit. He can stand on his own. It won't hurt him a bit but it would show Martin up for the imitator he really is. What does Harrison care about a lawsuit of that kind? Why should he kill a man over a suit he does not fear? On the other hand, Martin knew he would lose the suit and for that reason wanted Harrison out of the way. Don't you see it?" he ended eagerly.

"No, I don't," Burke replied.

"Look! It was dark up there on the platform. The murderer wasn't sure which man was which. The knife intended for Harrison was plunged into Martin."

"Umm." Burke considered.

"It could happen that way," Johnson suggested.

"Sure it could," Fields added.

"Have you located the person in the orchestra who received the message which you think came from Martin?" Burke asked.

"No, and I've been watching them all carefully too."

"You say Harrison was up there at the time of the murder?"

"Yes. He just steps to one side when a guest star is singing because he has to take over as soon as the number is finished."

"Who was near Martin and Harrison at the time of the murder?"

Maxie hesitated to answer that question.

"The musicians," Johnson answered. "The men in the front row of the band were the nearest. That fellow was directly behind Martin. He was the one who was holding Martin's body when the lights came up." He pointed at Scat Miller.

"Why did you knife him?" Burke demanded of Miller.

Scat, already pale, turned whiter and gulped.

"Come on!" Burke insisted.

"I didn't knife him. Harrison shoved the body toward me and told me to hold it. He said Martin had fainted. That's all I know."

"Didn't you try to do anything for Martin?"

"How could I in the dark? I just held him."

"Didn't you know it wasn't a faint? Couldn't you tell the man was dying?"

"I never saw anyone die. I didn't know. Martin was so still. I believed Harrison."

"Tried to steer me away from Harrison, did you?" Burke demanded of Maxie. "Where's this Harrison?" he bellowed.

"He's leading the band," Fields replied.

"Bring him in!" Burke ordered.

"But, Inspector," Fields pleaded, "if the band stops, this crowd will go wild on our hands. They know something's wrong. The band must keep playing!"

"Wait a minute!" Burke recalled the policeman who had opened the door letting in a burst of dance music. He turned to the others and asked, "Can any of you lead this band?"

Kingford, Stoner and Carlton jumped to their feet.

"I can," Kingford said eagerly.

"Sure he can," Chubby Carlton said. "He's always wanted to play here."

"Which one are you?" Burke asked Kingford.

"Rex Kingford."

"You're the fellow who didn't get along with Martin, eh? Where were you when Martin was murdered?"

"I don't know when he was murdered," Kingford replied, refusing to fall into Burke's trap.

"You heard him gasp, didn't you?"

"Yes."

"Well, where were you at that moment?"

"At the table with these men." He pointed hopefully toward the other band leaders.

"That right?" Burke asked.

There was a moment of hesitant silence.

"Was he with you or not?" Burke demanded.

Chick Stoner spoke. "He left the table the first time Martin sang. He may have come back but I don't know. You see, Inspector, the room was dark and I was watching the floor show."

"How about you?" Burke asked Chubby.

Substantially Carlton agreed with Stoner. If Kingford had a genuine alibi, it was ruined by the darkness of the room.

"You saw me, Dave," Kingford cried desperately.

"I don't remember," Dave Fields answered. "Do you think I was looking at you with all the things I had on my mind? I don't remember seeing you since you were at the table fighting with Martin."

That remark was of no help to Kingford.

"What were you fighting about?" Burke asked.

"It wasn't a fight," Kingford denied. "We were having an argument, that was all."

"They were always at each other's throat," Fields said maliciously as if he relished the opportunity of getting back at Kingford for his earlier remarks.

"You had a fight with Martin just before the murder. You left the table soon after he did and you can't prove an alibi. Where were you?" Burke insisted.

"I told you," Kingford cried. "I was at the table. They could say so if they wanted to," he accused.

Burke glanced at both Stoner and Carlton.

"I didn't see him," Stoner said.

"Neither did I," Carlton repeated.

"I'll keep you right here under my eye, Kingford. A man with a possible motive and no alibi is good material."

Kingford jumped to his feet and accused them all of trying to frame him. He was crazy, fighting mad.

"Don't get hysterical. Or do you call it temperament?" Burke sneered. "It won't help you any. Sit down and be quiet or I'll run you in right now."

Kingford, his rage spent, sank hopelessly into his chair.

"Hey you, the fat one!" Burke pointed at Chubby Carlton. "Go take a whirl at that band. Take him out, Johnson, and bring Harrison in."

Carlton beamed. "Now you're gonna hear music," he promised as he followed Johnson through the door.

CHAPTER FOUR

When they reached the edge of the dance floor Johnson pushed into the crowd like an ice breaker to cut a channel between the edge of the bandstand and the surging swaying crowd on the floor. Carlton wallowed in his wake, panting slightly from the exertion necessary to maintain his position. As they neared the center of the stand, the forward movement was somewhat retarded by the dense mass of couples.

Joan was standing directly in front of Hal talking up at him with venomous rapidity. Her feet planted firmly on the floor, slightly apart, her hands braced against the edge of the platform, she managed to withstand the buffeting onslaught of the human waves as they surged against her. Hal was doing his best to ignore her and her sharp speech.

"He would have the best looking girl in the place standing at his feet," Carlton mumbled.

Johnson made no reply. He was too busy with his forward attack. He paused for a moment after he had dislodged the final couple who separated him from Joan and her position in front of the microphone. He listened to what Joan was saying, then sidled up to her and said curtly, "Step aside, sister."

Joan was startled. She looked like a guilty child caught stealing jam when she realized that Johnson was an officer. Hal's eyes widened but he went on with his conducting.

"We want you inside, Harrison," Johnson called over the sound of the music.

Hal nodded in understanding as Carlton climbed up.

"Come on," Johnson called.

With a glance at the crowded floor Hal suggested, "Let's go this way. It's easier." He pointed toward the side of the stand.

Johnson's arm shot out and clutched at Joan, who had tried to melt into the crowd. "Not so fast," he growled; "I want you too."

"Me?" she cried in surprise.

"Yes, you! Get up there!" Without ceremony he gave Joan a boost which shot her up to the edge of the stand.

"Can't I be arrested without having you tagging along?" Hal complained as he caught her hand to steady her.

The dancers pressed closer to the stand, their eyes glued on the couple as they were led off by Johnson.

This little scene had not escaped the sharp eye of Mrs. Paxton, who had been watching them. She left her table and raced down the side aisle, colliding with a waiter who was carrying a large tray of filled beer glasses. She gave the startled waiter an accusing look as his load toppled to the floor and like an avenging goddess passed on, Joan's ermine wrap billowing from her shoulders, the spilled beer a foamy wake.

Breathless she reached the roped off enclosure and forced her way past a policeman just as the trio were entering Fields' office. "Wait for me!" she cried.

"You can't come in here, lady," Johnson denied.

"Then you can't take my daughter in there, either! Come, Joan!" she gasped, one hand on her heaving bosom as she fought for breath.

"Please, Mother, go away," Joan begged.

"I'll do nothing of the sort! The very idea! I never heard of such a thing!" She heaved between gasps.

"Let her in or lock her up," Hal suggested to Johnson.

"Who is she?" Johnson asked.

"The girl's mother. Just try to keep her quiet."

"Come in," Johnson said to Mrs. Paxton as he stepped to one side.

Mrs. Paxton fluttered through the door. At the sight of the body, which was at that moment being covered with a sheet preparatory to being carried away, Mrs. Paxton gave a little shriek, reeled and sank panting on the divan. "Isn't it simply awful?" she cried to the room at large. "But so—"

"Quiet!" Burke barked.

"But it *is* awful," Mrs. Paxton insisted, "and I don't care what you say!"

"Who are these women?" Burke snapped. "I sent you for Harrison, not his harem."

"Don't be ridiculous!" Mrs. Paxton cried. "I'm Mrs. Llewellyn Paxton and that's my daughter Joan."

"Why did you bring them in?" Burke demanded, trying to ignore Mrs. Paxton for a moment.

"The girl knows something about the murder," Johnson replied.

"She does not!" Mrs. Paxton denied, springing to her feet. "For if she did she'd have told me. She tells me everything. A girl should confide in her mother."

"Sit down!" Burke shouted.

Stoner, Mary and Hal were exchanging amused glances. Burke caught them at it. "It won't be so funny if I take you down to the station house," he growled. As the commotion died down he said, "Now, Johnson, tell me about the girl."

Johnson had been waiting for his chance to explain. He said, "As I moved up to the stand this girl was in front of the mike talking to Harrison. She didn't see me coming but he did and he scowled a warning at her."

"Ha!" Hal interrupted.

Johnson went on: "You know how a person does when they want someone else to stop talking. She didn't catch on, for she paid no attention to him and she didn't stop. I heard her say, 'I hope they hang you for this murder!'"

"Why, Joan!" Mrs. Paxton breathed in horror. "You didn't! Not hung! Not before he plays for the Benefit! How could you say such a thing?"

"I ought to know what she said," Johnson protested annoyed. "I heard her."

"And I know my daughter!"

"And I know this. One more word out of you and out you go," Burke stormed at Mrs. Paxton. "What do you think this is, a pink tea? We're investigating a murder."

"Yes, I know," Mrs. Paxton agreed. "I'm so thrilled. Really—"

"Quiet," Joan whispered a warning.

Mary Dale reached forward and put a restraining hand on Mrs. Paxton's arm. Mrs. Paxton nodded sweetly in understanding.

Hal's eyes were full of slumbering resentment as he watched mother and daughter. Joan flashed him a pert smile as she faced Burke waiting for him to go on.

"What did you mean by your remark?" Burke demanded.

"Nothing," Joan replied.

"Why did you say it?"

"I don't know. It just popped into my head," she replied.

"What made it pop into your head? Why did you connect Harrison with this murder? You must have had some reason."

"I did," Joan replied.

There was an astonished gasp from Hal.

"Just what was your reason?" Burke demanded.

"Well, you see—"

"What was it she said to him, Johnson? Repeat it, please."

"She said, 'I hope they hang you for this.'" Johnson quoted again.

"I thought you said 'this murder' before," Burke asked quickly.

"That's right," Johnson agreed.

Burke turned to Joan. "I can understand your saying, 'I hope they hang you,' but what I want to know is what made you add, 'for this murder'?" Burke insisted.

"We were quarreling," Joan answered. "I knew he'd be suspected, I suppose that's why I said it."

"What made you so sure that he'd be suspected?"

"Because of the things which were in the papers this morning and again tonight. I knew you'd suspect him the moment you remembered those things. And," she added quickly, "because he was refusing to do something that I very much wanted him to do."

"Were you asking him about the Benefit, darling?" Mrs. Paxton purred as if she knew the answer.

"No," Joan answered hesitantly. She turned to Burke. "I suppose you'd call it a lovers' quarrel." As she bent her head demurely, she missed Hal's sudden start. When she turned her glance to Burke's face once more her eyes were brimming. "You know how you say things you don't mean when you're angry with someone you like. You've heard husbands and wives, brothers and sisters saying awful things to each other. You have, haven't you, Inspector?"

He muttered something in recognition of the universal truth she had stated.

Joan smiled brightly. "You must believe me. It was just a jealous girl's bad temper."

Hal was dumfounded. He cried out, "Look here, Inspector—"

His speech was halted by a vicious kick on the shins slyly administered by Joan.

"I'm coming to you. Step aside," Burke ordered Joan. "What about this bad blood between you and Martin?"

"Just an old feud, Inspector. Professional jealousy," Hal answered evenly. "You don't like a man who tries to steal your stuff."

"Oh, you don't, don't you?" Burke scoffed.

"No, I don't," Hal replied with decision.

"So you killed him," Burke suggested, "to save yourself the trouble of a lawsuit!"

"Don't be ridiculous!" Hal cried.

"You can't say things like that to him!" Maxie burst in protectingly.

"I'll show you what I can do. I'll have him in jail in a half hour with a murder charge hung round his neck for good measure," Burke threatened.

"You can't put me in jail," Hal protested. "You have no evidence."

"That's what you think," Burke replied with grim satisfaction. "I have plenty of evidence that will satisfy any judge." He turned to Scat Miller, who, still pale and shaken, stood near the door. "Come here, Miller. Tell me again in front of him exactly what happened."

Miller repeated the story he had told earlier in the evening, ending with the words, "Hal said Martin had fainted."

"Oh, he did, did he?" Burke was gleeful.

"But I thought he had fainted," Hal protested.

"You tried to shift the crime on this man," Burke charged, pointing his finger at the totally bewildered Scat. "Tell me, Miller, what did you do with the body?"

"Nothing. I just sat there holding him up. It was dark. He was heavy and slumpy. I waited for Hal to finish the number. Martin was limp when I caught hold of him," Scat said vaguely. "When the lights came up I tried to shift him. He slid across my lap. Something dug into my leg. As I moved my hands, I felt the knife and then something soft and sticky—" He shuddered. His voice trailed away. With a sigh he collapsed to the floor.

Hal, realizing what was about to happen, caught Miller in his arms as he sagged.

"What a case!" Burke complained. "Hysterical women and fainting men! Take him outside and revive him," he instructed. As Miller was carried from the room he returned to hammer at Hal. "What did you mean by that statement in the paper?"

"Just exactly what it said," Hal replied.

"Martin was trying to keep us away from San Francisco. Don't you remember, I told you?" Maxie cut in.

"We think it was Martin," Hal interrupted quickly.

"Why should Martin want to keep you away from here?"

"Because he claims he originated my particular type of singing. He knew if I came here I would invite him to sing a number. It is always done by a visiting leader, a matter of professional courtesy."

"That's right," Fields agreed

"So what?" Burke asked.

"Martin knew that if we sang on the same program, it would prove conclusively that he was the imitator."

"He served papers on you, didn't he?"

"Yes."

"Then that doesn't look like the action of a man who was afraid. What proof have you that he didn't want you to come here?"

"A telegram received in Portland, a threatening telegram."

"I suppose you destroyed it," Burke sneered.

"No, as a matter of fact, I have it here in my wallet." Hal opened his billfold and produced the telegram, which Burke read and handed back with a grunt.

"Martin sent it all right," Maxie stated.

"What makes you so sure of it?" Burke asked promptly.

"No one else had a reason," Hal replied, scowling at Maxie to keep still in the future.

"So when you met Martin you accused him of sending it?" Burke suggested.

"No, I didn't mention the telegram or the summons."

"I suppose you met like old friends," Burke scoffed.

"No, business acquaintances."

"And everything was peaceful and friendly, was it?"

"No. Not exactly."

"What happened?"

"We had a little argument."

"Why?"

"He accused me of imitating him."

"And that was all?"

"That was all that mattered."

"Did the argument stop there?" Burke insisted.

"No, not right there. It sort of ran along. You know how arguments go," Hal replied.

"Tell me about it."

"I'd rather not."

Burke swung on Stoner. "You were at the table with them, weren't you?"

Stoner nodded. Prompted by Burke he gave a detailed account of the argument between Hal and Martin.

When Stoner finished, Burke turned to Hal. "So you wanted to beat him up. Threatened him, didn't you?"

"Yes," Hal admitted frankly. "He accused me of being a crook."

"But you didn't threaten him because of that. What were you afraid Martin would say there in front of those people?"

"I'd rather not answer."

"When you had your previous fight with him was it about the same thing?"

"Yes, but it could have nothing to do with this case," Hal replied.

"Why did you fight with Martin? I must know."

Hal refused to answer.

"Tell him, Hal," Mary Dale urged.

"Keep out of this," Hal warned her.

Mary jumped to her feet. "He's protecting me, Inspector. They fought because of me."

There was a general gasp of surprise. Mrs. Paxton fluttered to an awakened interest as she leaned forward in avid anticipation.

"A woman at the bottom of it. I thought so!" Burke said with satisfaction. "There's always a woman!"

"It's not what you think, Inspector." Mary spoke quickly. "Mr. Harrison has been nothing more than an employer and a good friend to me. I was in love with Phil Martin—"

"Don't, Mary!" Hal cautioned.

"You married him, didn't you?" Fields asked.

"Yes, secretly," Mary answered.

There was a flutter of surprised amazement at Mary's reply.

"We thought it best to keep the marriage quiet," she explained, seeing the shocked amazement in Hal's eyes.

Mary was excessively nervous. She pulled off her gloves and rolled them into a tight ball as she talked.

"It was your affair," Hal reassured her.

"Why did you keep it a secret?" Burke demanded.

"We—" She hesitated.

"Because you didn't want any trouble with Harrison, was that it?" Burke went on.

"No," she replied firmly.

"But Martin was jealous of Harrison's attentions to you?" Burke jumped at what seemed an obvious conclusion.

"No. Phil Martin never loved me," she answered bitterly.

"Have you been in communication with Martin?" Burke demanded.

"No. He deserted me immediately after he was discharged from the orchestra."

Burke swung to Hal. "Why did you fire him?"

"It will do no good to bring that up. It has nothing to do with the case," Hal said quickly.

"Unless you killed him or know who did, you'd better let me decide on the importance of things, young fellow," Burke condescended. "Why did you fire him?"

"He was blackmailing women." It was Mary who made the startling announcement. "That's why he married me."

"I don't see the point," Burke objected.

"He wanted me to threaten women with divorce proceedings and collect the hush money for him," she replied bluntly.

"And you refused to do it?"

"Naturally."

"Why didn't you divorce him?" Burke asked. Mary did not answer the question.

"Come, come!" Burke prompted. "You must have had some reason."

"I—er—" Mary hesitated.

"You'd better make a clean breast of it to save your own neck," Burke advised.

"Tell him, my dear. The truth's best in the long run, you know!" Mrs. Paxton urged, unable to restrain her desire to hear more scandal.

"I couldn't get a divorce," Mary stated.

"Why not?"

"Because Phil threatened to bring a countersuit against me, suing Hal for alienation of affections. You see, he didn't want to be divorced. He didn't want to be in a position where he might be forced to marry some girl. Also his blackmail threats had more force when his victims knew he had a wife. When he realized what I intended doing about a divorce he knew he could stop me by threatening Hal's career. At the same time he protected himself."

"And you preferred being tied to a man who did not love you than have the career of your—"

"Don't say that, Burke!" Hal warned, his fists doubled ready for action.

"It's bad business threatening an officer in this State," Burke reminded Hal with a glance at the doubled fists. He returned to Mary. "If Martin was so anxious to ruin Harrison, why didn't he go on with his suit?"

"Because he knew that Hal had damaging evidence against him which would be sure to come out in a trial."

"So you gave up your suit?"

"Naturally."

"Doesn't make sense," Burke blurted. "If you had the goods on Martin you had nothing to fear, did you?"

"I didn't want the disagreeable facts made public. It would have reflected on Hal and the whole orchestra. It would have given the band a bad name. It would have affected the prestige of all bands. It would have ruined my career. I would have had to leave the band," she replied honestly.

Burke switched to Hal and demanded, "Did you know about this threatened alienation suit?"

"No. I didn't even know they were married."

"Umm." Burke mused for a moment. "It's a nice case. Are you two lovers?" he asked with the suddenness of lightning.

It was Mary who answered first with an emphatic, "No."

"Of course, you'd deny it. I expected that. But what a chance for both of you! You were tied to Martin but couldn't get a divorce without hurting Harrison. Harrison was threatened with a million dollar suit and didn't want that kind of publicity. That's more motive than most people need to commit murder."

"So I killed him to get the worst possible kind of publicity!" Hal scoffed. " Ridiculous!"

The policeman on guard at the door interrupted to tell Burke that the fingerprint man was ready with his report on the knife.

The man came in with the knife, which he laid on the desk. "Not a print on it of any kind," he said. "The murderer must have been wearing gloves." He waited for Burke to look over the report.

"That's all," Burke said, dropping the paper on the desk.

"There's a couple of slight scratches that look new," the man said. "I thought you might like to know about them."

"What kind of scratches?"

"I don't know. They could have been made by almost anything."

"Would a ring do it?"

The man considered a moment. "Yes, a diamond or a loose setting might scratch through a hole in a glove."

"Okay," Burke dismissed the man. He turned back to Mary. "Let me see those gloves of yours which you rolled into a ball a moment ago."

Mary handed him the gloves. As he opened them he asked, "Do you turn your rings in toward your palm when you put your gloves on?"

"You can't get them on decently unless you do," she replied.

"Ah! I thought so!" Burke exclaimed with satisfaction as he inspected the glove for the right hand.

The group leaned forward trying to see what he had found in the glove to please him so greatly.

"There's a hole in this glove caused by wearing a ring," he said slowly, pointedly, "and unless I'm greatly mistaken this is a drop of blood."

CHAPTER FIVE

Burke's statement caused an excited stir in the room. He was cleverly weaving a net about the girl from which it would be exceedingly difficult to extricate herself.

"It's lipstick," she said.

"We'll soon check on that." He tossed the glove to a policeman and ordered, "Have that stain examined."

"She didn't kill Martin," Hal defended stoutly. "She was nowhere near him."

"There are no fingerprints on that knife. But there are some scratches on the handle. Mary Dale, you were wearing gloves. You were wearing a ring on your right hand which you admit you turn toward your palm. You were down front. You certainly had motive, and you had the opportunity. I charge you with the murder of your husband, Phil Martini"

"Wait, Inspector, please!" Joan cried.

"For what?"

"It's about Miss Dale. You ought to know this fact: The trio, including Mary, sang just before Martin was killed. When they finished their part in the program, they retired to the divan at the back of the platform. Mr. Harrison and I had to step aside to give them room to pass."

"I suppose you saw them in the dark," he challenged.

"It wasn't completely dark. It was semi gloom, a half light," she answered.

"Then you couldn't be sure Mary Dale passed you."

"But the three girls passed us and since there were only three girls on the stage and only three in the company, Mary had to be one of them. Isn't that right?" she appealed to Hal.

Before Hal could reply, Burke retorted, "She could have lagged behind. You wouldn't have known the difference."

"When you are forced into an abnormal position to permit someone to pass you, you subconsciously count the number who are to go by," Hal cut in. "I know all three girls went past me when their number ended. Miss Paxton is absolutely right, Inspector. Mary was nowhere near Martin at the time of his death."

The force of Hal's argument was augmented by the return of the policeman who had taken the glove. He handed it back to Burke saying, "Cotter says it ain't blood."

"Tell him I want to know what made those scratches on the handle," he ordered to hide his deflated spirits. He faced Hal. "Which brings us right back to you."

There was a commotion at the door. A policeman entered saying he had overheard a conversation which he thought Burke should know about. He ushered in a waiter. While all eyes were on the new witness, Joan thoughtfully studied the faces of Hal and Mary. Were they lovers? Had she killed her husband? Hal turned and smiled reassuringly at Mary. His glance was warm and friendly, nothing more, but Mary's reaction, her slight flush and the tenderness which filled her eyes convinced Joan that Mary was in love with Hal.

"What is it, Dugan?" Burke's voice cut across the room.

"While I was walking around outside, keeping me eyes and ears open, I heard this fellow talking to a couple of other waiters. They were talking about the murder and didn't see me. I heard this man say, 'I tell you I saw the knife in Harrison's hand!'"

There were amazed exclamations all over the room. Mrs. Paxton gasped in evident relish at this sudden new turn of events.

"That's absurd!" Hal protested angrily, facing the waiter.

"I did," the waiter said with sullen insistence.

"What's your name?" Burke asked.

"Pete Schwartz."

"Where were you at the time of the murder?"

"I was down near the bandstand. I stopped for a moment and looked out on the floor. The girls were dancing and Martin was singing. Just before he seemed to choke I saw something come between Harrison and Martin. It gleamed sort of blue like. You can't be exactly sure of what you see when the lights are low."

"Why didn't you come to me with the information?" Burke demanded testily.

"I didn't want to get mixed up in it. We were just wondering who did it when this man overheard us. I did see the knife," Schwartz insisted.

Burke beamed. "How do you like that?" he asked.

"The man's crazy," Hal cried desperately; "or lying," he added as an afterthought. "Who told you to say that?" Hal demanded suddenly.

The man seemed startled by the question, but Burke took no notice of that fact. Instead he bellowed at Hal, "I'm asking the questions!"

"Then find out why a man insists that he saw a thing which never happened," Hal cried.

Joan stepped forward. "Inspector, may I speak?"

"You've had your say," he growled, exasperated.

"Wait, Inspector. You don't want to make a mistake, do you?" she asked earnestly.

"I don't make mistakes," Burke stated, then with a change of mind asked, "What do you want?"

"To tell you something important. I, too, saw the knife."

"You what?" Burke gasped.

Mrs. Paxton tried to catch Joan's eye. Her lips shaped the words, "Remember the Benefit."

"What are you trying to do now," Burke demanded, "hang him or save his neck?"

"To clear Mr. Harrison of this false accusation."

"And a moment ago you said you wanted to see him hang. He's evidently quite a ladies' man," he sneered.

"You ought to know women well enough to realize that they often say things they don't mean."

"If I didn't, I seem to be learning it now!" Burke replied.

Joan was very calm as she faced the Inspector. Hal as puzzled by her statement and curious to know what her next step would be.

"You're just trying to cover up for him now that you know he's in danger," Burke accused. "I know women well enough for that."

"Before you jump at conclusions, why not hear what I have to say?" Joan insisted icily. "Mr. Harrison was with me from the moment the lights dimmed until Mr. Martin gasped. As a matter of fact," her eyes lowered for a moment shyly and she appeared to blush, "he had his arms around me. He couldn't have stabbed Phil Martin in that position, could he?" she asked brightly. She hurried on, "And furthermore, we were at least eight feet away from the microphone."

Mrs. Paxton gasped, horrified, "Why, Joan!"

Joan continued, paying no attention to her mother. "I saw the knife a second or two before Mr. Martin choked."

"I don't believe you!" Burke shouted, completely exasperated by the turn things had taken.

"I can't help that. I'm simply telling you that I saw the knife while Mr. Harrison held me in his arms," Joan repeated patiently. "The waiter is right. It did gleam blue like in the dim light. I suppose from where he stood it seemed to pass from Mr. Harrison to Martin."

"Why didn't you do something about it?" Burke demanded.

"I didn't know it was a knife," she answered, then added coyly, "I wasn't thinking of knives or murder." She turned adoring eyes at Hal, who scowled at her impishness. "It never occurred to me that I had seen the knife," she went on, "until I heard Schwartz make his amazing statement a moment ago."

"Who held the knife? Where did it come from?" Burke

demanded.

"It wasn't held. It seemed to float in the air," she replied.

"I suppose you're trying to tell me he was killed by a knife that just up and jumped into his back?" Burke growled in disgust.

"Somebody had to hold it!" Fields cried.

"Of course," Burke agreed. "Where was the knife when you saw it?" he demanded of Joan.

"Behind Martin, naturally, since it went into his back."

"How was it held?" he insisted.

"I don't know how it was held or who had it," Joan cried irritably. "I'm telling you what I saw and I know Hal Harrison had nothing to do with it."

Burke stared at Joan resentfully. Her testimony, if true, had snatched two likely suspects from his grasp. He admitted the value of what she had just said and knew how much weight such evidence would have in court. A jury would believe Joan, and if she were telling the truth not all the cross examination in the world would be able to erase the impression she would make. On the other hand, she could quite possibly be mistaken. If she had made a mistake about the three girls he would have to be able to prove that before he could arrest Mary Dale. If Harrison had his arms about Joan at the time of the murder he couldn't possibly have stabbed Martin, unless she was mistaken about their distance from the singer. That, too, was a point he would have to prove.

The group was restless and uneasy. They looked at each other with quick furtive glances. Mary Dale tried to assume a calm which the nervous fluttering of her fingers belied. Kingford glowered sourly at Chick Stoner, who was unconcernedly smoking a cigarette. Joan continued to watch Burke candidly. Hal's attention was divided between Joan and Mary. His glances toward each were highly speculative but they changed in quality as he shifted from one girl to the other. Mrs. Paxton studied each of the faces in the room and seemed to be deciding which one was the actual criminal. Maxie sauntered toward the door. Fields paced back and forth, his huge paws clasped behind his back.

It was Fields who finally broke Burke's thoughtful silence. "Are you going to keep us here all night and do nothing?" he demanded.

"The band must have a rest," Hal insisted "They must be dead! We'll have to run a long intermission," he said to Fields.

"You can all go back to your tables," Burke said, "but don't try to leave the building, any of you, until you get permission from me."

There was a general scramble for the door. "I'll tell the boys to take a rest," Maxie called.

"Bring the band in here," Burke instructed one of his men. "While they're resting I'll ask them a few questions."

"That's no rest," Hal protested.

"It's all they'll get tonight," Burke barked.

Hal shrugged, turned and followed the others into the corridor, where they clustered in a small group. "What are we going to do now?" Maxie demanded of Hal.

"Take Stoner and Kingford back to the table and buy them a couple of stiff drinks. I have a personal matter to attend to and will see you later," Hal advised.

"Come along, Joan," Mrs. Paxton called as she turned away from Mary, to whom she had just said, "For a moment, I thought he would hang you."

"Just a moment," Hal put a restraining hand on Joan's arm.

They had to step to one side to let the weary members of the band pass into Fields' office. As the door swung shut, one of the janitors approached Fields and said, "I can't find the gadget to fix the lights."

"Never mind." Fields tried to brush him aside.

"But you always said—" the man protested.

"With a murder on my hands you worry me about lights!" Fields cried. "Go away."

The man shuffled off mumbling under his breath. Fields trailed after him.

Hal took Joan by the arm and said gruffly, "I want to talk to you." He steered her down the corridor.

"Can't you talk to me here?" she asked.

"No," he snapped the answer.

Mrs. Paxton and Mary followed them. Hal paused at the door of the musicians' room. He put his arm about Mary for a moment as he said, "I'm sorry about all this, Mary. Why didn't you tell me?"

"It would have done no good," she answered simply.

"But it might have saved you this experience. You shouldn't have told him all the things you did. It put you in a dangerous position. Everything will be all right now; don't worry."

"I won't," she promised.

"And thanks for trying to help me. I appreciate it."

She smiled up at him. "It was nothing."

"Sez you." He bent forward and kissed her. He opened the door. "In here, please," he said to Joan. As Joan stepped forward he said to Mary, "I want to be alone with Miss Paxton for a few minutes. Will you see to it that no one disturbs us?"

Mary gave him an understanding look and moved into a position nearer the door.

"I'm going in," Mrs. Paxton said haughtily as Hal tried to shut her out. "I don't allow my daughter to run about unchaperoned."

"Very well, have it your way." Hal stepped aside for her to enter. He followed her and closed the door. Joan looked up at him expectantly. "You've certainly got us into a fine mess!" he accused.

"Mess!" she repeated blankly.

"Yes, mess! What was the idea of your lying like that? All that stuff about my having my arms around you? Just one lie right after another! And you put Mary in a jam, too," he accused. "Why couldn't you keep her out of it? What do you think Burke will do when he learns that you were nowhere near either of us at the time of the murder? What are you going to say or do when he learns the truth? Of all the stupid, brainless things for a person to do!"

"How dare you call my daughter stupid?" Mrs. Paxton flared.

"Be quiet, Mother," Joan ordered. "This is my affair." She whirled on Hal. "If you didn't like it, why didn't you stop me in there?"

"Because I was so bewildered I didn't know what to do."

"You were thinking of your neck, that's why. You liked my lies then. Now that you are safe you can afford to be indignant," Joan taunted.

"Lies!" Mrs. Paxton exploded into the gap of their conversation. "You mean that the things you said—that he didn't? Oh, Joan! I'm so glad. I thought--I was afraid that you had fallen in love—but you wouldn't, would you, darling? After all, he's nothing but a--Good gracious! Joan! This will be in all the papers! Do you realize that? Your name will be connected with his. People will say--I won't have it! I'm not going to have my little girl talked about! Thank goodness, I know what to do! Mother will protect you." She scurried to the door, her hands fluttering. "I'm going right out there and tell the Inspector."

"Mother!" Joan cried sharply. "Don't you dare!"

"Why, Joan! After all, I'm your mother. I know what to do."

"You'll do nothing!" Joan cried. "Do you want me to go to jail for perjury, accessory before and after the fact, and several other things?"

"They wouldn't dare put you in jail," Mrs. Paxton replied, but her voice was tinged with doubt.

"Wouldn't they?" Joan scoffed. "Burke would do anything this minute. He's up a tree right now and he doesn't know where to turn."

"Something must be done," Mrs. Paxton insisted.

"Let her go! Let her tell Burke," Hal said grimly. "He's finding it out right now. The boys in the orchestra know she wasn't on the stand with me. They'll spill the beans and we'll all be in jail. It's going to be such a nice party," he snapped at Mrs. Paxton.

"I never thought of that," Mrs. Paxton cried. "It will put Joan in such a bad light, won't it? Everybody will wonder why she lied to save you." She spoke as if it were all Hal's fault. "The newspapers will say terrible things. 'Society Girl Lies to Save Band playing Lover.' No, they'll probably say, 'Debutante Tries to Save the Dream Man.' That's it," she cried. "I won't have it. That Inspector is an awful man. He'll brand Joan as a liar!"

"Well, she did lie, didn't she?" Hal demanded. "And," he added, "no one asked for her help."

"She did it for me, didn't you, darling?" Mrs. Paxton fluttered to Joan's defense. "She knows how much the Benefit means to me and she didn't want you hung before you played for my Hands Across—"

"I'd rather hang than hear that name again!" Hal shouted, one degree removed from insanity.

Mrs. Paxton sailed for the door. "Not while Eva Paxton can help you."

"Where are you going?" Joan demanded.

"I'm going in there and warn the musicians to keep quiet." She opened the door and closed it after her with a resounding bang.

CHAPTER SIX

The members of the band were tired and hot after their long session without an intermission. They resented being huddled into Fields' office and showed it plainly. They were glum and unresponding to Burke's rapid questions. Because of their attitude Burke became less sure of himself and consequently less bulldozing as he proceeded. While he had no reason to doubt the veracity of the statements Joan had made, he felt reasonably certain that she could be wrong. He was well aware of the fact that eye witnesses are not too trustworthy. He had heard too many conflicting stories given by creditable witnesses as they attempted to describe the thing they had seen.

Burke's suspicions were still fastened on Mary Dale and Hal. If he could get at the truth he would have a conventional murder case. All the elements were there, love, hate, jealousy, and money. With Martin out of their way Hal and Mary could marry, the threatened suit would die a natural death. Burke knew the murder had been carefully planned. His long experience had also taught him that nine out of ten planned murders were involved with a sex problem in one way or another. This was no crime of passion committed in a consuming burst of rage. It was too subtle for that in spite of the spectacular way it had been done.

Burke decided to change his tactics. "I know you fellows are tired," he said, "but it can't be helped. We've a murder on our hands and it's up to me to solve it. I'm confident that the guilty person is still in the auditorium but it's like looking for the needle in a haystack. There are at least five thousand people here tonight but only one of them is the criminal. We can reduce our suspects to the people who knew and were near Martin at the time of his death. That statement is not an accusation pointed at any of you," he added quickly, "but since you boys were at the scene of the crime you should be able to help me."

Scat Miller, sitting on the divan, gulped. Joe Stevens gave the still pallid Scat a reassuring pat on the arm.

Burke went on. "Two reliable witnesses have stated that they saw the knife before it entered Martin's body. From the things they say it would seem that the knife floated in the air. Now we know that is an impossibility. The knife was on the stand and was used by someone who was right in your midst, possibly one of you."

"How could any of us kill him when we were playing?" Joe Stevens asked.

Burke essayed a smile before he answered. "That's what I'm trying to find out now. What song were you playing when it happened?"

"Goodbye forever," Joe Stevens answered. "It's Harrison's new song. He wrote it himself."

That gave Burke an idea. "Do you have a copy?"

"Sure, a complete score is on the piano," Stevens replied.

"I want to see it." Burke called one of his men and told him to bring back a copy of the score.

The men exchanged questioning glances, wondering what Burke had in mind. Art Mathews, the guitar player, shifted uneasily in his chair.

"Where were you sitting?" Burke asked Mathews.

"Down front on the side," Mathews replied promptly.

"Did you see the knife?"

"No."

"Could you see Martin from where you were sitting?"

"Sure. He was right in front of all of us."

"Isn't it strange that you saw nothing?" Burke asked with quiet insistence.

"Most of the time there's nothing for us to see but a lot of gaping faces and we get sick of that."

"But you couldn't see the faces during that particular number. I understand the room was in semi darkness."

"It was. I probably had my eyes closed," Mathews replied indifferently.

"Was Harrison on your side of the stage?" Burke asked innocently.

"No."

"Where does the trio stand when they sing?"

"In front of the microphone, of course," Mathews replied.

"And where was Martin while they were singing?"

"He just stepped aside for their number."

"Would there have been any time for any conversation between Martin and the members of the trio?"

"Er—" Mathews started to reply. His eyes flickered as memory tapped him.

"Er what?" Burke prompted.

"I was gonna say 'No,' but I just remembered there are a few bars of music between choruses," Mathews replied.

"And what else did you remember?" Burke urged.

"Nothing."

"Are you quite sure?"

"Well," Mathews hesitated a second, "it was nothing. Martin must have said something to Mary because I heard her say, 'I told you what I'd do.'"

"Was that all?" Burke had difficulty hiding his eagerness.

"That was all I heard because Martin took up the song."

"And what happened to the trio?"

"They went off, I guess; they always do,"

"But don't you know?"

"No," Mathews cried irritably. "How should I know? I wasn't watching them."

"But didn't you see any figures outlined between you and the light on the floor?"

"I don't remember."

Burke asked each member of the band that same question and they all refused to make a definite statement. Joe Stevens was the last one and he answered, "I can't see the front mike very well on account of the piano lid. I sit pretty far back."

Burke's patience was wearing thin. "You boys are trying to cover Harrison," he accused, "but it won't do you any good. I'm going to keep your band in San Francisco until I get the murderer if it takes a year, understand?"

The policeman returned with the score of the song. Burke looked it over quickly, separating the sheets and examining the individual parts. After his preliminary inspection he asked Joe Stevens to step forward. "What does this mean?" he asked, pointing to one of the sheets.

"These are rest marks," Joe explained.

"That means that the man wasn't playing, doesn't it?" Burke asked.

"That's right."

"What were you doing, Miller, during your rest period?" Burke demanded.

"Nothing."

"Weren't you interested in what was going on?"

"No."

"Why not?"

"I wasn't interested, that's all."

"Didn't you know that Harrison's life had been threatened?"

"No." His amazement was genuine.

"How long have you been with Harrison's band?" Burke asked.

"Three years."

"Then you knew Martin?"

"Yes."

"But you didn't like him?"

"Not particularly."

"Why not?"

"No reason."

Burke took a stab in the dark. "You knew about Martin and Mary Dale, didn't you?"

"Keep her out of this," Miller replied.

"She's in it up to her neck," Burke answered.

"She didn't kill him," Miller insisted.

"Then who did?"

"I don't know."

"You could have killed him," Burke suggested.

"But I didn't. I told you what happened."

"You told me what you wanted me to know. You had a long pause which came just at the time of the murder. You could have reached forward and stabbed him."

"I didn't!" Miller cried.

"Then you know who did. You'll talk better at the station house," Burke threatened.

"Just a minute!" Thurber, the first violinist, cried. "Miller couldn't have done it."

"Why not?"

"Because at the very moment Martin choked, Miller was picking something from the floor. He was bent over and I was wondering what he was doing. He was bent sideways facing toward me."

"Thanks, Thurber," Miller said appreciatively. "I'd forgotten all about that. Things happened so quickly right after it." He turned back to Burke. "I dropped the guard which fits over the mouthpiece and was fumbling for it in the dark."

"It's a good alibi for the moment." Burke turned his attention to Thurber. "Tell me, when Martin started to sing, what did Harrison do?"

"He moved away from the microphone. Band leaders always do that when a guest is singing."

"Did you see Harrison move, or do you presume he did?" Burke insisted.

"I saw him," Thurber answered. "I could see his body loom up against the blue light."

"Then Harrison was alone on the stand?" Burke asked eagerly, sure that at last he was getting what he wanted.

Thurber hesitated.

"Come on!" Burke prompted.

"Well, a girl climbed up on the stand beside him," Thurber admitted.

"I know all about her," Burke said, showing his annoyance.

Thurber sighed with relief. "Then, that's all right. You see, I didn't want to—"

"Nobody wants to give me any information," Burke growled.

"Well, a fellow doesn't want to get a girl mixed up in a case like this, but as long as you know about her—"

"Did you hear them quarreling?" Burke asked.

"No. Their voices were low."

"What were they doing?"

"I don't know; they were standing pretty close together."

"Did Harrison have his arm about the girl?" Burke demanded.

"Knowing Hal, I'd say it was likely," Thurber smiled.

"But did you see it?"

"No. The girl was up there with him. She's the one who has been following him all over the country. They were pretty close together. You know how it is," he added with a wise grin.

Mrs. Paxton had forced her way into the room just in time to hear Thurber's remarks about Joan. "Don't you dare say anything about my daughter!" she shrilled.

Burke exploded at the sight of Mrs. Paxton. He had had all of her he wanted. "I'll take care of your daughter's reputation."

"Thank you," Mrs. Paxton began to bubble. "I knew you were—"

"Get out!" Burke bellowed. "And stay out or I'll put you both in jail!"

A policeman took Mrs. Paxton by the arm and eased her through the door, shutting it behind her.

Burke went on grimly. "I'm not so sure now that one of you didn't kill Martin. You don't want to talk so I'll have to dig for facts, and I'll get them. You are not to leave the building until you get permission from me."

Dave Fields entered in time to hear Burke's last remark. "Can't they play, Inspector? The crowd's getting restless. We'll have a riot on our hands if we're not careful. They paid good money to hear music. It's been a long intermission and they're beginning to complain. They may wreck the place unless something is done."

"All right. Go ahead and play," Burke ordered, "but remember what I told you."

"Where's Harrison?" Fields wailed. "Why isn't he here? He could handle the crowds."

"I'll take care of the crowds," Burke promised. "Where's the mike? I want to make an announcement."

As the door swung open, Mrs. Paxton was babbling at Joan and Hal. Maxie hovered in the background.

"Get ready to play," Fields called to Hal.

"How about the people who tried to make getaways?" Johnson asked Burke. "I've got them waiting."

"After my announcement." Burke started across the floor, the musicians straggling behind him.

When Burke was out of earshot Thurber sidled up to Hal and asked in a whisper, "What's the dope about the girl? Burke's suspicious."

Quickly Hal explained Joan's lie. "Tell the boys to be careful, will you?" Hal asked. "Just spread it around. He's out to trap us if he can."

"Who did it?" Thurber asked. "The dame?"

"No!"

"Well, it would make it easier for us if she had. Burke says we've gotta stay in San Francisco until he gets the murderer."

Maxie groaned. "I knew this town was gonna be bad luck. Didn't I tell you?" he demanded of Hal.

"We may have to do a little detective work ourselves if we want to open in New York next Tuesday," Hal suggested.

"You mean if Higgins doesn't cancel the contract! That's what I'm worried about," Maxie groaned.

From the main floor of the building the calls of the crowds, their clapping and a measured stamping of feet vibrated through the building. Fields ran up, frantic with worry. "Hal, for God's sake, go out and show yourself, will you? They think you've gone home, been arrested, or something."

Hal swung toward the stand as Burke's voice boomed over the noise. "Quiet!" he called. "Quiet!" The noise continued. A roll of the drum demanded attention. Comparative silence followed.

"I want you to keep your seats and stay away from this end of the hall," Burke ordered.

"Why? We want music!" a voice cried. It was caught up immediately by hundreds of voices calling, "We want music! We want music!"

"You'll get your music," he promised as Hal took up his position beside him.

As Burke stepped down from the platform he was besieged by reporters demanding to know what had happened. He told them about the murder and promised to have the culprit for them before he left the dance hall that night.

The reporters scampered for telephones as the band began to play.

Burke, with Fields, began a tour of the area in and about the bandstand. When they reached the back of the stand, Burke asked. "What are the tracks for?"

"The stand rolls out onto the floor."

Burke grunted. "What's inside it?"

"Martin stores his instruments and stuff in there. I dunno," Fields answered without interest.

"Who controls the rolling mechanism?" Burke asked.

"Either the band leader or the sound engineer. They both have control buttons at convenient spots."

"Was it out or in at the time of the murder?"

"Out."

"Okay, work it for me."

"We can't. The dancers are all bunched before Harrison at the front of the stand," Fields objected.

"Let 'em get out of the way," Burke replied indifferently.

Fields led the way to the front of the stand. He stopped for a moment to tell two policemen to push the crowd back as the stand was coming out. They walked over to the microphone stand. Fields pressed the button and the stand began to roll forward like some giant juggernaut. The crowd gave way before its relentless slow advance.

"This is as far as it will go," Fields explained when the stand settled to a stop.

Burke looked about. He glanced up at the balcony. His eyes lit up. The balcony was broken, allowing a space for the stand when it rolled forward. On either side of the stand there were two boxes that were now well behind Hal. Burke stepped back several feet to gauge the distance better. He bumped into Hal, who stepped aside and grabbed the microphone to keep it from toppling over. "That's it! The girl was right, after all! The knife did come from the balcony! It was thrown! Come on!"

Burke had been so absorbed in his reasoning that he did not realize that every word he had said had been amplified and boomed throughout the hall.

CHAPTER SEVEN

While Burke's booming voice was echoing away, there was a clattering commotion in the upper corner box. Mrs. John Carter Dufrane, waiting uneasily for a chance to escape, had been terrified at what she had heard. She jumped from her chair so quickly that the chair upset, toppling over with a crash. Thinking only of escape she slipped into the corridor at the rear of the boxes and darted for one of the stairways. Like a hunted animal, she fled for safety to the crowds on the floor below. No one had seen her leave the box or descend the stairs. If she could mingle with the crowd she knew she'd be safe for a moment. She flew down the steps, barely touching the treads in her haste. She must reach the bottom before Burke came from the bandstand.

As she reached the bottom step, the crowd heaved back toward her, making it impossible for her to gain the floor. Burke and Fields were coming round the end of the bandstand and the crowd was giving way before them. The crowd moved back another step. With a sob of despair, Mrs. Dufrane was forced to step up one step, where she stood head and shoulders above the mob at her feet. Burke and Fields were moving toward her. The crowd began to open up. Mrs. Dufrane tried to flatten herself against the wall, hoping to be unnoticed. Then all hope vanished as she heard a voice calling her by name.

It was Mrs. Paxton calling at the top of her voice, "Hello! Hello! Mrs. Dufrane!" Mrs. Paxton was excitedly waving her right hand to attract her attention.

Mrs. Dufrane gave a sickly smile as Mrs. Paxton started to force her way through the crowd, calling as she came, using her elbows as weapons. "Imagine seeing you here! My dear, I meant to telephone you, but we haven't had a minute. San Francisco is such a fascinating place and we just arrived this afternoon. Isn't it thrilling? Wasn't it just my luck to get here in time for a murder?" With the final sentence she reached Mrs. Dufrane's side just as Burke and Fields reached the stairs.

Mrs. Dufrane's attempt at a smile died as running feet came down the steps and a hand was placed on her arm. A voice asked, "Why'd you run away, lady?"

"I wasn't running away, officer, I—" Fear shadowed her eyes.

"What's this?" Burke demanded of the officer.

"I saw this woman dart out of a box across the corridor and start down," the officer replied. "She seemed to be running away."

"But, officer," Mrs. Dufrane protested, "I wasn't running—"

"Certainly not!" Mrs. Paxton cried. "She came down to speak to me, didn't you, darling?"

"Yes. Of course," Mrs. Dufrane agreed eagerly, grasping at the only straw in sight.

"Well, maybe you did and maybe you didn't, but it was my duty to follow you just the same."

"Now, Inspector," Mrs. Paxton began.

"Keep out of this!" Burke growled at her. He turned to the officer. "Where was she sitting?"

"In one of them corner boxes, and the minute you mentioned that knife was thrown, up she got and away she went down the stairs. It seemed suspicious to me. I was at the other end of the corridor and couldn't get here any sooner. I was afraid for a moment I had lost her."

"What was your hurry?" Burke demanded of Mrs. Dufrane, who was a little more composed.

"Inspector, don't be ridiculous! This is Mrs. John Carter Dufrane—everybody knows her! You'll get yourself into trouble—" Mrs. Paxton warned.

"And so will you if you don't get out from under my feet! If it's not your daughter gumming up the works, it's you. If I catch you bothering me again I'll run you in for disorderly conduct. Understand?"

"But I was only trying to explain—" Mrs. Paxton cried.

"Explain inside." He turned to the officer. "Take them into the office. I'm going up to have a look at those boxes." With heavy tread he started up the stairs as the crowd opened for the officer and the two women.

Joan tried to struggle through the crowd to her mother but couldn't make it. She was worried. She wormed her way along the edge of the throng to the bandstand and stepped boldly up on the platform. She moved over to Hal, who scowled at her as she advanced.

"Turn that thing off," she ordered. "There's something you must know."

"What now?" he asked, doing as she instructed.

"They're taking Mother back to the office. I think we'd better be there. You never know what she'll say or do."

"It runs in the family," he retorted. With a nod at Joe Stevens to take over, he led Joan across the stand and up to the office door.

The policeman on guard tried to stop them. Hal said, "Inspector Burke sent for us." They were permitted to pass inside.

Mrs. Paxton was as frothy as a pan of soapsuds when she spied them. She called, "Joan, dear, you remember Mrs. Dufrane." Then she introduced Hal saying, "And this is Hal Harrison, who's going to play for my Benefit."

Any denial that Hal might have tried to make was cut short by the entrance of Burke and Fields. "Who are all these people?" Burke demanded.

"These are the people who tried to make getaways." Johnson indicated a little fat man, a luscious blonde, and Kelton the racketeer. "I don't know anything about these others. Sounds like a tea party to me."

"I know about them," Burke answered and stopped when he realized that Hal and Joan were in the room. "What do you want? I thought you were playing?"

"Something I wanted to say to you," Hal answered quickly, "but it can wait if you're busy."

"Unless it's important it'll have to wait." He turned to the three people Johnson had collected.

"What have you got to say for yourself, Kelton?"

"That I want to get out of here."

"Yeah, me too," the blonde added.

"What are you doing in a place like this?" Burke demanded. "And why did you try to make a getaway?"

"I don't like being mixed up in murders, that's all," Kelton said with a smirk.

"Then you must have something to hide."

"No. Music and women aren't my racket."

"Just what do you mean by that?" Burke demanded.

"What I said and nothing else. Ask this dame." He nodded toward Mrs. Dufrane. "She probably can tell you plenty. So could Dave, if he wanted to."

"I don't know what you're talking about," Fields denied quickly.

"Don't stall, Fields," the blonde cut in. "If you didn't know Martin was bleeding a lot of these society dames, then you're a bigger sap than I take you for."

"What's this?" Burke demanded.

"Aw! Don't be so innocent!" the blonde said harshly. "If you don't know what goes on in this dance hall, you're the only one who don't. What do you suppose this woman is doing here? Look at her! Does she look like a dance hall type?" She was merciless as she included Mrs. Dufrane in her denouncement of the dance hall.

"I come here because I happen to like this type of music," Mrs. Dufrane said steadily with obvious control of her nerves.

"Of course, so do I," Mrs. Paxton chimed in.

"Sure," Fields agreed. "A lot of nice ladies do." He turned to the blonde. "Listen, Charlotte, are you trying to give my place a bad name?"

"Ha!" Charlotte scoffed. "Don't make me laugh. You know how to spoil a bad egg, don't you?"

"Look, Inspector," the little fat man interrupted. "Please! I'm a night watchman and I gotta be on the job.

I'll lose my work. See! Here's my card. Let me go, will you?" As he waited for Burke to read the card he added quickly, "I tried to get away because I wouldn't want my missus to know I was here. I told her I was going to the Lodge."

"Go ahead," Burke said as he returned the card.

"How about us?" Kelton asked.

"What were you doing here, Kelton, since you don't like music?" Burke asked.

"Charlotte wanted to come."

"Did you know Martin?"

"Sure, I knew him."

"Ever have any business with him?"

"He used to come into my place once in a while until I told him to stay away."

"Why did you do that?"

"Because I don't like heels, never did."

"Is that why you tried to get out right after the murder?"

"We didn't like the show. Any crime in that?" Kelton asked.

"Why don't you do things right?" the blonde asked Dave.

"Keep out of this, you two," Burke growled. "Where were you sitting, Kelton?"

"Down at the back, since we couldn't dance."

"See anything?" Burke demanded.

"Nothing but a bunch of nuts milling around out on the floor like a lot of sardines."

"How do you happen to know so much about what goes on in a place like this?"

"It's my business to know things."

"You weren't trying to get a cut on any graft, were you?" Burke asked.

"Listen, Burke. You ought to know my reputation well enough to know that I don't mix business and pleasure. When I take a lady out for an evening, there's no business done. And what's more, I have my own way of doing things."

"So I understand. If Martin had a good racket you'd be interested, wouldn't you?"

"Not in this cheap blackmailing stuff."

"How do you know so much about it?"

"Martin was tight one day and told me."

"Why?"

"How do I know why drunks talk?"

"He didn't happen to owe you money, did he?"

"I don't let people owe me money."

"We've been wanting to get something on you, Kelton, and this looks like it."

"I was at the table all the time after the first dance Ask the waiter, he knows. That's if you think I need an alibi."

"I will. Thanks for the suggestion." He sent a policeman out with Kelton to check. While they waited, he said to the blonde, "Tell me how this blackmail racket works."

"There's no blackmail racket here," Fields burst in on the conversation. "She's trying to give my place a bad name."

"It's got it," Charlotte scoffed. "Listen, Burke. I'll tell you. These fellows get a dame interested in them. They play around with her nice and friendly like for a while. Then the first thing the woman knows she's invited to his apartment to see his etchings or something. Sometimes it's supposed to be a party. Anyhow, while the woman is there someone comes to the apartment and sees her. The first thing she knows she gets a telephone call asking for dough or her husband will be informed of her affair with Joe Doakes. Isn't that right?" she turned and asked Mrs. Dufrane.

"I really don't know," Mrs. Dufrane denied.

"That's how it works, nevertheless," Charlotte insisted. "And if there are letters, it makes it all the harder for the victim."

Kelton and the officer returned. "The alibi is all right," he reported.

"So do we go?" Kelton demanded.

"Go ahead," Burke dismissed them.

"Thanks for nothin'," Kelton said as he went through the door, the blonde on his arm.

"What a horrible man!" Mrs. Paxton breathed as the door closed.

"Now, Mrs. Dufrane." Burke paused for a long moment. He was worried by her importance in San Francisco society and the prominence of her husband.

"Yes, Inspector."

"Did you know this Phil Martin?"

"Yes."

"Were you on, let's say, friendly terms with him?"

"I knew him rather well but not intimately," she answered.

"Did you come here tonight to see him?"

"No. I came to hear Mr. Harrison play."

"Did you see Martin tonight?"

"Yes."

"Did you give him anything?"

"I don't understand."

"Perhaps this will freshen your memory." He went to the desk and from an envelope drew out a package of bills. "These were found on Martin."

He put the packet of bills to his nostrils. "They were probably carried in a woman's handbag as a faint odor of perfume still lingers on them."

"I know nothing about the money," Mrs. Dufrane insisted.

"Would you mind letting me see your handbag?" Burke asked.

"Certainly not." She passed the bag forward.

"I want to look inside," he explained as he took the bag.

"I don't mind."

Burke opened the bag and held it under his nostrils. "Smells like the same scent to me," he said with a smile.

"It's very popular," she said.

Burke rummaged in the small bag. He turned up the usual compact, lipstick, change purse, mirror, etc. He seemed to be seeking something very definite because he made a careful search. He produced a small flat folded checkbook, in a leather folder. He flipped it open and studied the stub. "Would you say it was a coincidence if I told you that the check you drew to cash this afternoon was for the exact amount of money that we found on Martin's body?"

Mrs. Paxton gasped.

"I certainly would," Mrs. Dufrane replied.

"Why don't you tell the truth?" Burke demanded. "You came here tonight to see Martin. You gave him this money. What did you expect him to give you in return?"

"I did none of those things."

"Then where is the money you drew from the bank?"

"Home in the safe, of course."

The two men who had been sent to search Martin's apartment returned, halting the investigation.

"What did you find?" Burke asked eagerly. Joan thought she noticed a sudden tenseness as Mrs. Dufrane watched the two men, who placed a small bag on the desk.

"Nothing much!" one man answered.

Burke sorted the things quickly. "Didn't you find any papers, notebooks, diaries, or memoranda?" he asked with evident disappointment.

"That's all there was!"

"He must have kept records somewhere," Burke mused.

"If he did, they're not in his apartment," the man insisted.

That halted Burke, but only for a moment. He turned to Mrs. Dufrane. "Why did you try to run away if you had nothing to hide?"

"She didn't run away," Mrs. Paxton cut in. "I told you she came down to see me."

"And I told you to keep out of my sight! Get out!" Burke shouted.

Mrs. Paxton hesitated a moment.

"Get out!" Burke repeated. With a flurry Mrs. Paxton made a scampering exit.

"And now, Mrs. Dufrane, will you answer my question?" Burke's voice was lowered once more.

"I didn't run away, Inspector. Had I been trying to escape, I could have vanished into the crowd. Your man told you that he had a long way to go to follow me. I did want to see Mrs. Paxton and I wanted to avoid the very thing that is happening now."

"What?" he asked uncertain of her meaning.

"I can't afford to have any publicity, Inspector. My husband, he'd—"

"Don't worry, Mrs. Dufrane," Fields broke in. "He won't let any of this get into the papers, will you, Inspector?"

"Not if I'm satisfied she had nothing to do with the killing," he replied. He turned back to Mrs. Dufrane. "Martin was killed rather curiously, Mrs. Dufrane. Two witnesses have testified to seeing the knife which they claim was suspended in mid air. There were no fingerprints on the knife. You could have thrown it from your box. I see you're wearing gloves."

Mrs. Dufrane looked at her hands helplessly for a moment before she said, "But I didn't throw it, Inspector. I couldn't throw anything and hit a mark—honestly!"

"Excuse me, Inspector," Hal said; "if both the waiter and Miss Paxton are right, the knife wasn't thrown. They said it floated in the air; they both saw the blue light gleam on it. The waiter said he saw it in my hand. He said it passed from my body to Martin's."

"Well, what are you driving at?" Burke asked sourly.

"If the knife had been thrown it would have flashed, not floated," Hal replied. "Also, it would have been on an angle on its way down. What does the medical examiner's report say about the direction of the wound?"

"That's a point," Burke admitted grudgingly. His assistant handed him a paper from the desk. Burke read:

"The knife entered the lower chest cavity under a rib and penetrated the heart. The wound indicates a slight upward thrust."

"I'm sorry, Mrs. Dufrane," Burke admitted. "Thanks to the medical examiner's report—which I haven't had time to read—I've been saved from making a grave mistake."

"May I go now?" Mrs. Dufrane asked, relieved.

"Just a moment, Mrs. Dufrane," Hal interrupted. "I'll take you out."

"What did you want in here anyhow?" Burke demanded.

"I knew you were interested in the balcony as a starting place for the knife and I wanted to remind you of the facts I just told you. I knew if the waiter and Miss Paxton were telling the truth that, well," he shrugged, "you discovered the same fact yourself. I was anxious to know the angle from which the knife entered the body."

"You didn't give me credit for any sense, eh?" Burke asked testily.

"Certainly. I was overanxious to help, that was all. Forgive my zealousness, Inspector. I want you to solve this case. I'm leaving San Francisco tomorrow night."

"That's what you think," Burke growled.

Hal took Mrs. Dufrane's arm. Joan followed. As they reached the door, Fields stepped up. "I'm sorry this happened, Mrs. Dufrane. I hope you won't let it make any difference."

"It's one of those things," she replied.

As the door closed behind them, Joan whispered in Hal's ear, "Who's telling lies now, little George Washington?"

CHAPTER EIGHT

As Hal and Mrs. Dufrane, followed by Joan, stepped into the corridor they were besieged by clamoring reporters and photographers. Mrs. Paxton, who had been hovering outside, darted forward. The startling, noiseless flares of photographers' bulbs flashed in front of them, blinding them for the moment. Mrs. Dufrane made a belated effort to conceal her face.

"What's the story, Harrison? Who did it? Was there a woman mixed up in it?" Jimmie Farr asked with the easy familiarity of a crack reporter.

"Sorry, I don't know a thing," Hal answered. He took Mrs. Dufrane by the arm and stepped forward.

"Hold it a minute, please," a voice called.

They hesitated for one second. Mrs. Paxton's eyes glistened as she smiled expansively. Mrs. Dufrane took an impulsive step backward, but Mrs. Paxton clutched her arm, holding her directly before the camera as the flash popped.

"No more, now, please," Hal begged. "I've got to get back on the stand."

Jimmie Fair tugged at Hal's arm. "What's the dame's name?"

Mrs. Paxton overheard the stage whisper. She drew herself up haughtily and said, "Dame! Young man, I'll have you know I'm Mrs. Llewellyn Paxton. P A X T O N."

"Thanks," Jimmie said and ignored any further information that might come from her. Hal and Mrs. Dufrane passed under one of the ceiling lights. "Oh, good evening, Mrs. Dufrane. I didn't recognize you for a moment. Friend of Mr. Harrison's?"

"Certainly not!" Mrs. Paxton cut in. "She's with me."

"And who are you?" Jimmie asked with an appreciative glance at Joan.

"I'm Joan Paxton."

"And why were you being questioned?" Jimmie asked glibly.

"I have nothing to say at this time." Joan turned away.

Hal reached over, jerked her arm and led the women toward one of the balcony stairs.

"What do you mean 'at this time'?" Hal demanded angrily the moment they were away from the keen ear of Farr and the other reporters. "You're going to say nothing more. You've said too much already. You're going up to Mrs. Dufrane's box and you're going to stay there!"

"I'll say what I please and I'll go where I please," Joan flashed.

Hal played a trump card then. He turned to Mrs. Paxton and gave her one hundred percent of the Harrison charm as he begged, "Mrs. Paxton, I appeal to you. We have so much at stake, you and I. I must leave San Francisco tomorrow night. We're in a precarious position, all of us, and the less said—"

"The soonest mended," she finished brightly. "You're quite right. Come, Joan! We must do as Mr. Harrison says."

Joan's glance accused Hal of playing an underhand game. She would have told him so but was interrupted by the excited arrival of Maxie. "Hurry up! They're calling for you out there. You've been away from the stand too much. You've gotta play!"

Hal excused himself and turned away.

As the three women mounted the stairs, Mrs. Paxton looked down at Hal as he hurried to the bandstand. "Isn't he the dear boy? He's going to play for my Benefit, you know."

When they reached Mrs. Dufrane's table the band was in full swing. "I do hope they move the thing-um a bob out again," Mrs. Paxton babbled; "I simply love to watch him conduct. He has such verve, don't you think?"

Mrs. Dufrane made no answer; she was occupied with her own thoughts. Joan watched the woman intently. Mrs. Dufrane looked up suddenly, catching the girl's speculative stare. Joan smiled understandingly. "Anything we can do?" she asked quietly.

"Er—I—"

"You seem worried," Joan went on. "I just thought—"

"You're kind, my dear. I—" Mrs. Dufrane hesitated, seemed to have arrived at some decision. "I am worried. This place, those pictures. They'll be a little difficult for me to explain to my husband."

"Jealous?" Joan asked.

"Very."

"Deliver me from a jealous man!" Mrs. Paxton launched into one of her long tirades.

Joan's clipped command, "Mother!" cut her short in mid air. Mrs. Paxton, affronted, gasped but the steady glint in Joan's eyes kept her quiet.

"He doesn't know you come here? Is that it?" Joan asked.

Mrs. Dufrane nodded.

"We'll help you," Joan offered. "You came with us because we're trying to get Mr. Harrison to play for Mother's Benefit. That will explain the pictures."

"Thank you, my dear. You're very kind. That's a load off my mind."

"Forget it," Joan answered. "Remember our story, Mother, and don't make any mistakes."

"As if I would!" Mrs. Paxton exclaimed. "I know just how you feel, my dear. I was involved once—"

"Now, Mother! We don't want to hear that story."

"But it was a murder, too," Mrs. Paxton insisted. "Not as odd as this one though." Her eyebrows arched suddenly. "How do you suppose this Martin person was killed?"

"Didn't the Inspector say something about a knife?" Mrs. Dufrane asked.

Mrs. Paxton leaned forward, eager to tell all she knew. "It was a knife! Sticking right out of his back! My dear, I was right there all the time. It was a horrible sight. Of course I know that dear boy had nothing to do with it although—"

"Mother," Joan warned.

"What were you saying?" Mrs. Dufrane asked politely without interest.

Joan shook her head at Mrs. Paxton, who caught the cue to say nothing about Joan's fabricated story.

She babbled on. "What I was going to say—before I stopped to think—it's so curious. No one seems to have touched the knife—but of course they could have been wearing gloves. That's why the Inspector suspected you for a moment, wasn't it? Imagine your doing a thing like that! Ridiculous, isn't it—but then I always say people never see the things that are right under their noses. Knives don't stab by themselves, do they? Someone had to use the knife. Now who could it have been? I'd like to solve this crime just to show that bellowing baboon of an Inspector—" Her voice trailed away.

"It seems such a peculiar murder," Mrs. Dufrane mused. "It's so spectacular. Had I wanted to kill Phil—" The moment she mentioned Phil Martin by his first name she realized she had made a mistake. She tried to cover her slight thoughtful pause by racing on, "—Martin, I wouldn't have picked a place like this, would you?"

"Then you did know him?" Mrs. Paxton asked. Without waiting for a reply she babbled on, "Tell us about him. Perhaps we can find a motive."

"I know nothing about him," Mrs. Dufrane denied. "Mr. Fields introduced me to him one evening when I requested a special number."

"Then we'll have to find some other source of information. I'll ask Mr. Harrison all about him when we arrange the details for the Benefit."

Joan, who had been listening with one ear to the conversation, interrupted, "Don't be too sure of that, Mother."

"I'll make him play. I have him in a spot. He can't refuse me now. You know, Joan, about the—" Joan's black scowl was a danger signal which she observed. "Well, anyhow, I know something about Harrison and he wouldn't want me to tell the police. I'll force him to play for that Benefit or else—"

"If I were you I'd have nothing to do with it," Mrs. Dufrane advised.

"But I've always wanted to solve a murder. You know they never do it properly even in books. They make you read three hundred pages just to discover a fact you knew at the very beginning."

"What do you know now?" Joan demanded.

"I know the man was killed with a knife," Mrs. Paxton retorted positively.

"But you don't know how it was done and you don't know why it was done here tonight in front of so many people."

"Oh, Joan," Mrs. Paxton sighed, "you know very well that the hardest thing in the world to do is to find a needle in a haystack."

"You've got something there," Joan agreed.

"Of course I have, but sometimes the way you act you'd give people the impression that I was an utter fool."

Joan made no reply to that unanswerable statement.

"Now I'll go a step further," Mrs. Paxton continued, a little intoxicated by her own seeming brilliance. "The murderer is a smart man. I say man, although a woman could have done it—two women who were questioned were wearing gloves. You and Mary Dale, that singing person," she said with emphasis.

"Mary Dale is an artist," Joan stated emphatically, "not a person."

"You're too democratic, Joan. Don't keep interrupting my trend of thought. Now, where was I? Oh, yes! This crime was planned carefully. Do you know why?" she asked brightly and paused as if she were playing a game. "Give up?" she asked.

"Tell us," Joan suggested.

"The murderer wanted someone else to be suspected!" She sat back expecting them to be impressed with her keenness.

"Unless I've been grossly misled, that fact is true of all planned murders," Joan stated flatly.

"Then you admit I'm right?" Mrs. Paxton beamed.

"You have reached an obvious conclusion, yes, one that all thinking people would know."

"You won't give me credit for a thing!" Mrs. Paxton complained. "If you're so smart, why don't you tell us how this Martin person was killed."

"I wish I knew," Joan replied thoughtfully. All through her mother's gushing talk she had been thinking about the knife. She felt certain that whoever had killed Martin had planned the crime so that Hal Harrison would be suspected. The murderer had had twenty four hours to perfect the plan. It was a person familiar with the Crystal Gardens, but that fact led her nowhere. A thousand people could be familiar with the Gardens. What puzzled her was the fact that she knew she had seen the knife before it entered Martin's body. Where did it come from and how did it get there? She looked up at the ceiling. There was no way for it to have been used from above. Then she remembered the examiner's statement. The knife had entered the body with a slight upward thrust. The knife came from below. One of the musicians could have done it or there was some way for a person who knew the building to get near enough to do it. She stood up and looked out over the floor. She tapped her foot to the tantalizing rhythm of the music.

"It's great music," she said, "I feel like dancing. Will you excuse me? I'm going down and find myself a gigolo."

"Don't, child," Mrs. Dufrane advised. "This place is—" Her explanation was cut short by the appearance of Dave

Fields, who looked into the box and asked pleasantly, "Everything all right?"

"See you later," Joan promised Mrs. Dufrane as she slipped from the box.

Joan had some ideas about the knife. She wanted to test them alone and unobserved if possible. She felt positive that it had floated in the air a moment before Martin had gasped his last breath. She wanted to prove something for her own satisfaction. Then, too, she knew that she must be prepared to defend herself if Burke discovered her lie. If Hal had any place in her thoughts, except resentment, she didn't admit it.

When she reached the main floor, instead of the crowd she expected, she found the place deserted except for the occasional passing of a waiter or bus boy. The morbidly curious had succumbed to the lure of the music and were back on the dance floor watching Hal. She passed Fields' office, where a policeman still stood guard, and, turning the end of the corridor, inspected the bandstand and the flat steel track upon which it rolled when it slid forward. The stand rolled back to its normal position as she approached. She decided to do some immediate investigating. She tapped the sides. They gave off a hollow sound as she rapped with her knuckles. Unconsciously she found herself keeping time with the beat of the drum. She stopped, fearful lest she be heard. At the back of the stand she found the door which she felt must be there. She looked warily in both directions to be sure that she would be unobserved before she tried the door tentatively and, with a final, cautious glance, stepped up and into the hollow space under the band.

She pulled the door shut and paused for a moment in the Stygian blackness. The tapping of the musicians' feet was deafening in her ears. She groped and stumbled forward. She bumped her head on a beam which jutted out from the right side and cried, "Ouch!" For a moment she was stunned as sharp, excruciating pain shot through her head. Her eyes watered as she bit her lips and patted the bruised spot tenderly. In a few seconds she became accustomed to the semi gloom. She began to see things quite clearly in the light which came through cable holes and the cloth covered grills. She paused, chilled by what she saw. For a moment she was terrified and stepped backward, then she laughed nervously at her sudden fright. A bass viol case loomed up in front of her and she thought it was a man.

Reassured that she was alone in the black pit, she stepped forward. Her gown became entangled in an old music stand, which clattered to the floor with an ear splitting crash. She held her breath for a moment, afraid the din had given her away, but the music and the feet pounded on overhead. She found it necessary to bend forward as she neared the front of the stand. At the very last tier of them all she had to get down on her hands and knees. She crawled to a cable hole and peered out onto the dance floor.

Just a few feet away from her Hal's swaying legs blocked her vision of the floor and the closely packed couples clustered in front of him. She wondered idly why all band leaders had to wiggle and sway their legs so much as they conducted.

As she looked through that hole she did some rapid calculating.

She was satisfied that her guess had been a good one. She felt confident that she now had an answer to the manner in which the crime had been committed. She didn't want to stop there, however, until she proved her point to her own satisfaction. If she could find something to thrust through that hole, something long enough to reach Hal and give him a poke she would know that she was on the right track. She looked about hopefully. If she could just find a long stick! She'd have given a hundred dollars for a thin fishing rod at that moment.

She slid back and opened a violin case and considered the bow. No. It was not nearly long enough. She was determined not to be beaten. She worked her way back, searching as she went. It was not until she was back in the high wide part near the door that her search was rewarded. A long thin piece of molding, forgotten by some carpenter, lay near the door.

Satisfied with her find, Joan crawled back to the opening, taking extra precautions to move slowly, for at that moment the music stopped. From outside the applause was deafening. With her eye glued to the little hole, she saw Hal turn and heard him say to his band, "All right, boys. Make this one a sweetheart number."

She knew what that would mean. They would play some popular waltz tune. The lights would be dimmed again. The baby blue spots would be used. The stand would probably be rolled out onto the floor so that King Hal would be able to give the audience full benefit of his melodious dreamy voice.

"He's awfully sure of himself," she thought. "Smug, that's what I'd call him. He turns his smile and his charm on and off like water from a tap. But it is a nice smile. It would be," she corrected herself, "if he wasn't so darned cocky. I'd like to take that cockiness away from him just once. Why not? I'd like to see him squirm."

With her mind made up, she worked hurriedly. She took a small diamond bar pin which she wore at her throat and pushed the point through the end of the molding. She tested it against her fingers to see if it would work. It did. She poised the long stick at the entrance of the hole and looked out. She cried out in exasperation. Hal had moved away from the microphone. With him gone from the spot, how would she be able to prove the manner in which the murder had been committed?

She was startled by a sudden whirring sound, but the next instant she realized that it was the motor moving the stand out onto the floor. She peeked through the hole intently as the lights began to dim. She sighed with relief as she saw Hal's legs come into view. He was clearly outlined against the blue spot on the floor. Quickly she pushed her rod through the hole. The weight of the pin made the thin molding sag more than she had planned. She needed extra support for the stick. She reached for the violin case she had inspected earlier, took the bow and when the stick and pin had gone about two feet through the hole she rested the stick on the bow, which gave the pin the angle she had wanted. Carefully she pushed the long rod forward.

Hal was giving "Good night, sweetheart," all he had. No popular singer's voice had ever had the same sweet, suggestively caressing quality. Joan smiled as the rod went forward. She poked it forward. Nothing happened. Annoyed, she gave the stick a violent upward jerk.

Hal was singing down into the microphone, his eyes smiling at the adoring girls packed before him. His head jerked up suddenly, his voice broke, then he cried, "Ouch!" in startled alarm. His hand went behind him. The force of his jerking arm moving backward so quickly threw him off balance. He tripped backward swinging his arms violently to keep from falling. Some of the women directly in front of the microphone screamed; one of them, made of coarser grain, yelled, "My God! They've got him too!"

Her throaty voice resounded through the hall amplified by the mike.

Hal continued to reel backward. He tripped over a cable and, in a last valiant effort to regain his balance, went down, landing on Scat Miller's lap. Scat's saxophone clattered to the floor with a bang as with a long suffering groan Scat collapsed for the second time that night. As Scat's body sagged, Hal was thrown to the floor.

During his backward gyrations, Hal's hand had clutched at the still painful spot. As he picked himself up from the floor he held Joan's pin in the palm of his hand. A sudden flood of memory identified it. He slipped it into his pocket, the light of revenge glowing in his eyes.

It had all happened very quickly. Hal's sudden cry of surprised pain, the screams and the one woman's exclamation. Even in the darkness, Joan heard all those things over the beat of the music. Then came the solid thud of a falling body.

Frightened at what she might have done, or caused, she hurried for the door behind her. She peered cautiously out and stepped to the floor, pausing for a moment to adjust her clothes. Something bumped her in the back. She gave a terrified squeal of fright. It was the stand rolling back to its normal position. She ran ahead of it and dashed across the corridor, headed for the stairs. A policeman saw her run and took up pursuit.

His composure regained, Hal kept the band playing. When the lights went on he was down in front carrying on as usual. Burke, Fields and the excited dancers followed the retreating stand until it settled to rest.

"What happened?" Burke demanded.

"Something stung me," Hal said sheepishly. "For a moment I thought I had been stabbed. Everything's all right now." He said nothing about the pin in his pocket. He would take care of that business himself.

"Better explain to the crowd," Fields advised. "They're pretty edgy."

Hal explained the circumstances to the crowd. There was some good natured laughter. Grinning, Hal promised them one last number.

On her upward flight, Joan passed Mrs. Dufrane on the steps as she hurried to the box. Without pausing she called, "We'll see you tomorrow." A moment later the pursuing policeman caught up with her and clapped his hand on her shoulder.

"What'ya running for?" he demanded.

"Can't a girl have any privacy?" Joan demanded.

"None of that. The Inspector will want to see you." He wheeled her on the steps and led her downward.

Mrs. Dufrane was waiting. "What happened, dear?"

"Nothing," Joan shrugged. "I guess the police are nervous tonight."

Burke and Fields crossed the corridor. The policeman called to Burke, who came forward and received the explanation of Joan's quick movements right after the excitement on the floor.

Burke looked at her quizzically for a moment and asked, "You wouldn't be knowing what stung him, would you?"

"Stung whom?" Joan asked.

"Well, never mind," Burke said. "Let her go, Steve."

After a second good night to Mrs. Dufrane, Joan joined her mother in the Dufrane box.

"What's the matter with your hair?" Mrs. Paxton asked as Joan fingered the tender spot on the top of her head.

"Nothing."

"What happened down there? For a moment I thought it was another murder," Mrs. Paxton remarked with obvious disappointment.

Joan did not reply. She leaned over the corner of the box and watched Hal. A smile played over her mouth as she thought of his discomfiture. As the band swung into the famous Harrison signature song, Hal left the stand and the applause behind him and raced for the stairs and Mrs. Dufrane's box.

Hal burst into the box. During the quick run up the stairs he had had plenty of time to become angry all over again. He stopped at the table, his face red, his eyes blazing and started explosively, "You meddle some little—"

Mrs. Paxton jumped to her feet. "How dare you? Benefit or no Benefit, I won't allow you to talk to my daughter like that!"

The mention of the Benefit added fuel to Hal's rage and for a moment diverted his attention from Joan. He glared at Mrs. Paxton and spent some of his rage on her. "I'm not going to play for your Benefit and I'm sorry I ever saw either you or your nit wit daughter!" He drew the pin from his pocket and handed it to Joan.

"Here's your pin," he growled.

"Did he steal it, Joan?" Mrs. Paxton asked quickly. "I've always heard—"

"No, no," Joan cut in quickly. She giggled up into Hal's irate face. "I'm sorry. I didn't mean to hurt you. I was just testing a theory."

"Theory be damned! You purposely made me make a fool of myself," he accused.

"That wasn't hard to do, was it?" she asked icily.

"Look here! If you—"

Mrs. Paxton made a regal advance. "Young man," she began, "stop it. I've had all the nonsense from you I'll stand. You are going to play for my Benefit, so make up your mind to that right now."

"I'll die first!" Hal denied.

"That's exactly what you will do if you don't agree to play for my Benefit here and now."

Hal moved toward the door.

"Do you agree?" Mrs. Paxton insisted.

"Certainly not!"

"Very well, then, I'll tell the police what I know. Either you play for the Benefit or you go to jail."

"I'll take jail gladly," he barked and fled the box. Joan was directly behind him. He started down the corridor, Joan at his heels.

"Go away from me," he ordered.

"But I want to tell you something."

"And I don't want to hear it." He increased his stride.

"You'll be sorry if you don't listen."

"That wouldn't surprise me in the least. I've been sorry about everything you and your mother have done to me."

They rounded the corner of the balcony and started down the long side. Joan was fairly running to keep up with him. "Mother won't tell the police," she offered reassuringly.

"Let her. I might get a little peace in jail."

"But I thought you wanted to get away from San Francisco tomorrow night."

"I do."

"Then listen to what I have to tell you."

"No, thanks."

"Very well, stubborn, go to jail. I'll see you hung before I tell you now. You ought to be in jail," Joan ground out. She turned on her heel and left him.

He watched her for a moment and then followed her. "I say, wait a minute. I was angry and consequently too hasty. I have a rotten temper. It's always getting me into trouble."

Joan paid no attention but increased her pace. He had to lengthen his stride to keep up with her. She started to run.

"Be reasonable, can't you?" he asked, trotting behind her.

"Go away from me," Joan ordered.

"But I want to hear what you have to tell me!"

"And I don't want to tell you now," she flung back. She darted around the corner.

Hal overtook her. Caught her in his arms and swung her against the wall. He placed his hands on the wall so that his arms made a cage. Joan was panting slightly from the exertion. Her eyes were flashing.

"Tell me," he insisted. "You're my prisoner now and a very beautiful one."

"And you're just a dumb band leader," she chided. She ducked under his arms and ran for Mrs. Dufrane's box.

She was surprised to see Jimmie Farr at the table talking very confidentially with her mother. Jimmie looked like the cat who had swallowed the canary. He jumped up when he saw Joan and seemed anxious to get away, but Joan planted herself squarely before him and demanded, "What's she been telling you?"

"Just social notes," he answered. He saw Hal come into the box and said, "Hello, Harrison. Have you anything to say now?"

"Not a thing," Hal answered. "What's going on here?"

"Nothing that need interest you now, Mr. Harrison."

"Any little notes you'd like to give me, Miss Paxton?" Jimmie asked.

"No."

"Then I'll toddle along. Good night."

"I can depend on you to tell the truth, can't I?" Mrs. Paxton asked, beaming at him.

"Absolutely," he said. "I agree with you. And thanks for the tip." Farr slipped around Joan and out of the box.

Hal was puzzled by the whole scene. Joan ignored him. "Will you tell me now?" he asked.

"No."

"Come, darling. We mustn't associate with jailbirds."

"Aren't you being a little premature, Mrs. Paxton?" Hal asked.

"Not as much as you think. I wish you'd stop annoying my daughter with your attentions. Can't you see they are distasteful to her? Come with Mother." She put a fluttering hand on Joan's arm and moved toward the exit door.

Hal didn't understand the strange turn things had taken.

As Mrs. Paxton reached the door she turned and said with withering emphasis, "I wouldn't permit a *murderer* to play for my Hands Across the Sea Benefit!"

CHAPTER NINE

Joan thought she ought to tell Burke about her discovery before she left the Gardens, but when they were ready to go he could not be found. Her mother was impatient to get away and Joan, not knowing that her delay would make any difference, decided to wait until morning and see Burke then.

Joan spent a restless night due to the excitement and the crowded events of the evening. She thought a great deal about Hal and their several clashes. Then, too, she kept thinking about the murder, wondering who had done it, and why.

Her sleep was marred by horrible dreams. Each time she closed her eyes she found herself imprisoned beneath the bandstand. It was dark and out of the darkness would loom a man who advanced toward her threateningly. As she gasped herself awake in horror, the man would vanish and for a fleeting moment she would see the bull fiddle case. The fiddle case haunted her sleep, and her waking moments were filled with thoughts of Hal Harrison. She vowed she would never see or speak to him again. The way he had talked to her! After all, she had only been trying to help, had been following that instinct so common to most of us, our own belief in our powers as a detective. Of course it was necessary to jab Hal with her pin to prove her point.

Her sense of humor was her salvation. She giggled as she remembered his flushed face as he had thrust her pin toward her. Instinctively he had rubbed his leg with his other hand. No wonder he had been angry. Then her mother had taken such an about-face regarding him! He had sufficient reason to be annoyed with them.

He had been very nice, really, when he followed her back to the box begging for the information which she had

been anxious to give him and then had so perversely held
back. Well, she was glad she hadn't told him. Did he
really mean it when he said she was beautiful? She'd tell
him in the morning if she saw him and he could explain
to Burke. Poor chap! She had given him an awful
evening. Enough to make him cross.

As she thought about the events of the preceding
night she was too thoroughly awakened to hope to sleep
again. It was already dawn. She slipped from her bed and
went to the window. The sky across the bay was tinted
with pink. The new bridges loomed large and mysterious
through the wispy fog in the half light. She shivered. The
air was cold. As she reached for her dressing gown one of
her mules rattled to the floor.

"Is that you, Joan?" Mrs. Paxton called from the
adjoining room. "Can't you sleep?"

"No."

"Neither can I." Mrs. Paxton sighed wearily. She
appeared in the door, a net on her hair, adhesive
crescents beside her eyes, a chin bandage holding her
extra chin in place.

"Guilty conscience?" Joan asked.

"Certainly not. Why should I feel guilty? I haven't
done a thing. I—" She yawned with difficulty due to the
bandage. The painful operation over, she asked wistfully,
"I wonder if it's too early for breakfast?"

"Good idea! I'd like some coffee myself. I'll call room
service. What will you have?"

"The usual—no, make it fruit, cereal and ham and
eggs this morning. And, Joan, tell them to send up a
paper. All the papers. I think it will be fun to read about
the murder over our coffee, don't you?"

As Joan turned from the telephone she asked, "Why
are you so interested in the papers? You know more about
what happened than the newspaper men. You were with
Burke when he was asking all the questions."

"You'll see," Mrs. Paxton promised archly.

Joan paid no attention as she absently pulled on a pair of stockings and then fluffed up her hair. Mrs. Paxton stood watching her. "We'll go home tomorrow, Joan," she said.

"But I thought you were determined to have Harrison play for you! What about your bet?"

"I'm willing to lose the bet. I don't expect to see Hal Harrison ever again."

"I must see him before we go. It's very important."

"You take Mother's advice and stay away from him. As a matter of fact, you must not see him again."

"And why not? You followed him across the United States, you know, and dragged me with you."

"Reggie wouldn't like it," Mrs. Paxton pronounced. "That reminds me, I think I'll wire Reggie that we're coming. How would you like to be married on a nice cool October day?"

"Not to Reggie," Joan said quickly.

"Now, Joan, Mother knows what is best for you."

"If Reggie is your idea, you don't, so let's not discuss it any further."

"But, Joan—"

"I won't marry Reggie and the sooner you get that notion out of your head, the better it will be for all of us," Joan flared.

Any further conversation was cut short by the arrival of waiters with the breakfast table and a neat pile of the morning papers. When they were alone, Mrs. Paxton hastened to the table and reached for the papers. In her hurry she brushed them to the floor. With a grunt she bent over to pick them up.

Paper in hand, she toddled toward the window for a better light and started to read. After a moment she cried, "Oh! oh! oh!" She sank into a chair, tears of anger and frustration filling her eyes.

Joan leaped across the room. "What is it?"

Mrs. Paxton couldn't speak. She pointed at the paper where Joan read:

BAND LEADER MYSTERIOUSLY MURDERED!
New York Society Girl Hoodwinks Police.
Pulls Wool over Eyes of Gullible Inspector
to Save Hal Harrison from Arrest!

Beneath a four column cut of Hal, Mrs. Dufrane, Mrs. Paxton and Joan, a caption read:

The local social leader, Mrs. John Carter Dufrane, and her New York friends, Mrs. Llewellyn Paxton and daughter, Joan, with Hal Harrison immediately after being questioned about the death of Phil Martin.

The story followed:

Joan Paxton, the New York debutante who has followed Harrison across the country, last night lied effectively to divert Inspector Burke's suspicions from the famous singer and band leader. This paper can prove this statement and offers the information to the police for what it is worth.

Joan threw the paper to the floor and stamped on it in a frenzy of rage. Her anger was overwhelming because there was nothing she could do about it. One doesn't choke one's mother if one is a normal person, no matter what the provocation might be.

"Joan, darling!" Mrs. Paxton cried tearfully. "Don't! You'll get a headache."

"I have a headache!" Joan cried. "Why did you do it? Why? Why?"

"I didn't want them to print anything mean about you," Mrs. Paxton explained tearfully.

"So you told that reporter things he'd have given his eye teeth to have known. And you just handed it to him. What do you think Burke will do to us now?"

"But I was afraid they might misconstrue things. That reporter promised me to word it all very carefully. He was just going to hint to the police. He said he'd be subtle."

"He was as delicate as a twenty four inch gun." Joan paced up and down the room.

Mrs. Paxton poured herself a cup of coffee. "Come have your coffee. You'll feel better. Oh, dear, the eggs are cold! The idea of their serving cold food!"

"There's one consolation in the whole business," Joan said heartfully. "This will be the end of Reggie. He'd never marry me now." She was seething, trying to vent her anger. She stopped suddenly, pointed an accusing finger at her mother and demanded, "What will he think of me now?"

"I'll explain it all to Reggie." Mrs. Paxton's faith in her ability to fix all things was astounding. "I'll tell him all about it."

"Reggie! I wasn't thinking about Reggie! I meant that conceited, egotistical, self satisfied Hal Harrison!" Joan strode to her dressing table with the tread of a soldier going into battle.

She took a comb and raked it viciously through her hair, crying, "Ouch!" as the fine teeth caught the scar which had formed as a result of her bump under the stand.

"What is it, dear?" Mrs. Paxton asked solicitously.

"Nothing, just that scar."

"You must be careful. You might get an infection. I knew a woman once—"

"Save it," Joan cut her short. "I'm not going to get an infection and I'm not going to die until I've told that reporter what I think of him." She threw down the comb. She jerked the belt of her robe firmly around her slim waist, tied it into an enduring knot. With lips set in a firm line, she picked up the paper. She opened the hall door and marched grimly down the corridor.

At the door of Hal's suite she knocked rapidly. There was no answer. She banged again. Still no answer. She kicked at the door, hurting her foot. She was clutching the injured toe when a sleepy voice asked, "What is it?"

"Let me in!" she demanded.

"Listen, lady, go away," Maxie's sleepy voice advised.

"I can't!" she cried.

There was no reply from behind the door. Joan leaned close to the jamb. "Wait!" she begged tearfully. "You must listen to me! It's important! Look at the paper! I'll slide it under the door. We've got to do something!" As she talked, she was pushing the paper under the door with the toe of her slipper.

It vanished suddenly. After a moment she heard a startled whistle, then the door opened and she stepped inside. "Where is he?" she demanded of Maxie.

"What's all this racket?" Hal asked from the door of his bedroom. He was dressed in silk pajamas, his feet tucked into the woolly slippers. When he saw Joan, he stepped back.

"I won't hurt you!" she called, "any more than I have. Come out here and learn the worst! You're in a mess and we're responsible for it."

"Who told you?" he asked.

"Don't let's start quarreling and haggling, please," she begged. "You've got to get out of here."

"It's serious, all right," Maxie agreed, holding the paper toward Hal.

Looking like a sleepy Cossack in his Russian pajamas, Hal crossed the room and read the front page quickly. "Did you do this?" he asked.

"Same thing. My mother did," she answered. "We had the papers sent up. If you hurry, you may be able to get away before the police arrive!" He stared at her incredulously. "You must hide!" she cried in exasperation. "You've got to do something!"

"What, for example?" he asked bitterly, letting the paper drop to the floor. "Everything else has already happened to me! I may just as well go to jail."

"Don't be like that! You're not going to take it sitting down, are you?" she demanded.

"There's nothing else to do."

"But you must get away."

"Where could I go? Where could I hide? I'm too well known. I've got to take it."

"But they'll arrest you surely now. Oh, dear! I've made an awful mess of things."

He shrugged, and lit a cigarette. "Sometimes I think jail would be quiet and restful. I think I'd enjoy it there. At least I wouldn't have women messing in my life and private affairs." He turned away.

Joan took an impulsive step after him. "Please, Mr. Harrison, I'm sorry. Really I am. I knew nothing about this. I'll do anything I can to make this up to you."

He wheeled. "Can I depend on that?" He strode toward her.

"Yes, anything." Her eyes were rimmed with tears of contrition as they looked up at him earnestly. Her lips were slightly parted. All her pert smartness was gone. She was just a very pretty young girl with tears in her eyes.

Hal was captivated by her woeful expression. She seemed so beaten by what had happened. He stared at her for a moment. His mood changed. He wanted to comfort this girl who was feeling the thing so deeply. Before he realized what he was doing he bent forward and kissed her gently.

Joan recoiled as if stung. A kiss was the last thing in the world she had expected. Being essentially a fair person she had honestly wanted to make amends for the terrible thing her mother had done. Instead of meeting her man to man, he had kissed her. She swung away from him, wiping his kiss from her lips.

Maxie's reaction was immediate. "Well, I'll be damned!" he exploded. "Are you crazy?"

"Not him!" Joan said scornfully. "He's not crazy! It's just his great lover complex."

Hal was surprised at himself. It was the last thing in the world he had expected to do as he crossed to her. "But—" he started to explain.

"You needn't say a thing," she retorted quickly. "It's quite all right. I left myself open for it. I'm to blame. I'll probably see you in jail."

"It can't be as bad as that," Hal said. "We'll find a way out."

"Maybe," Maxie said morosely. His eyes followed Joan's trim figure as she hurried toward the door.

"Wait a minute. You can't go out now!" Hal cried as he heard angry voices arguing in the hall. Joan hesitated. A forceful pounding sounded against the door.

Hal ran to Joan and grabbed her by the arm. "You've got to hide!"

"I've nothing to conceal. I'm not afraid."

"Then I am. I won't have people knowing that you were in my room dressed like that at this hour of the morning."

"I can take it if you can't," she answered defiantly and squared herself to face him.

Exasperated, Hal glanced wildly about the room. "Get in there!" he ordered, pointing toward a closet.

"I won't," she defied.

With a quick sweep of his arms, Hal gathered her up, crossed the room, dropped her into the closet and closed the door. "Be quiet," he ordered as he turned the key. In his haste, he closed the door on part of her gown. As she tried to pull the gown through, a bit of lace caught on a sliver of wood and tore.

With a glance back at the closet Hal said, "Let them in, Maxie, before they break the door down."

The fidgety little hotel manager, Mr. Belknap, entered with a large, irate man. The man was in his late forties, well groomed and obviously a gentleman. "Where's my wife?" he demanded.

"You've made a mistake," Hal said quietly.

Maxie cleared his throat nervously. "Yeah, we're all out of wives," he said in a dismal attempt at lightness.

"Don't get funny!" the man said heavily. He crossed to Hal's bedroom and glanced inside. He started toward Maxie's room, then stopped suddenly.

Inside the closet Joan was frantically trying to pull her gown through the crack. The lace was persistent and stuck. She couldn't hear the slight tearing sound but it had attracted the attention of the man. His hand flashed into his pocket and came out with a gun. He aimed it at the closet door and cried, "Come out!"

"Don't shoot!" Hal cried.

Belknap groaned and stuffed his fingers into his ears, waiting for the shot.

Hal jumped toward the man, who repeated, "Come out, I tell you!"

Hal was just in time to strike up the man's arm as the gun went off. The bullet splintered the upper panel of the door.

"You fool!" Hal raged and wrenched the gun from the amazed man's hand.

In a bound Hal was at the door. He yanked it open. An unconscious Joan tumbled lifelessly into his arms.

"That does it!" Maxie groaned as he ran forward. "This means the end of our contract with Higgins. A girl murdered in your room at this hour of the morning."

"Shut up! Call a doctor! Do something!" Hal cried as he carried Joan to the couch.

Belknap stared at Joan. His mouth dropped open in utter bewilderment.

"But—But—" the strange man stammered. Joan sighed, then recovering quickly said, "I'm all right, I guess."

Maxie gave a whoop of relief and turned to the man, demanding, "Who do you think you are, shooting up the place, nearly killing people?"

Hal was tenderly solicitous of Joan as she insisted upon sitting up. "I never faint," she assured Hal. "I didn't sleep much. I—"

"Should I call the cops?" Maxie asked. "What do you want to do with Jesse James?"

"Not the police," Joan cried and flashed a look at Hal.

The man drew a crumpled newspaper from his pocket and gazed at it, completely puzzled.

"You'd better go," Belknap suggested to him.

"Wait a minute," Hal cut in. "Who are you, and why did you come shooting your way into my suite?"

"This picture," the man began an explanation. "My wife! I thought she was here!"

"Why should she be here?" Hal demanded. "I don't know your wife."

"But the picture—" The man tapped it with his finger.

"He's John Carter Dufrane," Belknap explained. "He came raving into the lobby this morning waving the paper and insisting that his wife was here with you."

"She didn't come home all night," Dufrane said. His eyes were hollow spots in red rims as he looked at them. "I didn't know what to think. I was nearly crazy. I went out into the streets looking for her. I couldn't find her anywhere. Then I bought the morning paper. The first thing I saw was her picture taken with you." He laughed bitterly. "She has always had a weakness for orchestra leaders but she didn't think I knew it. When I saw the picture I thought—"

"Forget it. She's probably home now."

"But why didn't she come home earlier?"

Joan moved forward. "I can explain about the picture. Mrs. Dufrane was with my mother. We had a box together. She left us about twelve thirty."

"But she didn't come home," he insisted. "Was she alone?"

"Yes. When she left us she promised to join us for tea this afternoon."

"I don't understand it," he insisted.

Hal took him by the arm and led him unprotesting to the door. "You'll find your wife and we'll forget all this ever happened," he promised. He gave Dufrane a gentle shove into the hall. Belknap minced in their wake. At the door he turned and said, "All I have to say, Mr. Harrison, is that I'm surprised at you." He left quickly. Hal closed the door after them.

"Phew!" He leaned against the door as limp as a day old cream puff.

"Why don't you get dressed before the police come," Maxie suggested.

"Wait a minute," Joan said, "I must go."

"Why the rush?"

"Because we've brought you nothing but bad luck, Mother and I, but that's all over now. We're leaving for New York on the first possible train."

"And desert me with all my troubles?" Hal asked. "I'm not a sinking ship. I haven't foundered yet. We'd better talk this over first. I'm not so sure you'll be allowed to leave, you know. How about a cup of coffee?"

She looked at him a moment, smiled faintly, and replied, "Why not?"

Maxie was already at the telephone giving the order.

"You had a close call. I don't see how the bullet missed you. I was afraid to open the door."

"I was bent down, trying to pull my nightgown through the crack. Then I heard you cry, 'Don't shoot!' and I didn't know what was happening until the bullet crashed through the door over my head."

"He might have killed you." Hal was still concerned with that possibility.

"The man's crazy," Maxie suggested.

"She told me he was jealous," Joan said, "but I'd no idea he was a madman to boot."

"What do you suppose happened to Mrs. Dufrane?" Hal asked.

"I don't know. She seemed worried about something all evening. When she told me about her husband and mentioned publicity, I thought that was her trouble."

"We nearly had another murder on our hands," Maxie said.

"I'm hard to kill," Joan answered laughingly.

"I guess you are. I'd rather have your luck than a license to steal." Then he turned to Hal. "If you're up for the day, you'd better get going on your throat exercises."

"I'd forgotten," Hal answered. He felt of his throat for a moment and then hummed, "me, me, me, me, me me."

Joan giggled at the performance.

"What's so funny?" he demanded.

"Nothing!"

"All singers have to do this," he answered. "It's very important to have your throat opened. Me me, me, me, me me."

"While you're doing your me mes why not put your robe on before we have any more callers?" Maxie suggested.

With a nod to Joan, Hal went to his room. He combed his hair carefully, gurgling, "Me, me, and do, re, mi, fa, so, la, ti, do." He paused a moment to look at himself quizzically. He rubbed critical fingers over his fresh beard, shrugged, and went on with his scales as he slipped into his beautifully monogrammed dressing gown.

The coffee had arrived when he returned to the sitting room. Joan was on the couch, ready to pour. He was still loosening his voice, running the scales gaily. Maxie gave him a questioning stare.

"There's no reason for him to feel so chipper," Maxie thought sourly.

"Quite a lark in the morning, aren't you?" Joan asked as he sat down beside her.

"It has to be done. Quite necessary. It's a habit. I owe it—"

"To your public?" she asked impishly as she handed him a cup of coffee.

"Does it annoy you?" he asked casually.

"I wouldn't say that. It is no concern of mine."

"But it is. I'm going to make myself very important to you from now on. If my exercises annoy you after we're married we'll have to have separate suites."

Joan was startled by the bland statement, but poor Maxie was overwhelmed. He gulped, choked, and sputtered a fountain like spray of hot coffee across the room.

"And what of Mary Dale?" Joan asked.

"Mary and I are just friends," he answered. "I'm serious."

Joan's laughter rippled over the coughing sputterings of poor Maxie.

"Listen!" Hal cried. "I want to know something about the man who is waiting for you in New York."

"Mother was arranging that this morning. She thinks I ought to be married in October. Do you think that's a good time to be married?"

"Look here," he begged. "Don't josh so! I know we haven't known each other very long, but that doesn't matter, does it?"

"Do you expect me to say, 'This is so sudden,' and fall into your arms, filled with gratitude and thankfulness for the great honor you are paying me?"

Maxie, still choking, was trying to keep back the coughs so that he could hear the balance of their conversation.

"Do you think I'm as bad as that?" he asked seriously. "Can't you see the real me that is buried beneath this necessary front of public life?"

"I'm not criticizing you or your life. I'm just wondering why you've had this sudden change of heart. You did hate me last night, you know."

"I thought I hated you but I've changed my mind."

"You'll probably hate me again before we're through with this. We're not out of the woods yet. Wait until Burke sees the papers."

"Oh, hang Burke and the whole silly business!"

"I wish we could," she said thoughtfully.

"I will if you say so," he promised boastfully.

Before Joan could think of an answer there was a determined bang, bang on the door. Then without more ado it swung open and Burke and two officers walked in.

"So you lied to me, eh?" Burke barked at Joan. "You thought you'd make a fool of me in the newspapers, huh?"

Joan jumped to her feet. "Inspector Burke! We were talking about you. We were coming over to explain. It wasn't all lies. I—"

"I wouldn't believe you now on a stack of Bibles," he growled.

"But, Inspector—" Hal came forward.

Burke didn't even listen to what they were trying to say. He pointed at Hal. "Come on, Harrison. We're going down to headquarters to book you on a charge of murder. Get some clothes on."

"Why put me in jail?" Hal demanded. "I can't get away."

"Jail's where you belong and jail's where you're going! Get dressed! Go with him, Thurston, and see that there's no funny business. You stay in the hall, Smith, and see that no one leaves by any of the other doors."

Maxie groaned. He clutched Burke by the arm. "Don't do this, Inspector. He ain't done nothing. His sponsor'll go crazy if Hal gets mixed up in a scandal! It'll ruin his popularity. We gotta be in New York by Tuesday to start a new series of broadcasts!"

"That's just too bad," Burke replied coldly.

Hal shrugged. Followed by the policeman, he entered his bedroom.

"Will this affect his contract?" Joan asked Maxie.

"Will it? Higgins is the head of the Purity League. He won't stand for any nonsense and Hal knows it. We've got to get out of this somehow."

"We will," Joan assured him brightly.

"Not where you're going," Burke said grimly.

"Me?" Joan pretended a surprise she did not feel.

"Yes, you. Get some clothes on. I'm arresting you, too."

"On what charge?" Joan demanded.

"As an accessory after the fact, interfering with justice, and willfully shielding a criminal. You're going to jail."

Hal's door flew open. He was only partially dressed. "You can't take her to jail!" he bellowed.

"Can't! Who says I can't?"

"Well, she won't be of any use to you there," Hal said cockily.

"Oh, she won't, won't she?"

"No."

"And why not?"

"It's the law."

"You're telling me about the law!" Burke's face was reddening with rage.

Hal shrugged. "You know you can't make a wife testify against her husband."

"Wife?" Burke gasped.

Maxie gulped, suppressing a groan. He reached for his box of aspirin as Joan clapped a hand over her mouth to keep back a wild desire to laugh at Burke's surprise and Maxie's discomfiture. Burke whirled on Hal.

"So you're married? All right—who were your witnesses?"

"Who do you think?" Hal sparred for time. "Why—the judge's wife and Maxie."

Maxie shuddered as Burke looked at him. He managed to nod weakly in agreement.

"Where were you married?"

"Reno. We flew there last night." He retired into his room, throwing the balance of the conversation to Maxie and Joan.

Burke tugged his ear thoughtfully.

While he was thinking, Joan asked, "Will I have time to change, or will you take me like this?" She indicated her nightgown and robe. She sauntered toward the door.

"Get some respectable clothes on," he ordered.

"I'll go, but of course you know you're going to look awfully silly when the facts come out."

"Don't try to stall me, Mrs. Harrison!"

"Mrs. Harrison!" Maxie groaned.

"What's the matter with you?" Burke snapped at Maxie.

"He hasn't gotten accustomed to the idea yet, have you, Maxie? As a matter of fact, I'm not used to my new name myself, so don't be surprised if I don't answer you immediately when you call me Mrs. Harrison."

"Wait a minute! What facts did you mean just now?" Burke asked, suspicion tinged with anxiety in his voice.

"It wasn't all lies that story I told you. I was near Mr. Harrison. The only lie I told was about his arms being around me. They weren't and we were not having a lovers' quarrel. We were arguing about something else when I said I hoped he'd hang. I was trying to make him angry."

She told Burke about her mother's pending Benefit and their crazy dash across country in pursuit of Hal. She was a brilliant raconteur and added several embellishments which made him smile once or twice. She then hurried on to tell him about crawling under the bandstand and her experiment, the results of which he already knew. He laughed openly when she explained Hal's alleged sting which had so startled all the people in the dance hall.

"You see, Inspector, I'm sure that's the way the murder was committed. Don't you agree with me?"

"There's something in what you say," he admitted grudgingly. "Why didn't you tell me this last night? Why did you let that report get into the papers to make a monkey out of me?"

She explained her mother's desire to force Hal to play for the Benefit. "I wouldn't do a thing like that for many reasons," she added.

"It puts a different aspect on the situation," he conceded. "I'll have to think it over."

"I'm sure it does," she agreed. "I know the murderer was in there. He had to be."

"And you went in there messing around and ruined all our chances of finding any clues," he accused. "Fingerprints and all that sort of business."

"But the murderer was wearing gloves," she reminded him.

"That's right. But how was it done?" he asked thoughtfully. "How could a man balance a knife like that on a stick?"

"You'll find out," she said confidently.

"And you didn't see any stick or pole?" he asked.

"No. Nothing but the blue light gleaming on the steel."

"That's queer," he said slowly.

"Inspector—" Joan caught the lapel of his coat in her hand but he brushed it away. She paid no attention to the rebuff as she hurried on, "About the newspapers."

He stiffened as he remembered his own ridicule.

"You can make Farr look silly!" she promised. "Give a statement to all the other papers, telling them that Mr. Harrison, you and I agreed on that story because you didn't want the criminal to realize that you already knew how the crime was committed. Say that you now have evidence leading directly to the real criminal and expect to make an arrest sometime today."

"I have no evidence and you know it," he growled.

"But—"

"You think the crime was committed that way and I'm inclined to agree with you, but where's our motive and who did it?"

"But, Inspector, surely since you now realize that Mr. Harrison couldn't have done it, you will be able to see things with fresh eyes. There must be something out there at the Gardens which will give an experienced man like yourself the clue you need."

Hal came back fully dressed. "All ready, Burke?" he asked.

"For what?" Burke snapped.

"Jail, of course," Hal laughed shortly. "It's going to be a great publicity stunt. I'll pack 'em in for weeks on the strength of your mistake. You know I ought to give you a commission on my extra box-office."

"You're not going to jail, not yet! The little lady here has told me a couple of things."

Hal stopped near the piano. "But you said—" he remonstrated.

"Never mind what I said," Burke retorted.

Hal struck a note thoughtfully. "But I want to go to jail. I don't think you ought to deprive me of this publicity. It was your own suggestion, you know. I want to go to jail!" He looked gaily over his shoulder at Joan as he accompanied his last words with staccato notes. He liked the sound and continued singing, "I want to go to jail."

"Stop that nonsense! Say, what kind of a honeymoon is this?" Burke demanded.

"What's that got to do with my going to jail?" Hal demanded. "I'm an artist. I have my public to consider. My career comes first. Do I go to jail?" He punctuated his question with a chord.

"You may wind up there yet. Remember this, you two. Don't leave San Francisco again until I give you permission."

"We must leave tomorrow morning by plane," Hal said as his fingers floated over the keys.

"You'll leave when I give the word and not before!" Burke barked. "And stop that damned racket!" he shouted. "Come on, boys!" He started for the door.

"You'll solve the murder by midnight, won't you?" Joan begged, running after him. "It means so much to Mr. Harrison."

"I hope so," Burke flung back at her.

As the door closed behind the law, Joan moved over to the piano, where Hal was busy playing with one finger, "Tell me, pretty maiden, are there any more at home like you?"

Joan watched him speculatively for a moment, her foot keeping time with his playing. He finished and looked up with a grin. "We fixed that, didn't we?"

"We did." She spun on her heel. "We're even now!"

"What do you mean, even?" He followed her. "Where are you going?"

"To get a quick divorce. Talk about me getting you into a mess!"

He reached out and grabbed her arm. "Relax," he advised. "I did it to keep you out of jail. Who's going to find out about it?"

"Burke," she answered with assurance. "He isn't half as dumb as we think he is."

"But it gives us a little time. We've got to do something about this murder ourselves. We're in a mess. Unless we supplement the work the police are doing, our children will be native sons."

"You do jump ahead, don't you?" His remark startled her but she replied at once to hide her feelings. "Maybe you're right about turning detective. What shall we do?"

"Right? Of course I'm right! We'll all be on our way to New York tomorrow morning! Just you wait and see."

There was a discreet tap on the door.

"Now what?" Maxie groaned.

To Hal's "Come in" the door swung open. It was Mr. Belknap, the manager. He was full of smiles and contrition. "Why didn't you tell me?" he asked coyly. "I should have known. I'm sorry for what I said to you, Mr. Harrison, and I don't know what you think of me, Mrs. Harrison."

"What are you driving at?" Hal demanded.

"Oh, you know." He gave a half titter. "Inspector Burke told me about you. I took the liberty of ordering a wedding breakfast for you. It's my little present." His hand fluttered toward the door. He called, "Come in, come in."

A middle aged waiter rolled in a service cart. "Compliments of the hotel," Mr. Belknap beamed as he hovered over the table which a second waiter had carried in and arranged. Belknap fluttered about, adding deft touches here and there to the silver and cloth.

"It's just ducky, isn't it?"" Joan said to Hal.

His reply was prevented by an indignant, shrill voice in the hall demanding admittance.

"Mother!" Joan groaned.

"I most certainly will go in!" Mrs. Paxton shrieked as she backed into the room arguing with a waiter. As she stepped backward her heels caught in her negligee. A few more steps and she would have been denuded except for her nightgown. She stopped, kicked her feet free from the robe and, whirling round, pointed an accusing finger at Joan and demanded, "What have you been doing in here all this time? I couldn't believe my eyes when I woke up from my little nap."

Belknap looked at her reprovingly. "Madam!" he gasped.

She ignored him. "Joan, go to your room at once. I'll settle with this young man. To think that a daughter of mine—"

The march of incoming waiters bearing trays cut her short and forced her to one side of the room. "What is this?" she demanded.

Mr. Belknap gave her a sly nudge. "As if you didn't know!" he said coyly. He turned to Hal. "Will you want to see the reporters now, Mr. Harrison? They're here," he said. "I sent for the photographers, too," he added.

"Did you send for them?" Joan demanded angrily.

"No. I've no idea how they knew. They seem to know everything," Belknap cried as he hustled hither and yon.

"Burke," Hal's lips formed the word as Joan glanced toward him.

She flashed a quick understanding smile and shrugged.

"Photographers?" Mrs. Paxton exclaimed, puffing her hair up. "What for?"

"Don't be silly!" Belknap admonished as his fluttering hands indicated the young couple. "You know the papers love pictures of a bridal party."

"Bridal party!" Mrs. Paxton gasped. "Bridal—Joan! You—" She swayed forward and swooned in Belknap's arms.

CHAPTER TEN

Burke was not altogether pleased with the turn things had taken. He thought about Hal Harrison as he rode away from the hotel. Burke knew human nature well enough to know that Hal was a quick tempered young man who might do most anything on the spur of the moment. But this unreasonable murder had not been done spontaneously. It had been planned, carefully planned so that suspicion would be diverted away from the real criminal. Why?

He knew when he had answered that question he would have fairly clear sailing. It had all seemed so simple at first. Harrison and Martin were enemies. They had quarreled at the Gardens. Harrison had made that threatening statement. But someone had threatened Hal's life. For a few minutes, early in the investigation, he had believed he saw the end in sight. But it was not to be as simple as that. Instead of an open and shut case, Burke found himself involved in a murder that did not make sense. He hated ingenious murders. They were all right to read about in books, but in real life they were too complicated and meant too much hard, laborious work tracking down hundreds of wrong clues before the right one turned up.

He was perfectly satisfied that Hal Harrison had a reasonable motive for the murder. Suppose the girl was wrong? Had he been a fool to listen to her story? She was in love with Harrison. Perhaps she knew that Harrison had stabbed Martin and she had cooked up a story to save her lover's life. She admitted having lied to him. No; that didn't hold. He was inclined to believe Joan Paxton because the statement made by Pete Schwartz corroborated her story.

There was something fishy about the whole set up, however. None of the parts clung together. Why? He had been all wrong about Harrison and the Dale girl. He had jumped to the obvious conclusion that they were in love and wanted Martin out of the way. In nine cases out of ten, he would have been right and the case would have been over. This was the tenth case, however, and his theory had to be abandoned because of the marriage of Harrison and the Paxton girl.

Strange that Kelton should have been at the Gardens. It wasn't like Kelton, and yet, if he was in love with Charlotte it would explain everything. Even men like Kelton veer from the normal when they are in love.

There was the Dufrane woman, too. It looked bad for her for a while. Perhaps she was telling the truth about the money. Odd that it should be the exact amount found on Martin. Too bad the men had not been able to find any important papers in Martin's flat. A package of letters belonging to Mrs. Dufrane would write finis to the case at once. It would be so easy to reconstruct. She went out there to see Martin, gave him the money, but he refused to return her letters. Furious, she had killed him. There ought to be papers. Martin must have kept records. He'd have a look at that apartment later. The men may not have been thorough. He'd do that after he had looked over the Gardens in daylight.

Burke was annoyed with his suspects for not conforming to a pattern. He was determined to keep the case as simple as possible. With Kelton, Harrison and Mrs. Dufrane out of it, who was the next most likely suspect? The Dale girl, of course. She had some ax to grind. She admitted wanting a divorce from Martin. Perhaps she was in love with some other man and wanted to be free. It was just the sort of crime a woman could and would think of committing. How did he know that she didn't do it? Joan Paxton swore that Mary Dale had passed her just before Martin was killed. It had been dark there. The Paxton girl could be wrong. Mary Dale could have slipped round the end of the bandstand. If the Paxton girl crawled in there so easily, Mary Dale could have done the same thing. Once under the stand she killed Martin and then hurried back to the stand. She would have had plenty of time to have done it. When the murder was discovered she was there ready to scream, thus giving herself an alibi which would be hard to break.

It was a good and reasonable theory and he would have to do something about it and do it quickly. But how did she do the killing? What implement had she used to hold the knife? Whatever it was, it must be in the Gardens. She couldn't have taken it away with her. The instrument found, the case would be plain sailing from then on. Before he reached the station he convinced himself that he had the solution in the palm of his hand. Laugh at him, would they? He'd show them. He'd spread the story of Hal's romantic wedding to the newspapers, that is, all but the *Crescent*, Farr's paper. Try to make a fool of him, would they? He'd show the *Crescent*. Why hadn't they called him before they printed such a story? Afraid he'd stop them. Just like a newspaper, print the story first and get the facts later. He'd sue them. No, better not. He wasn't dead sure yet. Best to be careful and tread lightly in such cases. Wouldn't Farr be sore, though, when he woke up to learn that he'd been sound asleep and missed the news of the wedding?

Ten minutes later he was at his desk calling the San Francisco papers. He even followed Joan's suggestion and told them that the story in the *Crescent* was a cooked up job to give the real murderer confidence. No, he was not in a position to divulge the name of the murderer. He promised them all a good break later in the day.

CHAPTER ELEVEN

At the hotel Belknap was enjoying himself. He had roused the members of Hal's orchestra, inviting them all to the impromptu breakfast.

When Hal realized what Belknap had been doing, he had a hurried consultation with Joan. After considering the situation from all angles they decided to go on pretending that they were married, for the duration of the breakfast at least. Hal argued that the news might slip out and they would be caught in a second lie before they had had a chance to take any action whatever.

In spite of Belknap's efficient management and prissy fussiness, the feast lacked the sparkle and verve that should have been rampant on such a gay occasion. Mrs. Paxton, for once in her life, was comparatively quiet. The bride and groom were preoccupied. Maxie floundered about in a fog, colliding with reporters and photographers until he managed to shoo them from the room. Mary Dale sat back deep in thought. Joe Stevens tried to liven the party with a few impromptu melodies, but that didn't work because it was barely seven o'clock and some of the other hotel guests made irritable protests that could not be ignored.

At the very height of the forced gaiety, Mary Dale slipped away from the table and left the room. Joan followed her. There was an awkward moment as the two girls faced each other. Joan advanced impulsively and put her hand on Mary's arm. "I'm sorry," she said.

"So'm I," Mary replied honestly. "It's just one of those things. Life is like that, isn't it? Oh, well," she shrugged and busied herself with a compact, trying to mask her feelings with powder and rouge. As she snapped the lid closed, she said, "You won't ever tell him about me, will you?"

"Never," Joan replied quickly.

Mary kissed Joan impulsively. "I wish you luck! You're a good kid! It won't be easy at times being the wife of a man like Hal. You want to be happy, don't you?" she asked seriously. Joan nodded. "Then always remember he's a band leader. He lives at night when other people are asleep. It isn't a normal life but you've got sense enough to get used to it." She turned toward the door. "Let's go back."

Joan stopped her. "Mary, wait! I can't lie to you." Quickly she related the circumstances and Hal's lie to prevent her arrest.

"He's in love with you just the same," Mary said. "He'll marry you, too. If I were you I'd do it right away before the police learn of this second hoax. We're not out of the woods yet, any of us."

"What do you mean by that?" Joan asked quickly.

"There are so many complications." Mary's voice trailed away.

"It's none of my business, Mary, but you're worried about something. I've been watching you. What is it? Do you want to tell me? Are you afraid?" she asked bluntly.

"Yes, I am. I'm bound to be connected with the murder."

"But why?" Joan gasped.

"It goes back to the time I wanted my divorce. When I realized what Phil was planning to do, I wrote him a threatening letter in which I told him I'd kill him if he ever interfered with Hal in any way. I wrote the letter before I knew that Hal could keep Phil quiet and needed no help from me."

"That's nothing to worry about." Joan tried to laugh away her fears.

"You didn't know Phil. He kept that letter. If the police ever find it they'll arrest me."

"But they searched his apartment," Joan reminded her.

"That doesn't prove a thing. They didn't know Phil."

"Why didn't you tell us about it last night?" Joan asked. "We could have done something about it then."

"You had trouble enough of your own last night."

"Perhaps Martin destroyed it?"

"Not Phil."

"Try not to think about it," Joan suggested tenderly. "No news is good news. It hasn't been found, you can be sure of that. Burke was here, you know, and when he couldn't arrest us he'd certainly have turned to you if he had the slightest grounds for suspicion."

"That's the point. I must get the note. Once they find it they'll arrest me."

"Then we'll have to get it for you."

"If it isn't too late," Mary added pessimistically.

"It's never too late to try. Wait a minute." Joan went to the door leading to the sitting room and called Hal, who came immediately.

As soon as she explained Mary's predicament to him he said, "We've got to go over to Phil's apartment at once."

"But the police may be there," Joan objected.

"We've got to take that chance. We want to find his papers before the police get them. Burke would love to find something as definite as that. Remember how eagerly he looked through the things the men brought from Phil's apartment? Burke has reached an impasse. He had only one thing on his mind this morning and that was the story in the Crescent. When he stops to think, he's going to do things," Hal assured her.

"To us when he learns that we're not married," Joan suggested. "What are you going to do about that?"

"I thought we agreed not to tell anyone about the hoax," he said, surprised.

"Mary's different," Joan replied.

"I'll say she is. You understand, don't you, Mary?" he asked.

She nodded.

"Perhaps the note is in a safety deposit box," Joan suggested.

"No." Mary was positive. "He had his own hiding places for things. He prided himself on his ingenuity. It ought to be in his apartment."

"Then let's hope it's still there," Joan cried.

"It is unless there's someone else who knows him as well as I do," Mary replied.

"Come on," Hal urged, "there's no time to lose. Whatever we do we must do it quickly."

Hal didn't know how right he was. He had no means of knowing what was going on in Burke's mind or in the office of the *Crescent*, where the city editor was a raving maniac as he tried to rouse Jimmie Farr from what Jimmie considered a well earned sleep. Blissfully ignorant of the wheels which had been set in motion they started for Phil Martin's apartment.

They had no difficulty finding the building, because Mary remembered the address which Burke had asked for the night before. The street was deserted except for an expensive roadster standing at the curb. The building itself was old, suggesting a glory which had passed. The lobby with its frayed elegance was depressing. A rickety elevator, door open, stood at the far end of the long hall.

Hal paused before a long line of letter boxes to get the apartment number. When they reached the elevator Hal moved forward to press the button but Joan stopped him. "Let's walk up," she suggested. "We don't want to be seen."

"Right," he agreed and turned toward the stairs.

Martin's apartment was on the second floor. Outside the door they hesitated for several seconds, listening intently to make sure that there was no one inside.

"How are we going to get in?" Joan whispered.

"We'll try the simple way first," Hal said and carefully turned the knob. The door swung open quietly.

"See? Simple!" Hal said.

"Careless of the police, you mean," Joan said. "I'm going to lock it behind us. We don't want to be surprised."

"Good idea. Come on!" Hal cried and led the way inside.

On tiptoes they crossed the foyer toward the living room. At the door Hal stopped and whistled. The girls pressed forward eagerly. The room had been turned inside out. Drawers stood open—papers littered the floor. An open closet door revealed a topsy turvy interior.

"The police did a good job of it, didn't they?" Joan asked.

"The police had nothing to do with this mess," Hal avowed. "This was done by someone in a hurry, someone who searched without a system."

"Well, system or no system, they didn't miss much," Joan stated. "In fact, they haven't missed a thing. Too bad we're too late."

"It's no use," Hal said hopelessly, turning to Mary. "Joan's right."

"Phil didn't leave things in obvious places," Mary insisted. "I lived with him. I know. That's why the room is in such a mess. The person who was here before us didn't find the thing he was looking for. We must search again."

"Where?" Hal demanded.

"Mary's right," Joan agreed. "It won't take long. We know where we don't have to look and that's something."

"Then keep your gloves on," Hal cautioned. "And work fast. We don't want to be connected with this place in any way. We can't afford to be connected with anything which looks suspicious. Any hunt suggestions?" he asked Mary.

Under her direction they began a systematic search of all likely and unlikely places that had not already been inspected. When they were discouraged and ready to give up the search it was Mary who called Hal to the radio.

"Do you know anything about these machines?" she asked.

"Not much, why?"

"I can't get the box off. It looks like part of the set but I don't know."

"If it is, I've never seen such a contraption," he said, tugging at a box which might very well have been part of the mechanism.

"Pry it off," Joan suggested.

"What do you think I'm doing?" he asked resentfully. He tugged again and the metal cover slid up his fingers.

They gasped with delight when they saw a small package of letters, a memorandum book and papers neatly held together by a broad flat rubber band.

"Give them to me," Mary cried eagerly.

"Okay, but don't stop to look at them here. Let's get out," Hal advised.

As they crossed the living room toward the foyer, Joan stepped on something which crunched under her foot. Naturally she looked down to see what it was.

"Come on," Hal urged.

"Just a minute." Joan bent forward and rescued a bar pin from the floor. The weight of her foot had damaged the clasp.

"Are you crazy?" Hal cried. "Come on!"

"Unless I'm very much mistaken this pin belongs to Mrs. Dufrane," Joan said thoughtfully.

"What would it be doing here?" Mary asked.

"That's what I'm wondering. Do you suppose—"

Hal grabbed her by the arm. "Do your supposing somewhere else, can't you?"

Joan was thoughtful while they walked down the street and around the corner looking for a cab.

Once they were settled and on their way back to the hotel Hal said, "Snap out of it."

"I'm wondering about Mrs. Dufrane. No wonder she didn't go home last night," Joan replied.

"I don't follow you," he said.

"If you were a woman you might. Burke suspected her because of that money found on Martin's body. No wonder she was so upset. I'll bet there are letters of hers in that bundle. Poor thing. She's probably frantic with worry right this minute. Don't you see what happened? She went to Martin's apartment last night and tried to find her letters."

"She might have been there, but a woman wouldn't have left things in such a mess," Mary objected.

"Not even a frantic woman?" Joan demanded. "Suppose you had gone there last night, would you have been careful?"

Mary made no reply. She sat staring ahead of her, the package of papers in her hands.

CHAPTER TWELVE

Back at the hotel, safely settled in Hal's sitting room, Mary and Joan began a systematic search of Phil Martin's private papers.

"You can help," Joan suggested to Hal with warm inclusiveness. She was beginning to feel differently about Hal. He had put himself in a false position to keep her from going to jail. In spite of what Mary had said about his career he had put her first, thought of her safety instead of his precious public.

"If you don't mind," he said, "I'd rather leave it to you." His refusal came as a complete rebuff.

It wasn't what he said that nettled her but the way he had said it. In his tone she sensed a distaste for the whole business. Well, did he think she was enjoying it? She curbed an impulse to make a retort and went on with the papers. She watched him as he wandered toward the piano. Perhaps he thought they knew more about such things. Perhaps he had meant nothing and she was being oversensitive. She had reached a point where she was willing to make excuses for him.

Sitting down at the piano he struck a few chords. His face was troubled. There were lines of worry between his eyes. He gazed off into space as his fingers idly picked out a melody. He played softly, paying no attention to the girls as they went on with the search of the papers.

He didn't notice Joan's gasp of surprise as she said, "This must have been the reason."

"What?" Mary asked leaning forward. "Have you found it?"

Joan tapped the packet she held in her hand. They were letters written to Martin by Mrs. Dufrane. "Mrs. Dufrane was after these," she said quietly. "Poor foolish woman!"

"What will we do with them?" Mary asked.

"I'd like to return them to her, if you have no objections," Joan said. "I'll call her now and tell her not to worry."

While Joan telephoned, Mary went on with her feverish examination of the papers. When Joan returned she was tucking the packet of letters into her blouse.

"Did you get her?" Mary asked.

"No. The butler or someone said she was not at home. I left the number."

At that moment Maxie rushed into the room, waved a telegram at Hal, and cried, "Now what are you going to do?"

The girls looked up, interested in Hal's reactions to Maxie's excitement. Hal returned the telegram without saying a word.

"Well?" Maxie demanded.

Hal scowled darkly but Maxie refused to be silent and blurted, "Higgins wants a picture of the bride to run on his publicity posters for the new campaign. A fine mess we're in!"

"We'll take care of that later," Hal said indifferently and resumed his playing.

"From the poorhouse, I suppose you mean?" Maxie growled and turned on his heel.

As they continued the search, Mary became frantic as she went through paper after paper. Her desire for haste was transmitted to Joan who, too, worked feverishly.

"It must be here," Mary insisted when they were about half through the papers. "He'd never destroy a thing like that."

Hal sang softly as the search continued. His voice died away to nothing for a moment as a heavy pounding sounded on the door.

"It's Burke," Joan cried, "I know his touch. Quick, we must hide these!"

As the girls rustled the papers, collecting them in handfuls, from the floor, Hal played louder and sang lustily while the banging continued.

Feverishly the girls stuffed the letters and papers into the upholstery of the chair where Mary had been sitting. Joan lifted one of the rugs and scattered a handful evenly on the floor and replaced the rug.

"Open this door!" Burke's voice shouted.

Hal stopped playing and asked, "Did I hear someone at the door?"

"Open up!" Burke demanded.

"Pack your suitcase," Joan said to Hal as she crossed to the piano and took up the melody where he had left off. Mary took a powder puff from her bag and was dabbing her face as Hal unlocked the door.

"What's going on here?" Burke demanded as he entered the room followed by Jimmie Farr and the inevitable policeman.

"Just rehearsing a new song," Hal replied. "Been waiting long?"

Burke growled.

"What's on your mind, Inspector?"

"Plenty! What were you doing at Phil Martin's apartment?"

Shocked and surprised by the question, Hal and Mary exchanged quick glances. Joan continued to play softly.

"Stop that racket!" Burke bellowed. "Now answer the question."

"I wanted to tell you about that," Hal began. "You see, you told me I wouldn't be able to leave San Francisco until you had found Martin's murderer so I thought I'd do a little detective work myself."

"And why did you go there?" Burke demanded with emphasis.

"It seemed like a logical starting place."

"And what did you find there?"

"Nothing."

"What were you looking for?"

"Evidence—clues if I could find any."

Jimmie Farr had been leaning against the door-jamb enjoying the discomfiture of Hal and the girls. He was the personification of smugness as he said, "They're holding out on you, Burke! Don't let them get away with it."

"You've been holding out yourself," Burke replied testily. "You said you'd tell me something interesting when we had the three of them together. Well, here they are. Spill it! What do you know that I should know?"

"Well, to begin—" Jimmie started, slowly relishing the look of consternation on the faces of the group.

"Get going," Burke growled. "You're as bad as a woman."

"Ask them what they did with Mrs. Dufrane."

"Mrs. Dufrane!" Burke gasped. "You mean that society woman?"

"Sure! She's been reported missing by her husband. You've been so busy following this pair that you missed the report."

"Well, what about it?"

"My editor put me on the pan because of that story you gave the other papers. I had to do something to save my neck, to say nothing of my job, so I followed a hunch. When I learned that Mrs. Dufrane was missing, I began to wonder why. The answer seemed obvious. Mrs. Dufrane knew too much about what happened out there at the Gardens last night. She must have seen Harrison when he killed Martin. She wouldn't want to be involved in such a case so she tried to get away but was stopped by your man. Do you remember Harrison butting in on you last night just after Mrs. Dufrane was taken to the office to be questioned?"

"That's right," Burke agreed, checking back.

"Why did he leave his orchestra to rush into that room?" Farr demanded. "He was afraid of what Mrs. Dufrane might tell you, that's why. I don't know what he did in there, but he evidently managed to keep her quiet."

"That's not true!" Joan cried. "Mrs. Dufrane—"

"Wait a minute, Joan. Let him finish," Hal stopped her from making a statement.

"That's nice of you, Harrison," Farr conceded. Relishing the situation, Jimmie went on. "Ask them "why they tore Martin's place inside out this morning? Ask them what they found? Ask them what became of Mrs. Dufrane."

"Why should we know anything about Mrs. Dufrane?" Hal asked.

"Didn't you see her roadster parked at the curb in front of Martin's apartment?" Farr demanded.

"No."

"Well, it's there all right. Maybe you don't know that car owners must carry their licenses on the posts of their steering wheels in California."

"I know nothing about Mrs. Dufrane or her car," Hal repeated.

"Go ahead, Burke, ask your questions, and while you're at it ask them why they tried to make a fool out of you when you were here early this morning!"

"One thing at a time," Burke said.

"But you'll be interested to know that these turtle doves are not married. They lied to you about that. They didn't leave the hotel last night. I have good friends in Reno. I checked on that story and with all the airports here. I have a telegram from Reno saying that there was no such wedding last night."

As Jimmie talked, Burke's face changed from its customary pink to red. He was nearing the boiling point as Farr hurried on. "I wanted to tell you all this in front of them, Inspector. Look at them! Are they guilty or not? They've been playing you for a sucker, Burke, trying to pull the wool over your eyes to keep the facts of the murder quiet!"

"You're crazy!" Hal cried in desperation.

"Oh, he is, is he?" Burke finally boiled over. Words poured from his mouth, tripping one over the other. "You're all in this together, all three of you. I'm beginning to see it now. You did kill Martin and hoped to fool me with your lies if I'd been dumb enough to believe you. Why, you—" He advanced threateningly toward Hal.

"Easy, Burke," Jimmie cautioned. "You couldn't get away with an assault. He's too well known."

Burke stopped, fuming.

"You bungling fool!" Joan railed at Jimmie. "Why can't you mind your own business?"

"Easy, kid," Mary cautioned. "Keep quiet."

"The news is my business," Jimmie said, "first, last, and always."

"Come on, Harrison." Burke moved forward and snapped a pair of cuffs on Hal's unresisting wrists. "And you, too," he said as he turned to Mary and put the bracelets on her.

"And what about me?" Joan demanded.

"You're just a lovesick little fool looking for excitement," Burke answered her scornfully.

"Thought you could make a mug out of me, eh?" Jimmie asked Joan gleefully.

"Nature beat me to it," she replied.

"Call the wagon," Burke ordered.

"Wait a minute," Jimmie warned. "Better search this place, Burke. They must have found something in Martin's apartment."

"Go ahead," Burke instructed the policeman before he reached the telephone.

Joan went to the piano, worried about Mary's frightened eyes. She felt she must warn Mary lest their hiding places be revealed. She sat down and began playing, listlessly at first. Then improvising, she began to sing, "Your eyes, your eyes, your wonderful eyes may tell—"

"Stop that racket," Burke bellowed as he joined in the search.

Joan glanced at Hal. "Don't look now," she said lightly, "but I think these men are hunting for something."

Hal and Mary nodded in understanding. Their gaze avoided the rug and chair. Joan went on playing softly. They had practically finished with the room and she was beginning to feel a bit more comfortable when Burke clumsily tripped over the rug under which the papers had been hidden.

Mary gasped. Burke looked up quickly. Mary turned her eyes away. Burke balanced on one foot to flip back the upturned corner of the rug with his other foot. He paused in the operation. He balanced himself on the one foot teetering for a moment.

"Silence!" he commanded. He listened carefully while the others smiled at his awkwardness. Satisfied, he knelt down and threw back the rug. The next instant Burke, Farr and the policeman were on their knees avidly opening and sorting the papers.

With a paper in his hand, Burke rose stiffly to his feet and moved toward them.

"Mary Dale," he began weightily. Mary stepped forward. "I'm arresting you and you alone for the murder of Phil Martin."

"Hey! Wait a minute!" Hal cried.

Burke paid no attention to Hal but continued explaining his charge to Mary. "You hated your husband, as this note clearly proves. You were sore at him because he threw you down first and then wouldn't give you a divorce. You had the opportunity last night and so you killed him. You were down front and screamed to cover yourself and provide an alibi."

"What?" Jimmie gasped.

"Shut up!" Burke growled. "I know what I'm doing. I know a few things that you don't know. You've bungled enough. Why don't you newspaper men get your facts straight before you go off half cocked?" Burke tapped the paper he held in his hand.

"Look here, Burke!" Hal cried. "You're all wrong!"

"Keep quiet! You knew about this note. You were trying to protect her all the time. Just a Galahad, aren't you?"

"She didn't kill Phil Martin," Hal protested vehemently.

"This note says different."

"What is it?" Jimmie asked eagerly.

"Just a warning from Mary Dale to Phil Martin."

"That was written a year ago!" Mary cried.

Burke looked at the letter. "If it was, it ain't dated."

"But it was," Mary insisted hopelessly.

"It's all clear to me now," Burke said, pleased with himself. He turned to Mary. "Where were you last night?"

"You know that," she answered.

"How did you get back to the hotel?" he asked.

"In a cab," she replied.

"I'll warn you now," Burke said, "anything you say will be used against you. You didn't come back to the hotel in a cab. You left the Gardens in Mrs. Dufrane's car."

"Mrs. Dufrane's car!" Jimmie repeated.

"What of it?" Mary asked defiantly.

"You were the only person who knew where Mrs. Dufrane was last night."

"I know nothing about her last night. She brought me here to the hotel and left me at the entrance. The doorman can tell you that," Mary cried defensively.

"The one on the Montgomery Street entrance told me that. I asked him on the way in when I learned out at the Gardens that you had left with her. But what you don't know is that he saw you pass through the corridor to Market Street and get in a cab."

Burke turned to Jimmie. "You see, you were only half right. This girl killed Martin. Then when she realized that Mrs. Dufrane had probably seen her, she decided to make away with the poor woman to protect herself. She followed Mrs. Dufrane away from the hotel last night.

What she did with her we don't know, but we'll soon find out."

"It's ridiculous!" Hal cried.

Maxie entered just in time to get Burke's next speech.

"You saw Mary Dale kill Martin and, wanting to keep the reputation of your band intact, you tried to keep her out of the jam. It's as clear as ABC. Come on, both of you. I'm booking you, Mary Dale, on a charge of murder, and you, Harrison, as an accessory after the fact."

Maxie groaned.

Joan tried to stop Burke, but he shoved her away.

"Keep away from me," he growled. "I want no more of your lies."

"Get a grip on yourself, Joan," Hal said. "We need your help. You and Maxie work together. Get the best lawyer in town. Call Fields. Arrange for bail. See that Fields and the lawyer are at police headquarters immediately. We'll be back before you know it."

CHAPTER THIRTEEN

Between them Joan and Maxie kept the wires humming for the next ten minutes. Fields, amazed at what had happened, promised to stand bail and suggested they secure the services of Alfred Cartwright, a prominent criminal lawyer.

Cartwright agreed to go to headquarters at once, where Joan and Maxie hurried to meet him. They arrived before the lawyer. While waiting, they asked to see Hal and Mary but were refused permission. Burke did tell them, somewhat grudgingly, that they would be permitted to attend the hearing as soon as the Judge had looked over the facts of the case.

When Cartwright arrived, Joan gave him a rapid summary of the whole affair. She took particular pains to impress upon Cartwright the fact that Burke had done nothing about discovering the actual method used in the killing of Martin. She explained her connection with the case, her lie and the series of lies which followed in its wake. "I was there. I did see the knife and I know that neither Hal nor Mary could have killed Martin," she ended emphatically.

She was just finishing when Dave Fields rushed in, worried and excited. "What are we going to do?" he wailed. "My business! This will ruin me!"

"You'll pack the place tonight," Maxie assured him, "and you know it. What are you doing for Hal? That's the important thing."

"I can get bail all right. What did the girl do?" he asked.

"She's accused of double murder."

"Double murder?" Fields repeated.

"Yes. Burke has some crazy idea that Mary killed Martin and then made way with Mrs. Dufrane."

"Mrs. Dufrane! Why shoot her?"

"The man who killed Martin could tell you that," Joan replied. Then she proceeded to ask Fields a number of questions about the bandstand and the number of people who were actually acquainted with the hollow space underneath and the type of implement the murderer might have used.

"Who'd think of crawling in there?" he asked.

"Anyone who knew the construction of the stand. It's the only way he could have been killed."

"Have you told Burke?"

"Yes, but he doesn't believe anything we say any more," she replied disconsolately.

"He's had experience with this sort of thing," Fields temporized.

"Then why doesn't he get some real clues? Why doesn't he investigate a lot of things?" Joan demanded.

"Like what?" Fields asked.

"The Gardens. The things you permit to go on out there. Martin's activities, plenty of things."

Before Fields could answer, an attendant came and led them into a room where the Judge was already seated at his desk. He looked up from some papers, gave them a careful scrutiny, and then returned to his reading. Hal and Mary were brought in. Joan moved forward and took a chair near the two prisoners. Fields followed her.

The Judge, his reading finished, moved the papers to one side, folded his hands and looked at the group for a long moment. He glanced in the direction of the lawyer and asked, "Are you representing the prisoners, Mr. Cartwright?"

"Yes, your Honor. I've arranged for bail."

"I'm sorry, Mr. Cartwright, but I cannot grant bail after considering the weight of evidence presented against Mary Dale."

"But, Judge, I'll be ruined!" Fields cried.

"That is not under the consideration of the court," the Judge replied.

Joan's heart sank. How awful for them both to remain in prison!

"But, your Honor—" Cartwright protested.

"Unless you are able to present new facts, Mary Dale must be booked on the charge of murder and held without bail." He turned to Burke. "You know we can do nothing on the Dufrane charge unless you can prove murder. Has the body been found?"

"Not yet," Burke admitted.

"I have a witness here who can positively testify that Mary Dale could not have killed Martin," Cartwright stated.

The Judge arched his brows as Cartwright indicated Joan. "Your name," he asked.

"Joan Paxton," she replied. She stepped forward eagerly.

"Your Honor," Burke boomed, "the witness is not dependable. She is a friend of both of them. Her falsifications have already befogged the case and confused the issue. By rights she ought to be locked up with the pair of them."

"Do you want to swear out a warrant?" the Judge demanded, a smile crinkling the corners of his mouth.

"No," Burke replied. "I just don't want her telling any more lies about this case."

The Judge actually smiled as he said, "Sit down, Miss Paxton."

Cartwright protested again but the Judge interrupted him. "Your witness can have no standing in this hearing," he said patiently. "If you think I'm being unreasonable, I suggest that you read the morning papers."

"I'll get a writ of habeas corpus," Cartwright cried.

"Just a moment, let me go on. From the evidence presented to me, it would seem that Mr. Harrison was an accomplice and is involved with this Mary Dale, but the point is not proved. If you have arranged satisfactory bail for him, I will consider his release."

Fields stepped forward with Cartwright.

"Take the other prisoner back to her cell," the Judge ordered.

Mary stood up. Her face was pale but she showed no sign of the emotion she was feeling. Hal took her in his arms. "I'll get you out of this," he promised.

"I'll be all right," she answered bravely. "I haven't done anything."

"We'll prove you didn't, somehow," Joan promised as she put her arms about Mary and gave her a warm friendly squeeze.

Something hard pressed against Joan's body as the matron with a determined hand took Mary from her embrace. Joan's hand went to her breast. "Wait!" she cried.

All eyes were turned on her.

"Your Honor—" Joan ran toward the Judge. As she raced forward she was trying to get the packet of letters out of her blouse. "Don't lock her up, please. Not until I have told you about these."

"It is quite useless, Miss Paxton," the Judge said icily.

"But you want motive for a crime, don't you? Ask Burke if he wasn't suspicious of Mrs. Dufrane last night."

Burke nodded.

"Didn't you hope to find letters or something in the things the men brought back from Martin's apartment?" Joan demanded.

"Yes," Burke admitted.

"Your Honor, here are letters written to Martin by Mrs. Dufrane. She's missing. Perhaps she has run away fearing she will be connected with the murder."

She raced on and told the Judge about the money found on Martin's body, the stub in Mrs. Dufrane's checkbook, the strange familiar scent common to Mrs. Dufrane's bag and the money, all the points Burke had made the night before.

"And why are you just producing this evidence?" the Judge asked.

"I forgot about it in the excitement of their arrest," Joan replied truthfully. "I know Mrs. Dufrane was at Martin's apartment some time before we were. Look," she rummaged in her pocketbook and produced the pin she had stepped on. "This is hers. She was wearing it last night."

"It's all very interesting," the Judge admitted, "but it proves nothing. Everything you say could be true and yet the evidence we have against Miss Dale would stand as it is in court."

"But she couldn't have done it! She didn't!" Joan cried. "You're making a terrible mistake."

"Your Honor," a new voice interrupted. It was Jimmie Farr.

"Yes, Farr."

"I overheard Miss Paxton's impassioned pleading, but, as usual, she is wrong. Mrs. Dufrane has not run away to escape the consequences of a crime which she did not commit. Mrs. Dufrane was murdered. We found her body in the basement of the apartment house."

While his audience recovered from his startling news, Farr beckoned to a smiling Oriental who stood at the rear of the room. "Come here, Joe," he called. "This is the man who operates the elevator in Martin's apartment house. When I questioned him this morning, he gave me some startling facts which I'm sure have a direct bearing on the case."

"What are they?" the Judge asked.

"You knew Mr. Martin?" Farr asked the man.

"Yes."

"You recognized the body of the woman we found in the basement?"

"She come many time to see Mr. Martin."

"Did other ladies call on Mr. Martin?"

"Many times."

"You told me that a lady came last night, a lady who did not use the elevator. You told me that that same lady was at the apartment this morning with a man and a woman."

"Yes."

"Is that lady here?"

"That lady." He pointed his finger at Mary. "She come last night soon after lady who die and she come back this morning with this man and this lady."

Hal and Joan were astounded. "Deny it, Mary," Hal ordered.

"I can't. I did go there last night."

"But, Mary," Joan cried, "why didn't you tell us?"

"What was the use? I didn't go in the apartment," she spoke to the Judge, "but I don't suppose anyone will believe me. I heard someone inside. I was afraid to go in. I didn't know what to do. When I heard the elevator going to the floors above, I slipped out of the building."

"Did you see this lady leave the apartment?" the Judge asked Joe.

"Only see her come in," he grinned.

The Judge turned to the matron. "Take her away."

"It's an outrage," Joan cried, and wheeling on Jimmie she cried, "and it's all your fault."

"Be reasonable," he answered.

The Judge's gavel cut short any further altercation as he proceeded to make arrangements for Hal's bail. When the Judge told Hal that he was free to go, Jimmie Farr hurried from the room.

Cartwright asked permission to talk with Mary, which the Judge granted. When Cartwright and the Judge had gone, Fields turned to Hal and said, "I don't understand all this."

"She hasn't done a thing," Hal replied, "but circumstantial evidence has piled up against her." He explained about their trip to Martin's apartment and the finding of the bundle of papers in the radio.

"In the radio?" Fields exclaimed. He shook his head. "No one but a band leader would ever think of such a screwy place."

Hal continued. "We were looking for a letter Mary wrote to him over a year ago."

"Did you find it?" Fields asked.

"The police beat us to it. They came in on us before we had a chance to go through the papers."

"Maybe they think she killed him for his money," Dave suggested tentatively.

"What money?" Hal asked quickly.

"Didn't he always seem to have a lot? Maybe he had investments. Wasn't there anything like that in his papers?"

"I told you we hadn't seen all of them when the police arrived," Hal answered irritably.

"And they got them all?" Fields asked.

"No. Just some of them. We managed to hide a few, but unfortunately Mary's threat was in the batch they did get."

"Sure, sure! Too bad! Keeping papers is bad business. You'd better be careful with the others. It'll look bad if they are found on you," he cautioned.

"They're in a safe place," Hal assured him. "They may come in handy yet."

"I'd get rid of them," Fields cautioned. "You don't want to be in any more trouble than you are, do you?"

"We'll look 'em over first," Hal said.

Fields was called away to sign a bail bond. Hal, Maxie, and Joan started back to the hotel. They were an unhappy group riding silently until Maxie asked forlornly, "Well, whatta we gonna do now?"

"I'd like to throw Farr and Burke into the bay!" Joan cried. "Of all the unreasonable, blundering men—"

"Wait a minute," Hal interrupted. "You're being a little unfair. We can't blame Burke. It's our fault if we threw him completely off the scent at the start."

"Are you blaming me?" Joan asked. She still remembered the tender way Hal had embraced Mary at the police station.

"I'm not blaming anyone," he replied. "Just stating a fact."

"You both acted like nit wits," Maxie blurted. "First one and then the other lying like mad. You sounded as if you were both on a vacation from an insane asylum."

"O dear," Joan moaned. "I'm always getting into things that are none of my business!"

"We've plenty to do now," Hal said seriously. "We've got to get Mary out of this mess."

"And you must work fast," Joan added.

"Fast!" He turned and looked at her intently. "I won't have a minute's peace while I know she's in jail."

"We'll have to put Burke back on the right track again, won't we?" Joan asked.

"Unfortunately Burke won't believe a thing we say until we have some definite proof to present to him. Have you any ideas, either of you?" Hal asked as the cab drew up in front of the hotel.

"We can't do anything here," Joan said.

"We can plan our campaign. There's work for all of us. We'll save time if we have a system."

Joan didn't want a system. She wanted to get right into the thick of the thing and get going, but she had to admit to herself that he was undoubtedly right in his idea.

In Hal's sitting room, several of the boys were standing in front of the radio listening to a news broadcast. As they entered the room a clear voice was saying:

"There has been a new development in the murder at the Crystal Gardens. Hal Harrison and Mary Dale were arrested this morning on a charge of murder. Miss Dale was held without bond, but Harrison was permitted his freedom on bail. He left accompanied by Miss Joan Paxton. It is now reported that Miss Paxton and Harrison have not been married, as was previously reported. The death of Mrs. John Carter Dufrane, who was shot at Phil Martin's apartment, adds still another mysterious note to the already baffling mystery."

"Turn it off," Hal said. "Now clear out, boys, will you? We've got to do something about Mary and do it fast. We can't leave her here and we've got to be on our way to New York in the morning. If you fellows see or hear anything, let us know."

As the boys drifted away, Hal stopped Scat Miller.

"Listen, Scat, the knife must have gone right past you. Didn't you see anything at all?"

"Not a thing, Hal. You know how I am when we're playing. Most of the time I keep my eyes closed."

"Okay. We've got to clutch at straws then," Hal answered. "We'll see you later, Scat."

Joan had settled herself in an armchair and was lost in thought. Hal lit a cigarette and stood in front of her. She looked up and asked, "If you were Burke and all this business hadn't happened"—her hands made an impulsive gesture—"I mean me and the lies and all that, what would you have done to find the murderer?"

"I'd have run all the clues to earth," Hal answered.

"You weren't in the room with him when he was getting so suspicious of Kingford," Maxie cut in. "He wouldn't let Kingford replace you on the stand, Hal, he was that suspicious."

"Why not?"

"Kingford didn't have an alibi." Maxie gave them a quick summary of Burke's questions before they were brought into the office.

"Why didn't Burke follow up on Kingford?" Joan demanded.

"He may have done it, for all we know," Hal replied.

"He was still asking questions when you were brought in and that nutty dame began her spiel." Maxie stopped, embarrassed when he realized he was talking about Joan's mother so disparagingly.

Joan hid a smile. "Go on," she prompted.

"Well, when you all came in, Burke got interested in you first, then that waiter, Pete Schwartz, and he seemed to forget about Kingford."

"Why do you suppose Pete Schwartz testified against you?" Joan asked Hal. "Ever do anything to him?"

"What do you mean?" Hal retorted. "I never saw him before last night."

"Then why should he testify the way he did?"

"The cop overheard him," Hal reminded her.

"Sounds fishy to me."

"Sure it's fishy," Maxie agreed. "A man wouldn't get mixed up in a case like this unless he was crazy, or couldn't help himself," he added quickly with a sly look at Joan.

"What are you driving at, Joan?" Hal demanded.

"I actually don't know. There's something behind all this, if we can just put our finger on it. Kingford didn't have an alibi. Schwartz testified. That's two things. And how was the murder committed?"

"I thought you knew," he said with a reminiscent pat on his leg.

"The murderer didn't use an old stick he found under there! He couldn't. He had to have something that would hold the knife firmly. I know that's how it was done but I can't see how they did it."

"We ought to go to Burke and offer these suggestions," Hal said.

"But as you've said, he'll never believe us unless we can give him some definite proof," she cried. "But where to begin and what to do?"

"Why not start on Kingford and the waiter?" Maxie suggested. "I'll go nuts if I sit around here just talking."

His face broke into a semi smile. "Say, we're forgetting someone! Dufrane. He said he knew his wife had gone to the Gardens. He came in here with a gun and nearly killed you. Mrs. Dufrane was shot, wasn't she?"

"That's right."

"Well, what about him for a suspect?" Maxie demanded.

"Dufrane!" Hal exclaimed. "We've been blind, all of us. Maxie, you've saved the day!"

"Wait a minute," Joan cautioned. "We can't go off half cocked. Suppose Dufrane killed Martin. That gives us that. Now the question is this, was Mrs. Dufrane dead when Dufrane came in here and took a shot at me?"

"What has that to do with it?" Maxie asked.

"Joan's right." Hal stated. "It's important. We've got to find out when Mrs. Dufrane was killed."

"How are you going to do it?" Maxie demanded.

"We've got to get to Burke and tell him the things we know about Dufrane. I'll see if I can get him on the telephone."

Joan caught his arm. "Wait! Burke's too sure of himself. He won't believe us."

"Not even a doubtful Burke can deny that bullet hole," Hal replied grimly, pointing at the closet door.

"He'll want to know why we didn't tell him about it this morning. We've done everything wrong so far. Let's not make any more mistakes. There must be a right way."

"There is," Hal answered as he began to leaf through the commercial section of the telephone directory. "I'll get the best detective agency in town, someone who will believe us and work fast."

"I've a better idea," Joan cried, her face lighting up.

"What?" Hal asked.

"I'm going to get Jimmie Farr and make him work for us," she said.

"Have you gone mad?" Hal demanded.

"No."

"But you can't do that! You can't trust him!" Hal exclaimed.

"He'd sell his soul for a good story and I'm going to convince him that we have it. Now listen—" She sat in one of the armchairs. "While I go after Farr, I want you boys to do two things. Go to Martin's apartment and

check with that elevator boy. Begin where Farr left off.
See if he saw anyone else at the apartment last night. He
may have seen Mrs. Dufrane try to leave the building. I
don't believe she was shot in the apartment. He may have
seen her go out." They seemed skeptical. "It's worth a try,
isn't it?" she demanded. "Wouldn't you like to prove that
Mrs. Dufrane was alive when that wild man husband of
hers was here?"

They admitted that it was worth trying.

"When you get this information, see Kingford. Feel
him out. Burke may have worked on him last night. We
don't know. If he did, there's nothing more we can do, but
if Burke slipped up on Kingford then it's up to us to do
something."

"And what will you be doing with Farr?" Hal asked.

"I'm going to get him to locate Pete Schwartz for me."
She pushed her hands down the sides of the upholstery as
she beamed at them.

While Hal and Maxie argued against her plan, she
drew a little memorandum book from the chair. It was
the chair Mary had been sitting in when Burke arrived.
"Say," she exclaimed, "we forgot about this junk!" She
opened the book and ran through the pages quickly. She
stopped.

"What is it?" Hal asked.

"Martin owed Kelton a lot of money. What sort of a
place does Kelton run?"

"Gambling, I suppose," Hal replied.

She poked the book back into the chair. "Farr will tell
me."

"That stuff in the chair, don't you think we ought to
look it over?" Hal suggested.

"There isn't time. We've work to do."

"I still don't want to work with Farr," Hal objected.

"He's just the man I need," she went on, ignoring his
objections. "And I'm going to get him." Filled with
determination she crossed to the telephone. "Don't you
worry about him," she flung back over her shoulder as

she reached for the receiver. "When I go to work on a man—"

"He's done for," Maxie finished with just a taint of vinegar in his voice.

"Right," she agreed pertly. She asked the operator to get her the *Crescent* office. There was a delay after she asked for Farr. When he was put on the wire she asked, "Will you be in your office for the next fifteen minutes?" She waited for a moment then said, "Well, if you want to know something new about the affair at the Gardens, wait for me." She hung up and turned to the boys saying, "That'll hold him. He's as curious as an old woman right now. I'll meet you back here. I won't be long."

Hal intercepted her at the door exclaiming, "You're taking a chance with Farr. I don't approve of it."

"You'd do anything to get Mary free, wouldn't you?" she demanded.

"Yes," he answered fervently.

"Then trust me. If we can't work with Burke, we've got to work alone. We've got to be tough or we won't get a thing. Farr knows all the answers. I'll have him all wrapped for you when I return. Do your job! Don't worry!"

CHAPTER FOURTEEN

When Joan arrived at the *Crescent* office, she went directly to the city room and asked for Jimmie Farr. He was completely surprised to see her, and his amazement increased when she said, "Get your hat, newsbag. You're taking me to lunch."

"Not so fast," he managed to say glibly. "This invitation has all the earmarks of being a 'ride.'"

"I wish it were," Joan answered promptly. "I'd like to see you burning in oil."

"Nice girl. Finishing schools do good jobs these days."

"Are you coming?" Joan demanded.

"Sorry, but I have a date."

"And I'm it. I telephoned you a few minutes ago. I wanted to make you curious. Come along," she said brusquely, starting for the door.

Jimmie hesitated for a moment. "You mean that you—"

Joan did not stop.

Jimmie hesitated no longer. He leaped the office rail and made the door in time to open it for her. "What's it all about?"

"After lunch," she replied over her shoulder as her heels clicked against the cement floor.

Jimmie trailed behind her, asking numerous questions which she refused to answer. "Why don't you give me some idea?" he finally begged.

"Because I'm hungry. I didn't eat much of my wedding breakfast worrying about you," she accused.

"There's a pretty good place across the street," he said, giving up at last and falling into step beside her.

In the nearby restaurant, Jimmie was too curious to eat. He toyed with his food as he bombarded Joan with questions, to which she paid absolutely no attention. "Have a heart, won't you?" he begged.

"I have, but at the moment I happen to be busy."

Jimmie tried to be patient. When Joan finished the last of her dessert, he said, "Now, tell me."

"Give me a cigarette first," she replied. She took several puffs and gazed about the room. She caught the waiter's eye and asked for more coffee.

"Did anyone ever tell you that you can be most aggravating?"

"Yes. I've been called cagey, too," she added.

"And what do you mean by that?"

"I'm a good judge of human nature, so they say. I wasn't hungry, but I did need an excuse for watching you. I had to study you a bit to help me make up my mind."

"I'd hate to see you eat when you were hungry and had nothing on your mind," he replied with a glance at the check.

"Perhaps that can be arranged," she suggested.

"How?"

"That depends on you."

"Don't keep talking in riddles."

"I'm not quite sure about you yet."

"Tell me what you want and I'll help you out if I can."

"What would you do to get the real beat on this story?"

"I've got it," he replied smugly.

"You only think you have. I guess Hal was right," she said thoughtfully. "You're too satisfied with yourself. Too volatile—that's a good word, isn't it? I'd better get some reporter who will appreciate facts and not fly off the handle." She slid her chair away from the table and rescued her napkin from the floor. "Thanks so much for the lunch."

"Wait a minute!" he begged as she started to rise.

She paused as if she might be persuaded to sit down again. She settled back into the chair as she asked, "Answer me one question. Do you really believe Mary Dale killed Martin and Mrs. Dufrane?"

"Sure I do—on the face of the evidence," he qualified quickly.

"That's all I wanted to know." She stood up and turned from the table with an air of finality.

She knew that men are just as curious as women, perhaps more so. She also knew that Jimmie had swallowed her bait completely. She wanted to play him a little longer before she gave him her confidence. If he could be convinced that she had a new angle on the case, she felt positive that he could help them get Mary out of jail. She was determined to make him agree to her terms before she told him a single thing.

"Not so fast," Jimmie cried. "Don't you know that ninety nine times out of a hundred circumstantial evidence is true?"

"The exception proves the rule, always," she replied.

"But—"

"There's really no point in our talking any longer. You wouldn't have your heart in it. We'd never agree. I want a man who believes Mary Dale is innocent."

"If you say she's innocent, I'll believe you," he promised extravagantly.

"No. You see, I don't really trust you. I'm sorry to have taken your time."

"What do you mean you can't trust me?" he bristled.

"My mother trusted you and look what you did to us," she reminded him. Joan had a flash of inspiration. "I don't mean all this Burke business either. Because of your enthusiasm, I was very nearly killed this morning."

"Quit kidding," he scoffed.

"There's a bullet hole to prove I'm telling the truth." She stopped suddenly, giving him the impression that she was sorry to have said so much.

"Tell me about it."

"No. You were told one story in confidence."

"You'd have done the same thing if you were a reporter," he defended. "Listen, Miss Paxton. News is all in the day's work for me."

"I know. Honor and decency can go overboard as long as you get your story," she retorted. "That's why I'm saying no more. I've said too much already. I suppose it's useless to ask you to forget our conversation."

"I didn't even hear you. How's that? I know how you must feel, but you ought to remember that reporting is my method of making a living."

When he started making excuses for himself, Joan felt that he was finally hooked.

"Look," he went on. "The *Crescent's* been out front on every break of this story. I want to keep it there. It means a lot to me. Maybe I have been a mug but—"

"You're willing to go right on being a mug as long as your paper keeps ahead of the others. I know all about it."

"You don't. Unless you're kidding me, you're on to something that no one else knows. You ain't kidding, are you?"

"I could think of more entertaining things to do," she answered.

"I'd like to be the one to crack this case," he said wistfully.

"That's one of the reasons I came to see you. I knew that."

"It would mean a raise in salary and—"

"You could marry the little woman who is waiting for you. You'd settle down in Mill Valley, I suppose," she suggested with an unbelieving grin.

"It's on the level about getting married," he replied. "How did you know?"

"Because you were so wistful about that raise."

"Give me the break, will you?"

After a long moment of consideration she said, "I'll take a chance! But you must promise to curb that instinct of yours to tell all until we have the facts. No jumping at conclusions. You are to print nothing until I tell you to go ahead. Is that a bargain?"

"It is," he agreed and offered her his hand to bind it.

As Joan dropped his hand she said, "I'm going to trust you, but I want to warn you here and now. If you don't keep your word, I'll make a monkey out of you."

"I believe you would," he answered with an understanding twinkle in his eye. "Now tell me what you know."

"I have no definite facts, yet."

"But you said—"

"I said if you wanted to know something more about the affair at the Gardens, didn't I?" she demanded.

"Yeah. What about that bullet hole you mentioned? Who shot at you?"

"That will come later. We've other work to do first."

"What?"

"Get some information about a man, a waiter. Peter Schwartz, the man who works at the Gardens."

"Why?"

Joan explained the details of Schwartz' testimony.

"Fishy," Jimmie replied.

"That's what I thought."

"Wait a minute. I'll call Burke," Jimmie said as he took Joan's arm and steered her toward the cashier.

"I don't want Burke in on this yet," she objected.

"Neither do I, but I can get some dope from him." With a nickel in his hand he moved to a telephone booth. "You can listen," he said.

Burke was not at the station. Jimmie tried several places and finally, at Joan's suggestion, called the Gardens. After a long wait, Burke came to the telephone. After some preliminary conversation Jimmie asked, "Did you know that Kelton operated his numbers racket at the Gardens?" There were long pauses interspersed with meaningless remarks from Jimmie. "Is he there?" Jimmie asked. "Why not ask him? It's just an idea. You can never tell. I thought you might like to know that. Oh, you knew it. Then why didn't you say so in the first place? Anything new? Oh, he did? No. Not until I hear from you." He hung up.

"Burke's sore about something," he said as he led her from the restaurant and called a cab.

"What about?"

"He didn't say." Settled in the cab he asked, "What made you suspicious of Schwartz?"

"Desperation," she replied honestly. "His testimony seemed to be useless. How do we locate Schwartz?"

The cab drew up in front of the city hall. "Right here," Jimmie replied. "All waiters are registered by the Board of Health. We can get his address from the bureau. It's a cinch. Wait for me, I'll be right back."

As he scampered up the steps Joan felt quite satisfied that she had made a wise choice. He'd sell his soul for a good story. He was interested and still curious because he had not forgotten the bullet hole. In a moment, Jimmie came running toward the cab. He called an address on Van Ness to the driver as he yanked open the door.

When the cab pulled up before a modern, fashionable apartment house and Jimmie had verified the address, Joan asked, "What are you waiting for?"

"I was just thinking. This is a pretty swell front for a waiter. You've got something here."

"Aren't we going in?" Joan asked.

"It will tip our hand. We ought to do some checking first."

"We haven't time," she said impatiently. "We want to get that girl out of jail and Harrison must leave here on the morning plane."

"Okay! In we go!"

It took several minutes to rouse Schwartz. He was reluctant to open the door at all, but Jimmie said,

"The *Crescent's* making an investigation. You'd better open up if you've nothing to hide."

Schwartz, in a Chinese robe, sleepy eyed and badly in need of a shave, admitted them.

"Nice place you've got here," Jimmie said, looking around. "Must take all your tips to keep it going."

"It does," Schwartz admitted.

"What's your racket?" Jimmie asked.

"I've got no racket," Schwartz denied sourly.

"Come on, Schwartz. A waiter can't live like this. We want to get some information about the killing out at the Gardens last night. Better come clean or I'll write you up."

"I don't know anything about the killing."

"You said you saw the knife in Harrison's hand," Joan cut in. "Why did you say that?"

Schwartz hesitated, looking from one to the other. Finally he said, "Well, I did."

"Now, that's very strange," Jimmie said. "Because Burke has arrested Mary Dale charged with the crime. You'd better get dressed, Schwartz, and go down to headquarters with us and tell your story all over again."

"I told Burke," Schwartz replied.

"Better tell him again."

"I'll keep out of it."

"Why didn't you think of that last night at the Gardens? You weren't told to say that, were you, Schwartz?"

Schwartz made no answer.

"Come on, Miss Paxton. He doesn't want to talk. We'll see Burke and let him work on Schwartz. The police have ways of getting information that are denied to us." He sauntered toward the door.

"Wait a minute," Schwartz stopped him. "I don't want to get mixed up with the cops."

"Then who told you to say you saw the knife in Harrison's hand?"

"I can't tell you that. It 'ud be the end of me if I did. Be reasonable, can't you? Do you want me bumped off?"

"That's your headache," Jimmie answered indifferently. "Was it Fields?"

"No."

"Martin was running a nice racket out there at the Gardens and he had to have help with his blackmail schemes. This looks just like the set up for it too. You didn't happen to be the go between for Martin, did you, Schwartz?"

"No."

"I think we've got something," Jimmie turned to Joan. "It's better than we thought. Schwartz did the blackmailing for Martin and they split on a nice little business. Martin probably brought women to this apartment and then Peter here put the pressure on. Don't you see it?" he asked eagerly. "Pete, being a waiter out there, knew all about the place. He and Martin had a row and Pete wanted to get even. Last night in the dark, Pete, here, sneaked in under the stand, killed Martin and then told Burke he saw the knife in Harrison's hand. Oh, boy! Is this going to wow them when I put it in the paper?"

"And the pieces fit together so nicely," Joan added.

"I didn't kill Martin, you're crazy!" Pete cried, alarmed at last.

"You can tell that to the cops when you're explaining how you can afford to live like this." Jimmie's hand indicated the room and its luxurious furnishings. "You'll find jail a lot different, or perhaps you know all about that." He went toward the door. "Come on, Miss Paxton. We've got the case cinched."

"Wait!" Schwartz cried. "It ain't true!"

"Tell that to Burke."

"But listen, I didn't work with Martin."

"Then who did Fields?"

"No. One of the boys maybe, but it wasn't me."

"Don't you know?"

"No."

"Where do you get your money?"

"I can't tell you."

"Burke will make him talk," Jimmie assured Joan.

"Don't get me into this," Schwartz begged. "I was told to alibi a guy."

"Who?"

"If I tell you, he'll kill me," Schwartz cried in desperation. "I had to do as I was told. This guy came to me and said, 'I was up front there when Martin was croaked. I expect you to alibi me.'"

"And so you tried to send an innocent man to his death," Joan cried contemptuously.

"Listen, lady! You don't know nothing about—"

"I guess I don't," Joan answered.

"It's too bad you were in such a hurry, Schwartz. You gave the whole show away."

"I don't get you."

"You said you saw the knife in Harrison's hand, didn't you?"

"Yes."

"And then later you said that Kelton was sitting at your table at the time of the murder. You gave him a double alibi but they don't agree. If you were up front, you couldn't see the table, and if you were near the table, you couldn't have seen the knife. Too bad! Kelton's going to be awful sore."

"Don't tell him!" Schwartz begged. "Don't tell him!"

"You tell him," Jimmie suggested heartlessly. Joan opened the door and left the room. Jimmie hurried after her. "What's the rush?"

"We're going to see Kelton."

"Not so fast! Kelton's dynamite!"

"And I'm the little spark that's going to set him off!"

"Easy. We've got to watch our step."

"Are you afraid?" she demanded.

"No. Just cautious. If Schwartz should die suddenly, what would we have?"

"You don't mean that Kelton would—"

"Sure he would. We want a little more to pin on him so that we have him both ways before we spring our little surprise."

"But won't Schwartz tell Kelton?"

"Schwartz may leave San Francisco, he may commit suicide, but he'll never tell Kelton."

"Come back to the hotel with me. I have just the thing you need." She told Jimmie about Martin's memorandum book which was tucked away in the upholstery of the big chair in Hal's sitting room.

"I wouldn't have believed it," Jimmie said when she had finished.

"Why not?"

"To think that Martin was such a fool. I can understand his trying to double cross Mrs. Dufrane. That was easy, he had nothing to fear from her."

"She might have killed him," Joan suggested. "But she didn't because she was bumped off herself. No. Martin thought he could stall Kelton. Somehow Kelton knew Martin had received that money from Mrs. Dufrane and when Martin didn't hand over—Curtains."

"That's just swell. All we have to do now is to prove it," Joan said.

CHAPTER FIFTEEN

Joan tapped on the door of Hal's suite, fully confident that Hal and Maxie would be waiting for her. There was no answer. She tried the knob. The door swung open. "We're a little late," she cried as she surveyed the disorder facing her. She dashed across the room toward the chair hoping against hope that she was wrong and would find the little book tucked in the upholstery where she had left it. She was full of despair as she faced Jimmie, her hands empty. "Schwartz did tell," she moaned.

"Nope. There wasn't time," Jimmie insisted.

"Then why this?"

"Kelton probably heard you had papers here and sent someone over to have a look. Where's Harrison?"

"Checking on Kingford and the probable time of Mrs. Dufrane's death."

"Not a bad idea," Jimmie said as he roamed about replacing sofa cushions and other things which had been scattered by the person who had searched the room. "So that's the bullet hole," he remarked as he paused before the splintered panel of the closet door. "Want to tell me now?"

"I might just as well." She told him about Dufrane and his mad entrance into the room. "He might have killed them both," she ended, "if we can get the approximate time of Mrs. Dufrane's death."

"I'll get that," he promised.

"But what are we going to do about Kelton?"

"I'll see Burke and try to put him to work. I can threaten him with the story in the paper unless he does some investigating."

"But you won't print anything," she said quickly. "Remember your promise!"

"Want to come along?"

"No. I promised Hal I'd meet him back here. I can't understand what's keeping him so long. Keep me posted by telephone, will you?" she begged as he left.

"You bet. We'll know all about Dufrane when I get back. Why don't you take a nap? You look tired."

Joan followed Jimmie's suggestion. She left a note for Hal and then went to her own room expecting a storm of indignant complainings from her mother, but Mrs. Paxton was not in their suite.

Joan was tired but she found it quite impossible to take a nap. Her brain was too active. There were too many ideas milling about in her head. If Jimmie was right about Schwartz, how had Kelton known about the papers found in Phil's apartment? How did he know that Burke had missed some of the papers? Where was Hal? Why didn't he return or call her? What was taking so long?

She slid from the bed and called his room. There was no answer. Restless and uneasy she wandered about the room. She paused before her mirror and made a long critical study of her face. Mary had said that Hal loved her. How did Mary know? Perhaps she could tell because she herself was in love with him. Poor Mary! They must get her out of jail. Why hadn't she told them about her trip to Martin's apartment the night before? Why had she returned to town with Mrs. Dufrane? Unless they could definitely prove that someone else had killed Mrs. Dufrane, Joan knew they'd never be able to get Mary released. What would Hal do? Would he go on to New York and leave Mary alone to fight her battle? Why didn't he come back, anyhow?

She decided she looked a sight. She ran the comb through her hair and winced as the teeth came in contact with the spot which was still tender from the bang she had given her head under the bandstand.

At three thirty, Mrs. Paxton arrived. She was in a complaining mood. "Well," she began with a snort, "where have you been all day, leaving me alone in a strange city? I think it was very inconsiderate of you. I've been so worried, too, and annoyed as well. The reporters—" She paused at Joan's dressing table to apply some powder.

"Reporters!" Joan cried in alarm. "You haven't been talking to reporters again, have you?"

"Once bitten, twice shy. You must think I'm an utter fool. I simply told them the whole thing was a terrible mistake. That's all. I left them to figure it out for themselves. They took some more pictures," she added brightly. "I do hope they turn out well! You haven't told me what you've been doing."

"Just trying to help rectify the havoc we've wrought."

"We haven't done a thing. I don't see why you need be so upset. The idea of that person saying you were his wife. I told those—" She caught herself just in time, eying Joan to see if she had noticed.

"He did it to keep me out of jail," Joan replied.

"Why do you take this thing to heart so? Goodness! They're nothing but strangers, professional people. Why, when I was a girl I'd have been socially ostracized if people had known that I was interested in—"

"I know all about your matinee idol romance," Joan interrupted. "This is nineteen thirty seven and people's ideas have changed."

"I suppose so. Why don't we go for a walk and see the city?"

"I don't want to see the city."

"But, darling, they say the shops are adorable. Let's go window shopping."

"I don't want to go window shopping. Why don't you go alone, Mother? You'd love it."

"Well, I did want to go to Gump's and Chinatown. Do you suppose it's safe for me to go to Chinatown? You know one hears such things."

"Of course it's safe. Take a cab and if you go into shops have the cab wait if you feel uneasy."

"They say they have the loveliest Chinese things. I do love Oriental art, you know. I suppose it's really the pagan in me. You won't be lonesome, will you dear, if I go?" she asked as she bent forward to leave a pecking kiss on Joan's brow. "You look positively haggard. Why don't you rest?" she suggested.

"I will." Joan promised but the moment she was alone she dressed and went to Hal's suite to wait.

She went to the piano and began playing softly. Perhaps because the murder and its complications were uppermost in her mind she unthinkingly drifted into the melody of "Goodbye Forever." She was crooning softly, when a voice at her elbow startled her.

"You don't want a job, do you?" Hal asked with an appreciative smile.

Dave Fields and Maxie stood just behind him.

"Where have you been?" she demanded, ending the song with a crashing chord.

"Doing the things you told me to do. Why?"

"You've been gone so long. I couldn't imagine what was keeping you. Any luck?"

"Blanks all along the line. Kingford was as tight as a tick when we arrived at his apartment. It took a long time to get a story out of him. Burke put him through the wringer last night and squeezed him dry. He had been drinking to drown his sorrows he said."

"How about that elevator boy?"

"He didn't see her after she entered the apartment until Jimmie found the body this morning. What luck did you have?"

Joan related her adventures quickly and ended, "But I guess we were too late."

"So was Kelton if he was here," Hal grinned.

"What do you mean?"

"After you left we decided we'd better take the papers with us. I have them in my pocket."

"Be careful, Hal!" Dave warned. "You can't fool with Kelton. I know."

"Kelton doesn't know anything about the papers," Hal replied.

"Haven't you looked at them?" Fields asked.

"Only the book. We haven't had time. They'll keep until later. Now that we know what Kelton wants."

"Better let me have them," Fields suggested. "I'll put 'em in the safe for you."

"They're safe enough," Hal replied with a tap at his breast pocket to make sure they were still there.

"Well, I'll see you later," Fields promised. "I've got work to do. We're gonna have a big crowd again tonight. Be early."

He left just as the telephone started to ring. It was Jimmie Farr, who told Joan that he was in Burke's office and Burke would do nothing about Kelton because they had no proof.

"But we have!" Joan cried. "We have the book! Bring Burke over at once, please." As she turned from the telephone she cried, "We'll have some action at last."

"Then I won't have to offer you that job," Hal said.

"What job?"

"The one I offered you when I came in. You didn't pay any attention to me."

"I thought you were joking."

"I wasn't. I thought you might take Mary's place tonight with the trio, but that won't be necessary now. We'll have her out of jail, I hope," he ended.

"Why don't you rehearse her in case we don't get Mary out?" Maxie suggested.

"I couldn't sing in public," Joan insisted. "Don't be silly."

"You could and it's not silly." Hal went to the piano. "Come on, try it. At least it'll fill in the time until they come."

"Did you look through those papers?" Joan asked.

"No."

"We should. There may be something in them that's important."

Hal drew the packet from his pocket and handed them to Maxie saying, "You look, Maxie, while we rehearse." Hal vamped the opening bars and nodded to Joan.

When she was halfway through the song he stopped her and explained why she was wrong. She went on. He stopped her again. Finally after the fifth stop she turned away. "I told you I couldn't sing. I don't want to do it, anyhow."

"But you're good," he said. "Surprisingly good! Try it again."

They were stopped by a long whistle from Maxie.

"What is it?" Joan asked, the song forgotten.

"A partnership agreement between Phil Martin and Dave Fields. Phil owned a half interest in the Gardens. Did you know that?" Maxie demanded.

"No."

"It's a good thing we looked at those papers," Joan cried. "If Burke had found that he'd be doubly certain that Mary had killed Phil to realize on his share of the Gardens. Give it to me."

"I'll take it." Hal stepped up, took the paper from Maxie, read it, folded it, and put it in his wallet. "It'll be safer here. Don't say anything about it," he warned.

The arrival of Jimmie and Burke interrupted the second rehearsal of the song.

"What do you want now?" Burke demanded suspiciously.

"Hasn't Jimmie told you?"

"We can't make a case out of that," he denied.

"But won't this book help?" she asked, taking the papers and the book from Maxie.

"So you held out on me," he accused.

"Let's say you didn't find them when you were here before," she suggested.

Burke looked at the memorandum in Martin's notebook. "Men have hung for less," he said, "but somehow it doesn't seem like Kelton. He's too smart."

"But you must do something about it!" Hal broke in. "You can't keep that innocent girl in jail any longer. Can't you release her now?"

"Not on the strength of this. If I can prove Kelton had anything to do with the murder, I'll let her out. You can depend on that."

"When will you let us know?" Hal asked.

"As soon as I get anything." He started for the door.

"How about the scratches on the knife handle? Were they made by a diamond?" Hal asked.

"Our man couldn't say. He's working on the scratches and her ring now. He'll have a report for me within the hour."

"Don't you realize she couldn't have held the dagger in her hand and killed him?" Joan insisted.

"That's what you think," Burke answered with more kindness and feeling than he had shown since the beginning of the case. "I know you don't want to think she did it, and I don't blame you, but we can't get away from the facts. She had double motive. She hated him and she wanted to be free. He wouldn't give her a divorce so she killed him. Mrs. Dufrane saw her do it, so she had to get her out of the way too."

"She didn't kill him!" Hal cried.

"Why didn't she tell you that she had gone to Martin's apartment last night? If she had had nothing to hide, she would have told you all about it. I'm sorry for you, but facts are facts. I'll do what I can to follow up this lead you've given me, but I'm holding out no hope." With a grunt to Jimmie he turned and left the room.

"There's one thing more I'd like," Joan said as she followed him into the hall.

"What?" Burke demanded shortly.

"I'd like to see Mary Dale. I want to take her some things. May I?"

He hesitated for a moment. "Okay. You can see her at eleven o'clock. Ask for Collins when you get to the jail.

He'll have it all fixed for you. Mind what you take," he cautioned.

Joan tripped down the hall to her own room. While her bath water was running, she turned on the radio. A musical number was just finishing. She hummed as she disrobed and put on her dressing gown. A voice startled her. It said:

"The roads leading to the Crystal Gardens out on the South Meadows are already choked with cars. The greatest crowd in the history of the city is trying to get to the Gardens tonight to see Hal Harrison, who has been so prominently concerned in the murder which took place there last night."

Joan snapped off the radio.

She was bathed and nearly dressed when Mrs. Paxton returned. She was followed by two bellhops who were loaded down with packages and boxes of all sizes and shapes.

"Darling, I bought the loveliest things," she gushed as the boys deposited the bundles on the bed. "You must see them! Look," she squealed with delight as she lifted a jangling litter of silver chain and gadgets from a box and began a demonstration. "This is a toilet set. Isn't it darling?" She fingered one of the gadgets. "This is a toothpick! And what do you suppose this is?" she asked exhibiting a tiny silver article suspended from a chain. "An ear spoon! Isn't that just too quaint? The man said they carried them around in their belts. It was only twenty dollars. Wasn't that a bargain. And this—"

A tap on the door interrupted her. It was Maxie, inviting them in for a cocktail before dinner.

"Of course, of course," Mrs. Paxton accepted immediately. "It's just what I need after a shopping trip." She fluttered an explanatory hand toward the bed. "It's so tiring, you know."

"So I've heard," Maxie answered sourly. With a nod, he backed out of the door.

As she powdered her face, Mrs. Paxton said, "It's so nice of him to ask us."

"It is, after the things you've said and done," Joan reminded her.

"Perhaps I was wrong." Mrs. Paxton swung round to face Joan, scattering a thin cloud of powder from the puff. "But you must remember I did what any mother would do. After all, we're Paxtons. We must be careful. Isn't it odd? It took a little thing like a murder to bring us together! You know yourself he wouldn't even speak to us for the first three thousand miles! I always say you never know! He'll be glad to play for the Benefit now, don't you think?"

"I wouldn't ask him again if I were you," Joan advised.

"But darling! He can't refuse now." She gave Joan a quizzical glance. "Just think how envious those women will be! Not only about his playing for the Benefit, but the murder and all. Why, we were right in at the killing, weren't we?"

"Yes, Mother," Joan answered patiently. "Come along."

As they went down the hall, Mrs. Paxton bubbled. "We must go to the Gardens tonight. They do say the murderer always returns to the scene of the crime. Now, wouldn't it be thrilling if we—But she can't come back, can she? She's in jail."

"She didn't kill him," Joan answered in a savage whisper as she tapped on the door prior to opening it.

The room was littered with members of the orchestra. They jumped to their feet as the two women entered. Hal, followed by Maxie bearing a tray, stepped forward.

"I was just saying to Joan," Mrs. Paxton gushed, "that—"

Maxie thrust a glass into her hand and said hurriedly, "Take this, Mrs. Paxton. You said you needed a drink."

Hal hooked his arm through Joan's and moved toward the window.

Mrs. Paxton returned her empty glass.

"Have another," Maxie invited.

Mrs. Paxton beamed. "Do you feel the way I do? It seems to me that .since repeal the drinks are very weak. You really need four or five before you begin to glow. I always say there's nothing like a glow."

"That's right," Maxie agreed and signaled a waiter to advance with the tray.

"Oh, how perfectly scrumptious!" She took two caviar canapés, ate one and waved the other at Maxie as she burbled on. "I always say the hors d'oeuvres are a meal in themselves."

"That's right," Maxie agreed. "Don't forget your glow," he reminded her, producing the third drink. At the window Joan sipped her drink and gazed down on the city.

"There it is," Hal said. "The romantic city of the West. It's like fairyland, isn't it?"

"The ferries look like fireflies, darting across the bay," Joan said.

"The bridges are fairy lanes of jeweled lights leading one to glamour and romance." He moved closer to her.

"Where was the Barbary Coast?" Joan asked.

"Down there," he pointed vaguely. "Behind us somewhere is the Golden Gate. I wanted to see it all," he sighed regretfully.

"You'll have to come back some day," she suggested.

"With you?" he asked.

"Perhaps. If you don't play for—"

"Don't say it," he laughed.

A rolling giggle echoed over their shoulders. "We must get dressed," Joan said, turning back into the room.

Mrs. Paxton was having a gorgeous time laughing, sipping, chewing, giggling.

Joan advanced. "We must dress for dinner, Mother. It's getting late."

Mrs. Paxton stifled the first of a series of hiccoughs.

"All right, darling, all right. Hie. Don't rush Mother. This is the first good time I've had—hic–since we left New

York. We don't have to dress hic—do we?" She put a hand on Maxie's arm.

"Why not?" he asked uncomfortably.

"See? We'll all have dinner together, won't we, Mr. Maxie? Wouldn't it be—hic—jolly?"

Maxie winced. "It certainly would," he replied and then, alarmed at the way she beamed at him, he added hurriedly, "But not tonight. We couldn't under the circumstances, you know."

"It's just like living in a birdcage, isn't it?" she giggled.

"Please, Mother!" Joan urged her toward the door, where Mrs. Paxton paused and waved good by before she was eased into the hall.

"Joan!" Hal called. "Just a minute."

"Go ahead. I'll be with you in a minute," Joan promised her mother.

Mrs. Paxton waved good by again and twittered down the hall. When she had closed her door behind her, Hal asked, "Why did you run away from me just now?"

"Why not?"

He took her left hand, held it thoughtfully in his for a moment, and said, "Look, Joan—"

She withdrew her hand slowly and shook her head mockingly. "Don't tell me you want to make an honest woman out of me!" she teased.

"I'm not kidding," he answered quietly. "I mean it. Some things are hard to say."

Behind them the telephone shrilled insistently.

"I know," Joan replied. "It's a sort of protection we have until we're sure."

"I was never more positive of anything in my life."

She looked at him for a long moment. "Neither was I."

He bent forward and kissed her. Her arms crept around his neck holding him to her.

Behind them the door flew open. Maxie, with a fevered hand on his brow, exclaimed, "Thank God!"

They parted, surprised.

Maxie clutched at Hal's sleeve. "You're not fooling this time, are you? You're really going to marry her, ain't you?"

"What's the matter with you?" Hal demanded.

"You gotta marry her," Maxie cried frantically. "Higgins just called on long distance again. He says unless you give him your word that you'll marry Joan the contract is all off. He was sore because you didn't give him a definite answer the last time."

"The sponsor," Joan said slowly.

"Sure, the sponsor," Maxie cried. "He's sore about all this publicity. He says if Hal doesn't marry you, it'll be a scandal and will hurt his product. It's wedding bells or no contract."

"I see," Joan said and turned away.

Hal clutched at her arm. "But you don't! Fool!" he bellowed at Maxie. "Listen, Joan."

She turned and pulled her arm from his grasp. "I've heard enough," she said.

"But, Joan," he cried following her, "you're going to marry me, aren't you?"

"What for—your public or your contract?" She stifled a sob and fled down the hall, with Hal in hot pursuit. She slammed the door in his face. He pounded frantically, calling, "Joan! Joan! You've got to listen to me!"

"If you don't go away from this door I'll call the manager!" she warned.

"But, Joan—"

With an ear pressed close to the panel she listened but refused to answer. Her heart fluttered. The pounding ceased. Had he taken her at her word? Why didn't he break the door down? Was he giving up so easily? If he really cared, if he were truly in love with her it would take more than a door to keep him away. Through the door she heard a sigh. Then silence while she waited.

He really had taken her at her word. He had gone away. A fine Lochinvar he had turned out to be. She had been a fool, anyhow. Why should she think that he had fallen in love with her just because she was in love with him? Mary had warned her. He was a public figure. He thought of his career first, last and always. Perhaps he did like her. Or did he? Had he known earlier in the day when he had first kissed her that his sponsor would demand that they be married? Had he been playing on her emotions, trifling with her for the good of his career? She had believed him. She had let him know not five minutes before that she really cared. She had done the thing that she had vowed she would never, never do until she was sure that she was really loved.

With a gesture of repulsion, she wiped his kiss from her lips. Marry her for his contract, would he? His contract could go hang and him with it. The thought of hanging made her remember Mary. Poor girl, she had been in love with him for years. And for what? Did he think, because so many women made fools of themselves over him, that he could play fast and loose with any woman he met? She'd show him.

She turned from the door a seething mixture of emotions. She knew she loved him. She was disappointed in him and she was hurt. The more she thought about it the madder she became.

She vented her anger and hurt pride on dresser drawers and closet doors as she flew about the room, gathering perfume, soap, powder and other things that Mary might want. As she rifled her possessions, Mrs. Paxton asked, "Did you lose something, dear?"

"Yes, my temper!" Joan snapped, flinging a pile of lingerie on the bed.

"Just be calm, darling. Anger eats up the vital forces. It doesn't pay." She took a piece of tissue and wiped cream from her face. "What are you doing?" Mrs. Paxton demanded.

"Getting some things ready for Mary."

"But, darling! Don't you think she'd rather have her own things?"

"I suppose so. Did you buy anything that would make a nice present?"

"They're all presents." With a finger pressed to her temple, Mrs. Paxton surveyed the litter of her purchases. She moved to the bed. "Now let me think. There's the dearest little creamer and sugar. No, that wouldn't do, would it? How about a sandalwood fan? No." She fingered the pile. "I know, these silk pajamas. Every woman in the jail will be envious of these." She held them up in front of her. "They're just the thing. I'm so glad I—"

"Thanks," Joan said shortly, snatching at the garment.

"My, but you are in a temper! Is it—?"

"It is! I don't want to talk about him. Now or ever! I'm going over to the jail to see Mary."

"But the Gardens! I thought you said—"

"Oh, I'm going." Joan flung the gay pajamas over her arm and opened the door. "I'm going down to get Mary's things. I'll see you later."

"But dinner—"

"Don't wait for me. I'll eat out there." She banged the door behind her.

The door of Mary's room was ajar. As Joan opened it, Hal looked up from one of the dresser drawers.

"Excuse me," Joan started to back out.

"Joan, wait a minute, please! I want to take some things over to Mary. Help me pack, will you?"

"I'll pack. I'm going over there. I can take care of her things," she answered coolly. She put a small suitcase on the bed and folded the pajamas and tucked them in. She went to work on the dresser drawers.

"We could go together," he suggested hopefully.

"It's not necessary. I know the way." She crossed to the bed with an armful of clothes.

"But she's my responsibility. I must see her again. After all—"

"I'm just butting in, is that it?" she asked frigidly.

"I didn't say that."

"But you were going to." She packed Mary's toilet articles.

"I wasn't. If you'd only be reasonable. If you didn't fly off the handle! If you'd only listen," he begged.

"I've heard plenty," she said decisively as she closed the lid and snapped the lock shut. "Here's the bag. When you get there ask for Collins. Burke was expecting me. It's all fixed." She turned on her heels and left him standing there.

"Joan," he called and ran to the door.

She refused to answer or look back.

CHAPTER SIXTEEN

Hal was in a fog of gloom when he left the hotel. He was so preoccupied that he forgot all about his prop smile and professional manner. He hurried into a cab and gloomed all the way to the jail.

What could a man do with a girl like Joan? Why couldn't she be reasonable, or were all women like that? Didn't she know that he wouldn't think of leaving San Francisco until Mary was freed from the accusation which hung over her? What did he care about Higgins or his contract? He could get plenty of work. Why did things have to come in bunches anyhow? Why did he have to fall in love at a time like this when he had so many other things on his mind?

At the jail he tried to brighten up when Mary was brought in under the watchful eye of a middle aged person.

"It was sweet of you to think of these," Mary exclaimed as she opened the bag.

"I'll have to look them over," the matron said, stepping forward.

"It was Joan's idea, the things," he said.

"She's sweet, Hal. You're lucky," Mary said as the matron lifted the items out one by one. "Oh! What gorgeous pajamas!" she cried and reached for them, caressing the silk lovingly. "Where did you get them?"

"Joan."

"Wasn't that nice of her! She's so considerate."

"Not of me," he answered.

"What's wrong?"

"Nothing," he denied weakly.

"There is! Tell me."

"I didn't come here to burden you with my troubles. You've enough of your own."

"They can't keep me here," she replied bravely. "Burke will soon realize that he made a mistake. Tell me what has happened."

Briefly he told her about the clues they had tried to unearth and run down. "We thought we might pin it on Dufrane," he said, "but according to the medical examiner she had been dead for a long time. As a matter of fact, she must have been killed soon after you followed her there."

"Then that doesn't make it look so good, does it?" she said.

"No. To be perfectly frank with you, it doesn't. We're pinning our last hope on Kelton now."

"And if that fails?" she asked hesitantly.

"I guess they'll try you unless something else turns up."

"Do you know how the knife was held?"

"No, not yet. Burke promised to check on that once more."

"I'm not going to give up hope," she said stoutly.

"Neither am I. I'll get you out."

"You've got your work and your contract to worry about. I'll be all right."

"The contract has gotten me into enough trouble. I'd just as soon throw it in the lake as not."

"Hal, you mustn't do that! Think of your career."

"I've been thinking about it. Do you suppose for one minute I'd desert you here in a strange city facing a charge of murder which I know you didn't commit? I'm not leaving here until you can leave with me."

Mary's face glowed. Her eyes caressed him. "I'll be very miserable if you don't leave tomorrow," she said.

"I'm not leaving. You'd be a lot more miserable here alone with no one to see you, talk to you, or work for you. We won't argue about it, please."

"All right," she agreed. "Now tell me about you and Joan. What happened?"

He gave her the whole story. When he had finished she said, "You don't know much about women, do you?"

"I never said I did. What should I have done?"

"You gave up too easily. You should have smashed the door down, done anything but go away."

"But she said—"

"Of course she did, but she didn't want you to believe her. When a girl is in love she wants to be possessed. She wants her knight to come riding, overcoming all obstacles in his way. She wants to be lifted up and carried off even if it is against her better judgment."

"How can you do that when she won't listen to you. She ran away!"

"You've got legs, too, haven't you? Run after her. Make her listen. She wants to listen, Hal."

Hal's face softened. "You mean I should have been more aggressive?"

"Since she had some cause for her resentment, yes. Your giving up so quickly would make her doubt of you justified."

"Gosh, I never thought of that! Doubt is a terrible thing, isn't it?"

"While we're on the subject," Mary said quietly, "I have a confession to make."

The matron leaned forward alert.

"What about?"

"That telegram you received in Portland. I received a wire from Phil in which he advised me to keep you away from San Francisco. I typed that message and gave the boy a dollar to deliver it to you. I'm sorry; I shouldn't have done it."

"It's okay, Mary. It's nice to know that there isn't anybody gunning for me. Forget it."

The matron straightened up, disappointed. She checked the wall clock with her wrist watch. "Your time's up," she warned.

"I had to tell you," Mary said.

"Forget it. We'll have you out of here in the morning," he promised.

"See Joan. She must be very unhappy."

"You bet I will. Thanks for the good advice." He watched as the matron led her through the door.

In the lobby of the building he spied a telephone booth. He called the hotel and asked for Joan. When she answered, he said, "This is Hal. You're having dinner with me and I won't take No for an answer." There was some spluttering reply but he did not wait to listen, he banged the receiver on the hook and dashed out of the building and into a waiting cab. A black car followed.

He looked at his watch. It was a few minutes after seven. "I'm going to be late at the Gardens," he said to himself, "but I don't care."

At the hotel he dashed into the lobby and down the hall to the elevators.

The black car which had been following him continued past the entrance and parked in a vacant spot near the alley.

When Hal reached his floor and swung down the corridor, Joan and her mother were just leaving their suite.

"Didn't I tell you to wait for me?" he demanded, dashing up to them.

"I do as I please, not as I'm told," Joan retorted.

"Then things will be different from now on," he replied, wondering just what he would do and how he would manage things. Mrs. Paxton definitely was not in his plan.

"My daughter is through with you," Mrs. Paxton said haughtily.

Just then the door of the service elevator opened and a waiter trundled a dinner cart and some provisions into the corridor.

"Hold it," Hal called to the operator, who stuck his head into the hall to see who it was who had spoken to him. Hal bent over, scooped a surprised Joan into his arms and started for the elevator.

"Young man! Put her down at once. At once! Do you hear me?" Mrs. Paxton shrilled.

"Oh, go sit on a tack," Hal yelled back as he stepped into the lift. "Down, and make it in a hurry," he called to the startled operator. "There's a five in it for you."

The door banged shut, falling away from Mrs. Paxton's shrill cries and poundings.

Joan had been squirming but not too violently. "Let me down," she finally demanded.

He slid her to her feet.

"Now, let me out of here."

"Tonight's my turn. I didn't want you in here last night but you came and stayed. Tonight I happen to want you here and you're going to stay until you listen to me."

The call buzzer kept ringing. "I guess it's the lady upstairs," the operator said.

"She'll rouse the house. Let us out on the ground floor the same as last night," Hal advised, digging into his wallet for a bill.

The operator stopped the car. Joan was ready to dash out.

"Not so fast!" Hal cried. Once more he scooped her up into his arms and dashed down the hall and through the door into the alley. When he reached the sidewalk he looked for a cab. The cab stand was at the opposite end of the street. A liveried chauffeur with cap pulled down over his eyes jumped from the black car and asked, "Car, sir? I've an hour to spare."

"My friend has a bad ankle. Take us for a ride," Hal said as he poured Joan into the back seat. She slithered across the seat and had reached the handle of the opposite door when he caught her foot and said, "No, you don't."

The car slid away from the curb. Joan turned her back to him.

"You're going to listen to me now," he said. "I love you and I'm going to marry you." He leaned forward and tapped on the glass, "Take us to the nearest airport," he ordered the driver. "You have to wait in California," he said. "We'll go to Yuma where they marry you first and ask questions afterward."

"You won't marry me in Yuma or anywhere else," she said.

"Unless you're blind to reason, I will," he insisted. "I've been waiting for you for years. I love you. Didn't I tell you so?"

"No," she denied. "You never said a word about love."

"Didn't I tell you we were going to be married this morning? Didn't I?" he demanded.

"That had nothing to do with love."

"Didn't I ask you again tonight just before Maxie—"

"Spilled the beans," she reminded him.

"Well, I did, didn't I?"

"You never told me you loved me. Do you think I'm a mind reader? You never said it until a minute ago after you nearly broke my foot yanking me back into the car. If you think this is the way to convince a girl that you love her, you're sadly mistaken."

"If this won't convince you, I give up," he cried in desperation. "I love you, I love you, I love you. There, have I said it enough?"

"Say it again," she said impishly as she turned toward him. "I like to hear it."

He took one long look at her before he folded her into his arms tenderly. "I love you," he whispered in her ear.

The car swerved and bumped over a bad road but they were not conscious of it for several minutes. It was Joan who became practical. "We can't go to Yuma. You've got to play tonight."

"The hell with contracts," he laughed.

"Your career comes first," she replied. "We're going to the Gardens." She leaned forward to tap on the window and called to the driver, "We've changed our minds. We don't want to go to the airport, after all. Take us to the Gardens."

They were traveling a murky smelly water front road out on the meadows.

"That's the Gardens over there," Hal said, pointing across the meadow.

They crossed a bridge over a creek and then turned into a narrow road. The car lurched to one side.

"It's bumpy," Joan cried as she rolled toward Hal, who, with a laugh, caught her in his arms.

As they neared a small shack, the driver went into second gear. He drove cautiously as he hit a pool of water. The car lurched sideways and slid in the mud. It stopped.

"What is the matter?" Hal asked as the driver climbed out and walked to the rear of the car.

"I don't want to get mired," the man answered.

Hal jumped out and stood beside the driver looking at the left rear wheel, which had sloped off the road. The driver bent down. So did Hal. Joan looked from the rear window. She saw a man advancing toward Hal from the shack. He was walking cautiously. His hand was raised. "Look out, Hal!" she cried. She tried to slide from the seat as she saw the man's hand fall and Hal sink to the ground. The next moment something struck her on the head. A companion of the driver, who had been slouched in the front seat, had tapped her over the head with a billy.

"Take him inside and give him the works," the driver ordered.

"How about the dame?" his companion asked.

"We'll take her up the line and dump her out. You didn't hit her hard, did you?"

"Just sleeping quietly," the man replied.

The car backed toward the shack and without lights retraced its way to the main highway. They stopped at the bridge and lifted Joan out.

"She might roll into the creek," the companion said.

"If she does, she won't be able to tell them anything. Come on, let's get out of here."

"Boy, was that a snap! Fell right into our laps, didn't they? I thought we might have to kill a cab driver or something," the companion said as he climbed in beside the driver and with lights on they went back toward the city.

CHAPTER SEVENTEEN

A police car with siren open speeded along Third Street away from the city.

"Why would a guy wanna kidnap a dame and take her to a place like the Gardens?" a policeman asked his companion who was driving. "It don't make sense."

"How do I know why guys wanna do the things they do? Why did that dame murder the guy out there last night? That didn't make sense either, did it? Would you bump a man off in front of five or six thousand people?"

"No."

"Neither would I. It don't make sense, but the guy was killed and they got the dame in the cooler."

"There's something on the bridge," the companion cried.

"Then let it get out of the way. Maybe it's somebody fishing." With a hand on his siren button he tore toward the bridge.

"Take it easy," the companion warned. "Whatever it is, it's struggling or something. Slow up, will you?"

Joan was recovering and trying to raise herself to her elbows. With a grinding shriek of brakes the police car slid to a stop about a foot from her body.

"It's a dame," the driver cried and bounded from the car.

"It's the dame we're looking for, I betcha," his companion cried. He knelt beside Joan and raised her in his arms. "What's the matter, lady?" he asked.

"Where is he?" she moaned.

"Who do you mean? The guy who hit you?"

"No, Hal. Where is he?"

"What did I tell ya? Hal Harrison. That's his name. This is the dame, all right. He must have thrown her out of the car thinking she'd roll into the creek. The dirty—"

"No," Joan moaned, "he didn't. He's hurt. We must find him."

"We'd better get her to a hospital," the driver said. "She's raving, poor kid."

"I'm not raving," Joan insisted with a slight return of her spirit. She struggled to get to her feet.

"Your name Paxton?" the driver asked.

"Yes."

"Where's Harrison?"

"That's what I've been trying to tell you." She rocked unsteadily on her feet.

"Take it easy," the policeman advised.

"We can't take it easy. We must find him," Joan cried frenziedly.

"Where is he?"

Joan told them what had happened.

"Near a shack here, you say?" the driver asked. She nodded and winced at the pain which shot through her head.

"There's no shack here," the policeman said.

"Then we must look for it. I remember crossing a bridge just like this. Then we turned off the road and ahead of us we could see the Gardens."

"It's the back road leading to the Gardens. The one the bootleggers used to use before repeal," the driver cried. "It's just up ahead here. Come on!"

While they were talking on the road, Hal returned to consciousness in the shack. He made an effort to sit up. His head was splitting with pain. He was on a bench. As he struggled to rise, he rolled from the bench to the floor. He lay there for a few minutes unable to move. He called for Joan. The echoing darkness filled him with terror for her. "Joan!" he cried, struggling to his hands and knees. He crawled to the door and pulled it open.

Across the meadows the lights of the Gardens sparkled through the thin fog which had trickled over the mountains in the distance. On his hands and knees he searched the cabin. In despair, he struggled to his feet and took a halting step toward the door and the beckoning lights. His knees sagged under him. He clutched at the jamb and by sheer force of will managed to remain erect. He waited a moment before taking another step. Halting, stumbling, he moved into the road and looked blankly at the spot where the car had stood.

He called for Joan. The night voices of the marsh life were the only answer. He turned and trudged toward the lights of the Gardens. He paused to rest. Behind him he heard the sound of a horn. Then lights swung toward him. He stood in the middle of the road and cried for help as he waved his arms in the air.

Their reunion was punctuated by matter of fact questions from the police, who first wanted to know why he had tried to abduct the girl.

"He didn't," Joan denied.

Then the police wanted to know about the car and the driver.

As they rode toward the Gardens, Hal explained what had happened.

"It was a dumb thing to do," the policeman remarked bluntly. "You played right into their hands. How much money did you lose?"

"I never carry much," Hal replied.

"My rings are gone," Joan cried, rubbing her hands together, "and a diamond pin."

"The pin?" Hal asked.

"Yes."

"I'm sorry about that. It was the thing that sort of brought us together," Hal said.

"What are you two talking about?" the policeman demanded.

"Our losses," Hal answered wearily.

The driver brought the car to a grinding stop opposite the kitchen entrance of the Gardens. Even there in the yard, they could hear the wild commotion which was going on inside. There was shrill whistling and a steady stamping of feet which echoed through the long building.

"We've got to hurry," Hal said to the policeman. "That mob is getting wild."

"You can't play looking like that," Joan reminded him. "You're mud from head to foot."

"If something isn't done soon there'll be a riot. Hurry!" He started to run forward but slowed to a quick walk because of the throbbing of his head. They mounted the steps to the kitchen and burst in on a surprised force. The steward came forward.

"Are you in charge here?" Hal demanded. At the man's nod Hal cried, "Tell Fields I'm here. Get my manager and a doctor to dress my head. How can I get to my dressing room without being seen?"

The steward barked orders. Men scuttled away.

"I'll report you've been found," one of the policemen said and went in search of a telephone.

Fields came dashing in, followed by Maxie and Mrs. Paxton, who was doing her best to play the role of a frantic mother.

"Where have you been?" Fields demanded. "Why didn't you get here on time? The place is a madhouse."

"How'd you get so dirty? Why didn't you tell me what you were going to do? It's a good thing I brought your clothes out. Look at you!" Maxie complained.

Mrs. Paxton flew to Joan. "My darling!" she cried as she tried to envelop Joan in her fluttering arms.

"I'm all right, Mother. Hal's been hurt. Where's the doctor?"

"Right here," a voice replied.

Mrs. Paxton stepped away from Joan. "I've had such a shock. I thought—Oh, Joan! I think I'm going to faint."

"Hold it!" Maxie commanded and gave her a resounding slap over the buttocks.

Mrs. Paxton gasped in shocked horror but she didn't faint. "Why—why—" she spluttered.

"What do you mean trying to kidnap the girl?" Fields was demanding of Hal.

"Go away," Hal answered wearily. "Go out there. Make an announcement. Tell 'em I'll be out in ten minutes. Get the boys on the stand. Do something."

Fields made a hasty exit.

Mrs. Paxton's inclination to faint had ebbed with her indignation at Maxie. Her role of frantic motherhood had been stripped from her ruthlessly, or rather slapped away from her, forcing her into the background, a place she did not relish. She went forward to where Joan, anxious about Hal, bent over watching the doctor dress the open cut on his scalp.

"Your hair, Joan. You're wounded. Why didn't you say something about it? You poor dear!"

"What's the matter?" Hal asked quickly.

"Matter!" Mrs. Paxton cried. "This poor child hurt her head last night. I told her to have something done about it. The wound is open. She's covered with blood from head to foot."

"Mother!"

"Now, darling. You've been bearing your pain in silence, I know, but his wound is no worse than yours. Doctor!"

"Look at her head," Hal ordered the doctor.

"Keep right on with what you're doing," Joan counterordered firmly. "It's nothing. He must be ready to play in a few minutes."

The doctor returned to the dressing of Hal's scalp.

"Isn't that the woman of it? Sacrificing herself for the man," Mrs. Paxton remarked to no one in particular.

"You were lucky," the doctor remarked as he finished the dressing. "You'll be all right."

Hal jumped to his feet. "Don't forget you're to sing with the trio," he said to Joan.

"I can't."

"Don't be like that. You're good. Mary would like it. Maxie will tell you when it's time to go on. I'm depending on you. Come on, Maxie, get me into some decent clothes. See you later," he called to Joan as he left the room.

"Now, I'll take a look at your head," the doctor said, helping Joan into the chair vacated by Hal.

As the doctor worked, Mrs. Paxton chattered away. "What's this about singing? What did he mean?"

Joan explained.

"I never heard of such a thing! A Paxton a public entertainer!"

"Why not, since I'm going to marry one?" Joan retorted.

"You're not!"

"It's all settled."

"Now, Joan. I won't let you do it, not even for my Benefit. That's why you're doing it, isn't it? I won't let you sacrifice yourself for me. No, don't say a word," she cautioned as Joan was about to speak. "I know divorces are easy and all that, but I won't let you do it. So there!"

Fields returned to see how things were going. He overheard Joan's explanation to her mother and the following conversation. "Why not let her do it?" he suggested. "Sounds like a great idea to me."

"It would," Mrs. Paxton said scathingly. "Come along, Joan, if the doctor's finished with you."

"Where's Hal?" Fields asked.

"Dressing," Joan replied.

Mrs. Paxton started for the exit. "Come, Joan."

"Why didn't you let me know ahead of time?" Fields demanded of Joan. "I could have given you a lot of publicity."

"I've had it," Joan reminded him as she followed her mother.

In the corridor, Mrs. Paxton was weaving a story to Jimmie Farr of the near tragedy from which Joan had miraculously escaped. "There were five men," she exaggerated as Joan joined her.

"Now, Mother," Joan remonstrated. "There were not more than three."

"What happened?" Jimmie asked eagerly. "Of course I knew you hadn't been kidnaped, but tell me what really happened."

"Give me your news first. Any luck?"

Jimmie shook his head.

"Tell me about it anyhow," Joan insisted.

"I've a table all reserved," Mrs. Paxton bubbled. "I want to hear too. I don't know a thing you've done this livelong day," she accused Joan.

Mrs. Paxton, clucking like a brooding hen, seated them at her table. "Such a din," she complained. "This place is very badly managed."

The noise was terrific. The crowd laughed, chatted, gave cat calls and stamped their feet. There was a concerted banging of mugs and glasses on table tops. The members of the band had taken their places but were waiting for Hal to appear. Someone shouted, "We want Harrison! We want Harrison!" Just as they had done on the preceding night, the crowd took up the call. "We want Harrison!"

A young lad jumped onto the floor followed by several of his pals. They started a snake dance. Girls joined in. The line grew instantly as they raced down the long floor toward the bandstand crying, "We want Harrison!" The line swung in front of the stand. The leader, thoroughly enjoying himself, started back down the hall. In a few minutes there was a long, twisting, swirling mass of humanity crowding the floor.

Fields dashed by Mrs. Paxton's table wringing his hands, barking incoherent orders at special police, waiters, and bus boys. "Get Burke," he cried, "before they wreck the place!"

"There's Hal," Jimmie said, glancing toward the platform.

The crowd on the floor was too busy and too intent on its own performance to notice Hal as he raised his baton and swung into his famous signature. The band played for several minutes before the crowd realized the music had started. Gradually the snake line broke into segments, the couples joining to sway with the music. A semblance of order reigned once more.

"Well," Mrs. Paxton cried. "I never—" She stopped to overhear what Jimmie was saying.

". . . And so you see Kelton was a blank. It was a good idea but it didn't work."

"Then it wasn't Kelton's gang that held us up?" Joan asked.

"Couldn't have been. Must have been plain yeggs. Say," he considered for a moment, "that didn't just happen. They must have been waiting for you."

"That's why I thought it was Kelton's men," she answered.

"It was blanks all around," Farr went on. "Dufrane might have killed Martin but it's a cinch he didn't kill his wife. She had been dead for hours."

"Thanks a lot for all you've done. I'm sorry. I thought we'd get something. I'll make it up to you some day," Joan promised.

"You're not quitting, are you?" he demanded.

"No. Just stymied for the moment. Do you mind if I do some thinking?"

At that moment Maxie hustled by. Joan stopped him. "How's Hal?" she asked.

"I dunno. He's glum over something. He wouldn't tell me. I left him alone for a moment and Fields said or did something to him that's got him all upset."

"But what could it have been?" Joan asked.

"Look at him. He looks as if he'd lost his last friend."

Hal was a solemn looking young man as he faced the crowd and led the band.

Maxie started away but was stopped by Mrs. Paxton, who put a restraining hand on his arm. "Have a drink. Turn about is fair play, you know," she said.

"Give me a rain check," Maxie answered. "I've lots of things to do." He scampered away.

"I was so sure we'd uncover something," Joan sighed. "Where's Burke?"

"He's around somewhere. He said he'd promised to do some checking for you."

"He's been decent after the way we treated him," Joan said. "If you see him, tell him I'd like to thank him."

"You sound as if you thought this was the end of everything," Jimmie said reprovingly.

"We've got to start over again," she replied.

"I must say, I'm disappointed," Mrs. Paxton chimed in. "I've always heard it said that the murderer returns to the scene of the crime."

"Suppose he never left it?" Joan asked thoughtfully.

"For mercy's sakes!" Mrs. Paxton cried, annoyed. She swung round and glared at a janitor who was pressing close to her chair. "What are you doing?"

"Sorry, lady. I gotta catch up on my work. A lot of bulbs get shorted out." He thrust a pole toward the ceiling and caught a dead bulb in the prongs at the end of the stick. With a couple of twists, the bulb was released. He lowered the pole, dropped the dead bulb into a bag, inserted a fresh one and attached it to its socket in the ceiling. The operation finished, he moved down the aisle.

"That," cried Joan, "is the answer to how it was done! Get that man back here!"

Jimmie, his eyes alive with interest, bounded from the table, overthrew his chair and collided with a waiter as he went in pursuit of the pole bearing janitor.

"I've got my work to do," the man was protesting as Jimmie dragged him back.

"It'll take but a minute. I want to see the end of that pole," Joan said sweetly.

Reluctantly the man lowered the pole for Joan's inspection. His expression clearly indicated that he thought them stark staring mad. He assumed an air of patient boredom as Jimmie and Joan examined the prongs.

"You've hit it," Jimmie cried gleefully. "Why didn't I think of it myself?"

"Why didn't any of us think about it?" Joan replied.

"Now the thing to do is to see if it will hold a knife," Jimmie suggested eagerly.

"I gotta get me work done," the janitor complained.

"My good man," Mrs. Paxton began, "don't be so impatient."

He gave her a disgusted look.

"It's important," she whispered. "It's about the—"

"Mother!" Joan cried a warning as she realized that the occupants of near by tables were interested in what she and Jimmie were doing.

Mrs. Paxton caught herself, smiled at the janitor, and went on, "It's about the 'you know.' Last night." Her eyes twinkled with the delight of a secret shared.

"I couldn't find the pole last night," the janitor answered in disgust.

"That's right, you couldn't," Joan said. "I remember you were looking for it. I wonder what happened to it?"

"I know what happened to it," he replied with an air of importance.

"Do you? What?" Jimmie asked quickly.

"It was put on the rubbish heap and burned. I found the end of it there this morning."

"Now who would do a thing like that?" Joan asked quizzically.

"I dunno. Somebody was jealous of my job, likely," he answered. "Mr. Fields is very particular about keeping the place in order and he's a crank about the lights. If he sees one has burned out before I do he lets me know about it, he does. 'Are you slipping, Al?' he'll say. He's a great one for asking questions, he is."

"It was a mean trick stealing your pole," Joan sympathized. "Don't you have a regular place where you keep it?"

"Sure I do. I keep it locked up in my broom closet and I'd have sworn I locked it up last night, but I can't be sure because we were very busy with the crowds pouring in on us and all. I had a lot of extra work to do," he volunteered, becoming more voluble as he sensed his importance to the little group who were so interested in him and his work.

"Perhaps you left it somewhere," Jimmie suggested. "That's an easy thing to do, particularly if you're very busy."

"Now, that's one thing I don't do," he boasted "I'm very particular about my tools. I never leave them scattered about the way some men do. I get that from my father. Trained in the old country he was, and particular like. If he'd catch me leaving things lay he'd give me a clout, he would. Sharp-like."

"But if it was locked up?" Joan insisted.

"I'm not sure about that, lady. You see, when I went looking for it the closet door was open and the pole gone."

"Didn't you look for it?"

"Sure I did. All over the place, but I couldn't find it anywhere. It's a lucky thing for me there was some excitement here last night or Mr. Fields would have fired me sure."

"Can't you remember where you left it?" Joan asked.

"Me mind's a blank," he replied.

While they talked, Jimmie had been inserting things into the prongs and testing their strength. "They're strong, all right," he assured Joan.

"Sure they're strong," the janitor agreed. "I've even put a paintbrush in the prongs to paint a spot on the ceiling that I couldn't reach with a ladder. You'd be surprised at the things you can do with one of these poles."

"I am surprised," Joan assured him.

At that moment, Maxie came dashing up to the table. "The trio is going to sing next," he cried. "Hal wants to know if you've changed your mind."

"Joan, you're not going to sing!" Mrs. Paxton cried.

"Of course I am." Joan stood up. "Keep your fingers crossed and keep going," she said to Jimmie. "We're getting hot."

"Such language," Mrs. Paxton shrilled. "I can't understand you. You've changed so. It's that man!"

"The girls are waiting for you in the musicians' room," Maxie said to Joan. As she passed him he whispered, "Try and cheer Hal up a bit, will you?"

"I'll have great news for him," she promised. "Get Burke. I want to see him as soon as the song is ended," she told Maxie.

"What's up?"

"A couple of ideas."

"Can't you tell me?" he asked.

"Not yet. I've got to think, remember back, and fit pieces together."

"Are you going to do that while you're singing?" he teased.

She shrugged and turned away.

"It's dull here," Mrs. Paxton complained to Maxie, who had become interested in Jimmie and the janitor.

"Huh?"

"I said it's dull here after last night," she repeated.

"Seems lively enough to me," he replied. "You don't want another murder, do you?"

"Anything but this boredom! No one pays any attention to me. Joan doesn't obey me. No one asks me to dance," she whined.

Maxie sensed what was coming and tried to get away, but Mrs. Paxton was too quick for him. "Mr. Maxie!" she cried. "Dance with me!"

He began a refusal but he didn't have a chance.

"Now, don't tell me you're busy. All work and no play, you know!" She rose and took hold of his arm. "We'll leave Mr. Farr to play with his fishing-pole," she said contemptuously as she tugged Maxie floorward.

"You said something," Jimmie muttered after her. "Fishing is right." He returned his attention to Al, the janitor.

CHAPTER EIGHTEEN

Mrs. Paxton was a "hopper." Maxie was a "foot dragger." The combination of their particular types of dancing produced a weird effect. As they swung, gyrated and bobbed along the floor toward Hal, he could think of only one thing to describe their progress. Mrs. Paxton looked like an ambitious little tugboat towing an unwieldy barge through turbulent waters.

As they neared the stand Maxie called to Hal, "It's okay. She's gonna sing."

With a nod of understanding Hal ended the number. When the applause had died down he announced: "There will be a short intermission. After that we have a surprise for you. Miss Joan Paxton, of New York, will take the place of Miss Mary Dale in the trio."

"Just when I was having such a good time," Mrs. Paxton pouted. "That man has a way of frustrating me."

"He can't play forever," Maxie said defensively.

"Wouldn't it be wonderful if you could just go on dancing forever?" she breathed.

"Maybe so," he agreed fearfully and steered her toward her table.

On the stand, Hal was besieged by crowds of autograph seekers who poked albums, cards and menus up at him to be signed. He wrote automatically. His prop smile was gone, his professional manner had vanished. His famous personality was definitely lacking, lost in the maze of his preoccupation.

"That's her," he heard someone in the crowd say.

Hal swung round. Joan and the girls were going up to the divan to wait for their number. "That's all," he said and turned from the crowd.

He beckoned to Joan as he moved over to the end of the platform. She came down from the divan to meet him. "Are you nervous?" he asked.

"Of course I'm nervous. Who wouldn't be? If I go sour I expect you to cover me up."

"Okay."

"What's the matter? Does your head hurt?" she asked anxiously.

"My head's all right. It's what's inside," he replied.

"What are you talking about?"

"You."

"What have I done?"

"Nothing, yet. I've been warned in time. I'm glad I still have a few friends."

"Why don't you come out with it?"

"Fields overheard you and your mother talking. So you're going to marry me to get me to play for that Benefit and then divorce me, are you?"

"Don't be ridiculous!"

"Did you ever say you loved me?" he demanded. "Did you?"

"I don't remember."

"Well, I do." He swung on his heel and went back to the microphone.

"Of all the—" Joan started to reply.

Hal tapped for attention. The band began to play, the floor filled with dancers while Joan stood where he had left her trying to make up her mind what she should do. The girls came down and joined her. "What's up?" one of them asked.

"For two cents I wouldn't sing in his old trio."

"You can't leave us flat now," the girls said. "Save it and take it out on him later. Did he say something mean to you? He's nervous, and no wonder. He didn't mean it."

Hal looked in their direction and nodded for them to come down. The girls took their position in front of their mike. Joan was ready when the cue came. She was to sing the verse of the song. She forgot to be nervous. She was boiling mad at him for upsetting her just before she was to sing. She put her rage and venom into the opening words as she said, "You said you loved me, I believed you, but you lied—"

Her voice demanded attention throughout the hall. The band's interest quickened. They nodded to each other that she was all right. Joe Stevens' fat face broke into a smile. Scat Miller opened his eyes and watched her attentively. Most of the boys had believed that Hal had completely lost his reason when he told them that Joan was going to take Mary's place in the trio.

The three girls were singing the chorus when Maxie hurried up to the microphone and handed Hal a note which read:

"Tell Joan to hurry back to her mother's table. The guy she's engaged to has just arrived."

Hal nodded an okay to Maxie as he finished the number. The applause was terrific. The girls shoved Joan forward to take a bow alone. The applause continued. "Do it over," Hal ordered tersely and began a replay of the entire number.

When they finished he handed Joan the note to read. "Who's being ridiculous?" he demanded.

"You are," she retorted and turned away. She raced across the platform to the side, where she was met by Fields. She paid no attention to the applause.

"You're a hit!" he cried. "I'll give you a contract. What do you say?"

"This is my first and last public appearance. I'm going back to New York where I belong." Joan wanted to get away. A good cry would have been a relief.

"Quitting the detective game, eh?" a voice asked coming from behind Fields. It was Burke who stepped into view.

Burke had a black eye, a perfect match to the one which adorned Fields' eager face.

"Maybe," Joan answered, "but first will you tell me how you got that black eye?"

"You gave it to me," he answered sourly.

"You can't blame that on me," she denied. "I haven't seen you for hours. Do you mean it was Kelton?"

"No. A beam. Under that damned stand which you were so insistent I investigate. I banged smack into it."

"Then I did give it to you," she laughed. Out of the corner of her eye she caught Fields unconsciously fingering his own discolored upper cheek.

"Listen to that applause!" Fields cried. "Let me sign you up?"

Joan jumped down from the platform and stood between Burke and Fields. She looked first at one man and then the other.

"What's going on?" Burke demanded.

One of the trio came to the edge of the platform and called, "We've got to go back. Hal says to hurry."

"Lift me up," Joan asked Burke.

As he lifted her she whispered, "Go to Fields' office. I'll be there in a few minutes. I'm sure I know who the murderer is now."

"You what?"

"In a few minutes," she called back and walked down front with the other girls.

"Sing the whole thing," Hal suggested. "We'll make it a blue number." He stepped aside, motioning the girls to use his microphone.

Joan took her position in the center of the group, directly in front of the microphone as Hal stepped aside. The lights dimmed as Joan started the song for the third time.

With the three girls so close to him, Scat Miller felt crowded. He shifted his chair back and to one side during his rest period after the chorus had started.

As the girls moaned the last few bars of the song, Scat cried out in alarm and pain. He slid to the floor. His stand crashed forward. One of the girls stifled a scream.

"What is it?" Hal cried, jumping forward to clutch Joan. "Are you hurt?"

"No. Quick! He's tried it again. Get Miller out before the lights come up!"

Because of his distance from the microphone, Scat's cry had not been amplified sufficiently to disturb the entire hall. Those down in front had heard it and were pressing forward as Hal tugged Scat to his feet.

"Who's tried what?" Hal asked quickly.

"The murderer. He probably knows I have found him out."

"You have! Who is it?"

"Not now. Hurry!"

"I'm all right," Scat mumbled. "Something struck me."

"I'll say it did," Hal replied. "Your side is all sticky. Come on, get offstage before the lights come up."

"I can make it," Scat answered and stumbled for the edge of the platform.

"Go to Fields' office," Hal whispered. "I'll be there in a minute."

As the lights came up, the girls took their bow and started from the stage. Hal reached for Joan with his free hand and whispered, "Don't go. I can't leave for a minute."

"But I'm catching the murderer," she answered and kept going.

"Take over, Joe," Hal called and followed her off. He caught her arm just as she stepped behind the column. "You're not running away from me again. Just now I thought—"

"I didn't love you—" she started.

She didn't finish. She was smothered in his arms, his lips finding hers. The piano player struck a wrong chord. An alert saxophone gave them a horse laugh. One of the trombone players pulled his horn apart as he watched them, his eyes bulging. A clarinet went off key. The bull fiddle forgot to play. Joe banged his baton helplessly, trying to hold the band together.

The dancers stopped and waited. One of them said, "This band is lousy."

Joan, the unseen cause of all the commotion, freed herself from Hal's embrace. "You mustn't forget your public," she chided, "nor the fact that I'm engaged to another man. Also, Burke is waiting for me to name the murderer."

"I can't leave you alone, ever again. You're so irresponsible. God, if I had lost you!" he cried.

"What are you talking about?" she asked, drinking in the words.

"Don't you realize that the murderer tried to kill you just as he killed Martin? If Scat hadn't moved over—you might have been—"

"But Scat did move over. I'm all right. Nothing can happen to me now."

"I'll say it can't. I'm going to watch you like a hawk!"

"And I'll like it."

"What happened?" Fields dashed up to ask.

"Just a slight accident," Joan replied.

"Another attempt at murder," Hal said.

"NO!" Fields was unbelieving. "Where's Burke?"

"In your office."

"Hadn't we better tell him?" Fields suggested.

"I'm going to tell him, plenty."

Joan darted across the corridor pursued by Hal and a wondering Fields. From the corner of her eye Joan saw Maxie and Jimmie hurrying toward them, with her mother in their wake. Behind Mrs. Paxton she saw a very tall, overly stout, bewildered young man trying to follow with his customary dignity. She smiled tolerantly.

"Have you any men here?" she demanded of Burke as she burst into the office. "Get the janitor who fixes the lights in the ceiling. Send someone under the stand to find, if possible, a long pole with prongs on the end of it."

The others surged into the office, forcing Burke back for a moment by their advance. Scat was in a chair holding his side. As Burke started through the door Joan called, "And get a doctor."

"What's all this?" Fields demanded. "What's going on?"

"It's the windup of murder," Joan replied.

"We got it, eh?" Jimmie cried.

"Yes."

"Well, I said you can't come in!" Burke snapped at someone at the door. He slammed it shut with a vicious bang. "Now," he turned to Joan.

"What have you done now?" Mrs. Paxton demanded. "More disgrace? Haven't you done enough? I was never so mortified in my life!"

"Who's the murderer?" Burke demanded.

"Fields," Joan replied.

Mrs. Paxton withdrew from Fields' side as if she had been bitten.

"What's the joke?" Fields asked.

"It's no joke, Fields," Joan replied. "If I'm wrong, you can soon prove it."

"Better be careful," Burke cautioned.

There was a knock on the door. Burke admitted the doctor, who went to Scat's side at once. Then the janitor came in, his eye on his precious pole which a policeman was carrying.

Joan took the pole from the policeman and handed it to Burke. "This is what the murderer used last night, or rather one like it. He tried it again tonight, why, I do not know."

"I can answer that question," Burke said. "Fields, eh? He was the only person in this place who knew what you whispered to me when I lifted you back onto the stand. I told him as we walked away. You said you had business to attend to, didn't you?"

Burke demanded of Fields. "It was murder you meant."

"Are you going to believe this nit wit girl who has done nothing but make a fool of you?" Fields retorted.

"Who's a nit wit?" Hal jumped forward, fists clenched, forgetting that a short twenty four hours before he had given Joan the same title.

"I'll take care of this." Burke stepped between Hal and Fields.

"Hold your temper!" Maxie cautioned.

Light began to dawn in that spot Mrs. Paxton called a brain. "You mean to say that he tried to kill my daughter?" she shrilled.

"Never mind, Mother," Joan silenced her.

"It's an outrage!" Fields stormed.

"You're under arrest, Fields. Be quiet!" Burke barked.

"On a charge like this? Where's your proof?" Fields cried.

That, of course, was a poser for Burke; he had no definite proof. He knew that Fields knew that Joan had promised to name the murderer for him but he had no facts. He turned toward Joan and said gruffly, "You made the charge. Back it up."

"Yes. Tell us about it, darling. Don't be shy! She's so modest," she explained to Burke.

"So's the Venus de Milo," he retorted.

Mrs. Paxton gulped. "Go on, dear. Tell us step by step. I didn't even suspect. I might have helped you but you never said a word to me. Now, the time I was involved in a murder—"

"Tell us," Burke begged with a worried look in the direction of Mrs. Paxton.

A policeman opened the door and called, "The reporters want to know what has happened."

"Keep them out," Joan cried to Burke. "This is Jimmie Farr's story. He helped."

"Clear the corridor," Burke commanded. "Now, Miss Paxton."

"We made our first discovery quite by accident," she began. She told Burke of her despair of ever hoping to free Mary and then the arrival of the janitor fixing the light bulbs.

"That's right. I remember," Mrs. Paxton cut in.

"Quiet!" Burke snapped.

Joan turned to the janitor. "You lost your pole last night, didn't you?"

"Yes, ma'am."

"Didn't I hear you telling Mr. Fields about it?"

"I dunno about that, ma'am. But I did tell him."

"And what did he say?"

"He said for me not to bother him. He didn't care if the lights were out. I was to leave them alone."

"Where did you get the new pole?" Jimmie asked.

"I bought it myself."

"Why?"

"Because when I was leaving last night I asked Mr. Fields for a new one and he told me not to bother with the lights for a few days."

"Why did you do that, Fields?" Farr asked.

"I had other things on my mind," Fields grumbled.

"Like murder, for instance?"

"But how did you connect the crime with Fields?" Burke asked Joan.

"You did it for me," she answered.

"I did?" He was puzzled.

"Yes. Your black eye. I had been trying to fit the pieces together ever since Farr and I realized that the pole was the implement used. When you came up to the stand with that black eye of yours, you gave me the whole answer. Last night when I went in under the stand I banged my head. Here's the mark. See it?" She bent forward for him to see.

"Now, if you'll stand up straight, you'll realize that the top of my head is on an exact level with your eye." She moved over and stood directly in front of him.

"That's right!" Mrs. Paxton cried.

"Now you and Fields are just about the same height. Stand together."

Burke moved over and stood beside Fields.

"She's right again. So observing!" Mrs. Paxton commented.

"What's all this nonsense got to do with her crazy charge?" Fields objected.

"You had a black eye last night," Joan reminded him.

"I got it before last night and I can prove it," he growled.

"But you bruised it again last night," she reminded him. "Just after Martin's murder the skin under your eye was badly broken."

"It's reasonable," Burke agreed, "but what about his motive?"

"Phil Martin owned half of this place," Hal exclaimed.

"That's a lie!" Fields cried.

"How about the partnership agreement between you and Martin?" Hal demanded.

"What's this?" Burke asked.

"In those papers we found in Martin's apartment, there was a partnership agreement between Fields and Martin. I have it in my pocket."

"Then produce it!" Fields cried.

Hal felt of his breast pocket where he usually carried his wallet. "I can't," he cried, "because you took it."

"I've been a very busy man according to you," Fields sneered.

"How'd you get so much mud on your shoes?" Joan asked, pointing down at his feet.

"Come clean, Fields," Burke warned.

Fields refused to answer.

"I'll tell you," Hal cried. "Fields knew about the bad blood between Martin and myself. He decided to take advantage of that situation. The statement I allowed to appear in the paper probably made the whole thing seem very simple to him. Since I had threatened Martin, I'd naturally be the one to be suspected. But Fields went further than that. He wanted to be sure I'd be suspected, so he planned the murder so that I couldn't have possibly escaped if it had not been for Joan's sharp eyes."

"And when he knew she was on to him he tried to kill her in the same way," Burke added.

"Why not search Fields?" Joan suggested. "If he doesn't have the paper on him it's probably in his safe."

While Burke and a policeman went through Fields' pockets, Hal turned to Scat. "How are you, fellah?" he asked.

"He's all right," the doctor replied. "It was a flesh wound which scraped one of his ribs."

"I'm feeling fine," Scat smiled. "I guess we go back to New York on time, eh?"

"It's not here," Burke said, disappointed, as he placed an arm holster and gun on the safe behind him. "He may have burned it."

"Can't you get a fence on the job?" Jimmie asked. "If we can locate anything that was stolen from Miss Paxton we can arrive back at the man who hired the boys to do the job."

Following the suggestion, Burke went to the telephone and gave minute instructions to headquarters.

"It's a frame up to get that girl out of jail!" Fields cried.

"While you're telephoning, Inspector, can't you arrange to have Mary released?" Joan suggested.

"I'll wait until I'm positive, if you don't mind," he said cautiously.

"How you gonna prove I shot Mrs. Dufrane?" Fields stormed at Joan. "Did you forget that there is a double charge of murder in this case?"

"Not for a moment; thanks for helping me out." She turned to Burke. "This morning at the jail when none of us knew where Mrs. Dufrane was or how she had died, I was talking to Fields. When I mentioned Mrs. Dufrane to him he asked me, 'Who shot her?'" She spun round to Fields. "How did you know she was shot? How did you know she was dead?"

"Well, when she didn't turn up you'd naturally think," he evaded lamely.

"Is that why you were so interested in the papers we took from Martin's apartment? Is that why you told us not to give the balance of them to Burke? Were you afraid if we turned the papers over to Burke he would find that agreement between you and Martin and so have a motive on which to work?" She turned to Burke. "He's the only person outside of ourselves who knew that there were papers in addition to the ones we gave you this morning. Hal even showed Fields where he was keeping them; in his inside coat pocket. After I found the memorandum book and had gone out, Hal discovered the agreement between Martin and Fields."

"Why didn't you give it to me?" Burke asked sourly. "We'd have had proof then."

"Because you still believed that Mary Dale was guilty. You would have considered that piece of paper as evidence against her rather than a motive for anyone else."

"Yeah, and I heard her admit that she was at Martin's apartment last night. She followed Mrs. Dufrane there," Fields cut in.

"Did you see her?" Joan asked quickly.

But Fields was not so easily trapped.

"How could I see her?"

"But you saw Mrs. Dufrane, you killed her because she surprised you," Joan accused.

"How long are you going to let this nonsense go on?" Fields demanded.

"Until I've had a look in your safe," Burke replied. He nodded toward one of the men to make a search. The safe was locked.

"Open it," Burke commanded.

"You haven't got a warrant."

"It's open it, or jail," Burke threatened. "Which do you prefer?"

"I'll open it, but I'll make you pay for this," Fields grumbled.

He knelt down before the safe. His fingers fumbled as he spun the dials.

"Come on, quit stalling," Burke insisted. "Get it open."

"I won't do it," Fields cried.

"Then we'll open it. What have you got to hide? We'll get you sooner or later. You can't escape."

There was a slight distracting commotion at the door. During that second, Fields' hand went up to the gun where Burke had placed it on the safe. With the gun in hand he bounded to his feet. "Don't move, any of you. Stay right where you are." He stepped backward, bumping into Mrs. Paxton, who squealed. "Get out of my way!" Fields growled and pointed the gun at her.

"Don't shoot, don't shoot!" she cried and collapsed in a heap on the floor. As she went down, she fell in Fields' path. He stepped back trying to avoid her fallen body and reach the window. He stumbled and tripped backward. He made an instinctive effort to save himself, but could not check his backward fall. His great bulk crashed through the low window.

Even though trying to escape a death sentence for murder, his sense of self preservation was so great that he called frantically for help as he disappeared from view.

Burke sprang to the window and looked down. The drop was about twelve feet. Fields lay sprawled on the ground. "Go down and pick him up," he called to one of his men. He went to the telephone and called headquarters, telling them to release Mary Dale from jail. "That seems to wind things up," he said as he faced Joan.

"You don't want to keep me here now, do you?" Jimmie Farr asked.

"You'd better telephone if you want the beat," Joan advised.

"Right as always." Jimmie made a dive for the telephone.

There was a determined commotion at the door. Trying to fight his way through the protecting police, the tall, overly fat young man by sheer force of size and weight was gaining ground. "I've got to go in there," he kept insisting.

"Reggie!" Mrs. Paxton gasped. "I forgot all about him! Poor boy!" She ran to the door. "Let him in!" she ordered.

The police stepped aside at a nod from Burke. Reggie, his moon face a deep pink, plodded into the room staring blankly at the gathering.

"This is Reggie Gardner, Joan's fiancé," Mrs. Paxton announced with a return to her social flutter.

Reggie bowed a bit more hurriedly than decorum required and rushed across the room to Joan, who was standing beside Hal. "Joan," he cried, "am I in time?"

"That all depends," she replied.

"But I took a plane the minute I heard you were not married to that band fellow." He was short of breath and exploded the words at her with irregular puffs.

"We're as good as married," Hal cut in. "We will be tomorrow."

"Congratulations," Reggie cried with a puff of relief. He took Joan's hand and pumped it several times. He even glanced at Hal and mumbled, "I hope you'll be very happy."

"But, Reggie—" Mrs. Paxton began.

Reggie ignored her. "Joan," he cut in, "now that you're married, there's just one thing I must ask

"Here's where I get properly disengaged," she whispered to Hal. "Yes, Reggie?"

"It's about the—Well, Mother thinks—and so do I, but Mother said you wouldn't want to keep that ring I gave you."

Joan hesitated.

Reggie continued. "She said that no girl of breeding— no matter what scandal—no matter what she might do, would think of keeping a ring after—Well, I guess you get the idea?"

Slowly, wordlessly, she slipped the ring from her finger and handed it to him. Fortunately, it was not one of those that had been stolen from her.

He sighed with relief. "Thanks a lot! This will be a load off Mother's mind." He turned and walked toward the door. "I can get a plane back to night. Good by."

Mrs. Paxton followed him with unbelieving eyes as the door closed behind him. She cried, "Well! I never in all my life!"

"His mother has nothing on me," Hal sighed. "That's a load off my mind."

"Then you don't think I was trying to double cross you?"

"If I had cared less, I would have known better," he replied. "We'll be married in Reno tomorrow."

"Still thinking of your sponsor?" she asked impishly.

"You bet your life I am! I'll have a wife to support now. Where's Maxie? Wire Higgins. Tell him I'll be married tomorrow."

"And so they lived happily ever afterward," Jimmie beamed at them. "It's on the level this time, isn't it?"

"Dead on the level," Hal replied.

Mrs. Paxton, who had been wide eyed and a trifle incredulous of what she had been hearing, suddenly remembered why she was in San Francisco. "Now you can't refuse to play for that Benefit," she cried.

"The answer is still 'No,' " Hal replied as he bent forward to kiss Joan

THE END

Resurrected Press Books in *The Chief Inspector Pointer Mystery* Series

Murder at Bridge

When an afternoon bridge party attended by some of Hamilton's leading citizens ends with the hostess being murdered in her boudoir, Special Investigator Dundee of the District Attorney's office is called in. But one of the attendees is guilty? There are plenty of suspects: the victim's former lover, her current suitor, the retired judge who is being blackmailed, the victim's maid who had been horribly disfigured accidentally by the murdered woman, or any of the women who's husbands had flirted with the victim. Or was she murdered by an outsider whose motive had nothing to do with the town of Hamilton. Find the answer in... **Murder at Bridge**

One Drop of Blood

When Dr. Koenig, head of Mayfield Sanitarium is murdered, the District Attorney's Special Investigator, "Bonnie" Dundee must go undercover to find the killer. Were any of the inmates of the asylum insane enough to have committed the crime? Or, was it one of the staff, motivated by jealousy? And what was is the secret in the murdered man's past. Find the answer in... **One Drop of Blood**

AVAILABLE FROM RESURRECTED PRESS!

THE EDWARDIAN DETECTIVES
LITERARY SLEUTHS OF THE EDWARDIAN ERA

The exploits of the great Victorian Detectives, Poe's C. Auguste Dupin, Gaboriau's Lecoq, and most famously, Arthur Conan Doyle's Sherlock Holmes, are well known. But what of those fictional detectives that came after, those of the Edwardian Age? The period between the death of Queen Victoria and the First World War had been called the Golden Age of the detective short story, but how familiar is the modern reader with the sleuths of this era? And such an extraordinary group they were, including in their numbers an unassuming English priest, a blind man, a master of disguises, a lecturer in medical jurisprudence, a noble woman working for Scotland Yard, and a savant so brilliant he was known as "The Thinking Machine."

To introduce readers to these detectives, Resurrected Press has assembled a collection of stories featuring these and other remarkable sleuths in The Edwardian Detectives.

- The Case of Laker, Absconded by Arthur Morrison
- The Fenchurch Street Mystery by Baroness Orczy
- The Crime of the French Café by Nick Carter
- The Man with Nailed Shoes by R Austin Freeman
- The Blue Cross by G. K. Chesterton
- The Case of the Pocket Diary Found in the Snow by Augusta Groner
- The Ninescore Mystery by Baroness Orczy
- The Riddle of the Ninth Finger by Thomas W. Hanshew
- The Knight's Cross Signal Problem by Ernest Bramah

- The Problem of Cell 13 by Jacques Futrelle
- The Conundrum of the Golf Links by Percy James Brebner
- The Silkworms of Florence by Clifford Ashdown
- The Gateway of the Monster by William Hope Hodgson
- The Affair at the Semiramis Hotel by A. E. W. Mason
- The Affair of the Avalanche Bicycle & Tyre Co., LTD by Arthur Morrison

RESURRECTED PRESS CLASSIC MYSTERY CATALOGUE

Journeys into Mystery
Travel and Mystery in a More Elegant Time

The Edwardian Detectives
Literary Sleuths of the Edwardian Era

Gems of Mystery
Lost Jewels from a More Elegant Age

E. C. Bentley
Trent's Last Case: The Woman in Black

Ernest Bramah
Max Carrados Resurrected:
The Detective Stories of Max Carrados

Agatha Christie
The Secret Adversary
The Mysterious Affair at Styles

Octavus Roy Cohen
Midnight

Freeman Wills Croft
The Ponson Case
The Pit Prop Syndicate

J. S. Fletcher
The Herapath Property
The Rayner-Slade Amalgamation
The Chestermarke Instinct
The Paradise Mystery
Dead Men's Money

The Middle of Things
Ravensdene Court
Scarhaven Keep
The Orange-Yellow Diamond
The Middle Temple Murder
The Tallyrand Maxim
The Borough Treasurer
In the Mayor's Parlour
The Saftey Pin

R. Austin Freeman
The Mystery of 31 New Inn from the Dr. Thorndyke
Series
John Thorndyke's Cases from the Dr. Thorndyke
Series
The Red Thumb Mark from The Dr. Thorndyke Series
The Eye of Osiris from The Dr. Thorndyke Series
A Silent Witness from the Dr. John Thorndyke Series
The Cat's Eye from the Dr. John Thorndyke Series
Helen Vardon's Confession: A Dr. John Thorndyke
Story
As a Thief in the Night: A Dr. John Thorndyke Story
Mr. Pottermack's Oversight: A Dr. John Thorndyke
Story
Dr. Thorndyke Intervenes: A Dr. John Thorndyke
Story
The Singing Bone: The Adventures of Dr. Thorndyke
The Stoneware Monkey: A Dr. John Thorndyke Story
The Great Portrait Mystery, and Other Stories: A
Collection of Dr. John Thorndyke and Other Stories
The Penrose Mystery: A Dr. John Thorndyke Story
The Uttermost Farthing: A Savant's Vendetta

Arthur Griffiths
The Passenger From Calais
The Rome Express

Fergus Hume
The Mystery of a Hansom Cab
The Green Mummy
The Silent House
The Secret Passage

Edgar Jepson
The Loudwater Mystery

A. E. W. Mason
At the Villa Rose

A. A. Milne
The Red House Mystery
Baroness Emma Orczy
The Old Man in the Corner

Edgar Allan Poe
The Detective Stories of Edgar Allan Poe

Arthur J. Rees
The Hampstead Mystery
The Shrieking Pit
The Hand In The Dark
The Moon Rock
The Mystery of the Downs

Mary Roberts Rinehart
Sight Unseen and The Confession

Dorothy L. Sayers
Whose Body?

Sir William Magnay
The Hunt Ball Mystery

Mabel and Paul Thorne
The Sheridan Road Mystery

Raoul Whitfield
Death in a Bowl

And much more!
Visit ResurrectedPress.com
for our complete catalogue

About Resurrected Press

A division of Intrepid Ink, LLC, Resurrected Press is dedicated to bringing high quality, vintage books back into publication. See our entire catalogue and find out more at www.ResurrectedPress.com.

About Intrepid Ink, LLC

Intrepid Ink, LLC provides full publishing services to authors of fiction and non-fiction books, eBooks and websites. From editing to formatting, from publishing to marketing, Intrepid Ink gets your creative works into the hands of the people who want to read them. Find out more at www.IntrepidInk.com.

www.ingramcontent.com/pod-product-compliance
Lightning Source LLC
Chambersburg PA
CBHW071257250626
47159CB00004B/1230